SO YOU SHALL REAP

A NOVEL

By Marilyn Pauline Donovan

AuthorHouse™
1663 Liberty Drive
Bloomington, IN 47403
www.authorhouse.com
Phone: 1-800-839-8640

First published by AuthorHouse 07/08/2011

ISBN: 978-1-4634-2225-7 (e)
ISBN: 978-1-4634-2223-3 (dj)
ISBN: 978-1-4634-2226-4 (sc)

Library of Congress Control Number: 2011910051

Printed in the United States of America

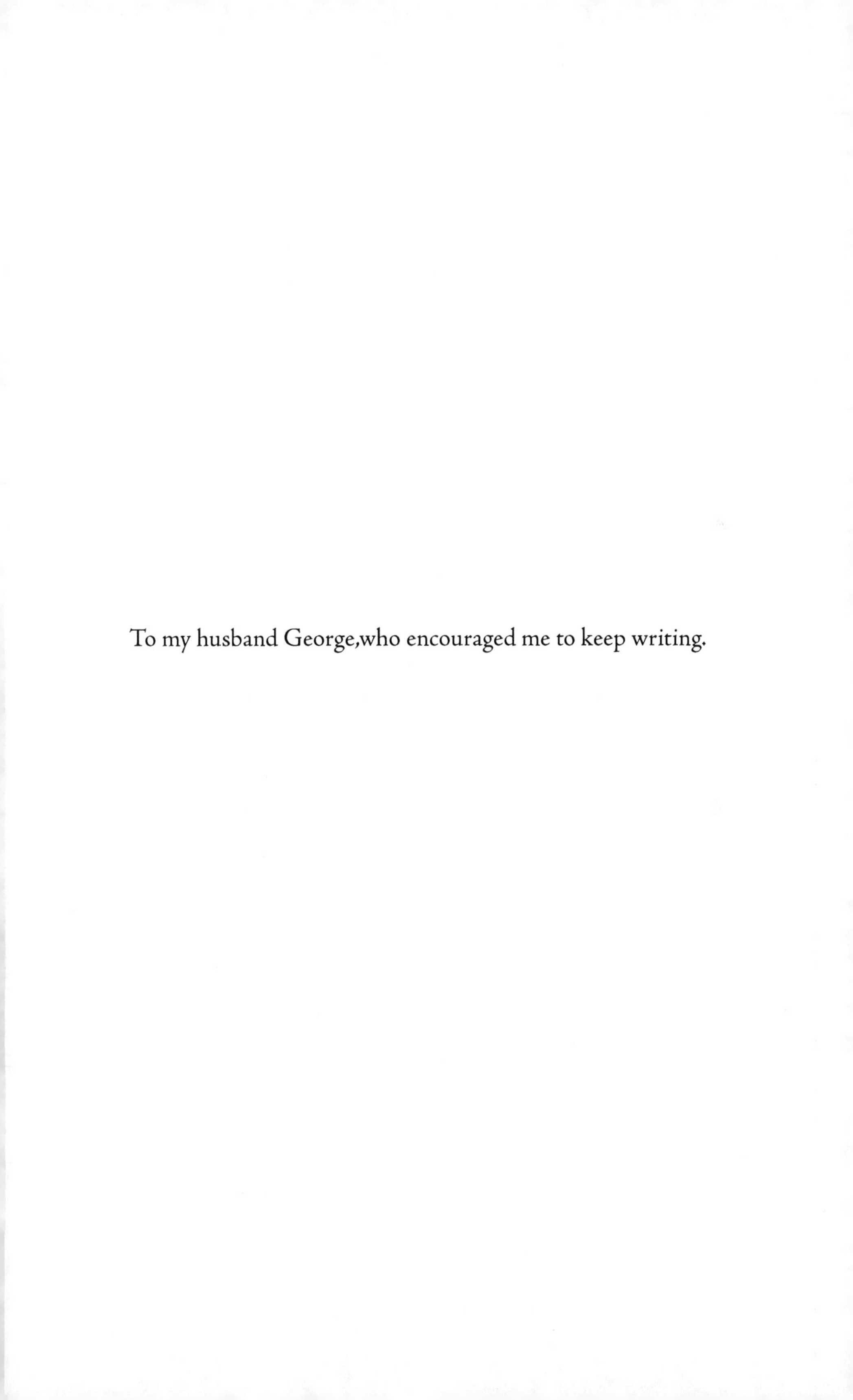

To my husband George,who encouraged me to keep writing.

And to my dear friend Eugene Woolcott, who helped me through the technical struggles, and the creative process.

CHAPTER 1

Ruth left Baker's Bookstore, grousing silently about how poorly Mr. Baker had treated her today. *But then,* she thought, *he's not nice to me at any time..* She was so engrossed in her thoughts that she wasn't paying attention to her surroundings as she walked.

The big, black Cadillac sped down the darkened streets. As it turned left and rounded a corner, the headlights fell on Ruth stepping off the curb. The sound of screeching brakes and the thud of something hitting the car was followed by a thin wail and then sudden silence that left the man behind the wheel stunned. It seemed an eternity before he could move.

Jon Malcolm opened the car door and stepped out. He walked slowly, afraid of what he might find. He saw a body on the ground and almost panicked. He had an almost uncontrollable desire to get back into the car and drive away but then the figure on the ground moved. A sense of relief surged through him, leaving him trembling. "Jesus!" he said when he heard the person moan. "She's alive!" Jon quickly composed himself and knelt beside the young woman on the ground.

"Please let me help you. Can you move? No, don't get up!" he exclaimed.

"I'm all right," she said, "just a little shaky."

"I was so scared. I thought I'd killed you."

"It was partly my fault," she said. "I shouldn't have stepped off the curb without looking. I think I walked into the side of your car just as it stopped moving."

He helped her to her feet but, when she tried to stand, her ankle buckled under her and she groaned at the sudden pain. He quickly swept her up into his arms to keep her from falling.

"You are hurt," he said. "I'd better take you to the hospital."

"No, please. It's not necessary. I'm all right, really I am. It's my ankle. I must have turned it as I fell. Please, put me down."

He became aware of her nearness. She was so small and slender, like a feather in his arms. He couldn't see clearly in the dimness of the streetlight, but what he did see was lovely. Her hair appeared dark and was very long. He was close enough to smell the clean, sweet, scent of it. He could only guess at its color. Her lips were full, her voice soft, and he wondered what color her eyes were.

"I said put me down, please!" she said adamantly.

He set her down gently. For a moment they faced each other and their eyes met and held. Startled, he realized he had been staring. She looked away first.

"Well, at least let me drive you home," he said. "I can't just leave you here." He was sincere in his need to help this person.

"I assure you I'm quite all right."

"Please, for my sake," he said.

"If you insist but you don't know where I live," she replied.

"You're going to tell me, aren't you?" he said with a chuckle.

Jon opened the car door and helped her sit down before he walked around and sat behind the wheel. "Now, where do you live?" he asked, as he started the engine.

"I really don't want you to trouble yourself. I'm perfectly all right, really I am."

"Look Miss..." He paused and smiled. "May I ask your name?"

"Lawson, Ruth Lawson."

"Miss Lawson, I am prepared to sit here, all night if necessary, until you agree to let me see you safely home."

"All right, you win. I guess that would be best. My ankle is throbbing a little. I live at 25 Station Street."

As the big car moved slowly forward, she relaxed a little. Her ankle was quite painful but she tried to conceal her discomfort.

"By the way, my name is Jon. Jon Malcolm."

"Pleased to meet you Mr. Malcolm," she said.

He looked at her, chuckled and shook his head.

Ruth didn't understand. "What's so funny?"

"It takes a stretch of the imagination to consider this a pleasant meeting, Miss Lawson. I did almost run you down. I think you're being courageous and I like that about you."

"Oh, I see what you mean." Then, she was laughing too. The uneasiness she felt disappeared as she relaxed.

Ruth glanced around. Trying hard not to stare, using her peripheral vision, she studied the well-dressed young man beside her and the beautiful automobile. Instinctively, she assumed that he must live in Brandon Hill, the beautiful part of town with gorgeous homes and spacious grounds; a part of town inhabited exclusively by the wealthy. He didn't seem to be at all snobbish, quite friendly in fact.

The big car turned a corner and, as it continued down the street, Ruth began to feel uncomfortable again. The houses began to show signs of neglect, becoming shabbier and shabbier as they approached her neighborhood. The streets became darker and in her mind seemed to get narrower until she felt everything was closing in on her.

Finally, Ruth told Jon to stop the car. They were in front of an old, brick, two-story building. It was just as shabby as the other houses on the block, with nothing to set it apart, except for the light in the hall tonight, which was very seldom lit because the light bulbs were always being stolen.

It had become a game with Ruth to see how long each bulb would last. Just once, the same bulb remained in its socket for two whole weeks. The only other light available was a street light on the corner, which was almost in front of the house. It wasn't very bright and colored everything yellow, but it was enough to make coming home at night a little less scary.

As usual, feelings of depression surged through her the moment they reached the building where Ruth lived with her father. Tonight, the depression seemed much worse. Maybe it was the big beautiful automobile or the handsome man sitting beside her. He was so obviously used to the best of everything, to all the luxuries that life had to offer, things that Ruth could only dream about. Tonight, for a very short while, she had been in his world, at least in her mind. Now, Ruth was back in the world she despised, one in which she was ashamed to have to live.

Jon was about to get out of the car but Ruth put a restraining hand on his arm. "There's no need for you to get out. I can make it from here. Thank you for driving me home."

Before he could protest, she opened the door and climbed out as fast as she could. She limped quickly up the two steps leading to the front door and hurried into the hallway. She heard him call, "Ruth! Ruth, wait!"

She quickly switched off the hall light so he wouldn't try to follow her and leaned against the door. She didn't want Jon to see the horrible conditions in which she was forced to live. A minute later, she heard the car pull away.

Her ankle throbbed painfully as she slowly made her way up the stairs. Ruth opened the door to the flat and limped to her bedroom as quietly as possible. Her father was sleeping soundly now; she could hear his labored breathing. The least little noise could disturb him and hearing her move around would mean another long evening of talking and Ruth wasn't in the mood to listen to another minute of redundant conversation. She didn't even turn on the lights because that might awaken him, too.

The moonlight shining through her bedroom window gave enough light to keep the room from complete darkness. As she undressed, she tried to recall everything that had happened this evening, but she was very tired and the bed looked so inviting. "I'll think about it in the morning," she mumbled, climbing into bed. As her eyes closed, her father began to cough. She waited but he didn't call her name as he'd done so often lately. He was still asleep.

When she awoke, sunlight was streaming through the window. She stretched, adjusted the sheet and squinted at the light. She felt the sun's warmth, magnified by its trip through the glass, on her face and slowly opened her eyes, blinking at the bright sunlight. Stretching lazily, she turned over and looked at the clock on her bedside table.

"Oh, my goodness," she cried and jumped out of bed. It was eight o'clock and she had to be at the shop at nine. She hurried to the bathroom and splashed cold water on her face, filled the basin with warm water, put her elbows in, soaped and rinsed under her arms. She dashed back to the bedroom for some clean clothes. While putting on her shoes, she remembered last night and looked at her ankle. It wasn't the least bit swollen and the pain was completely gone. *That's a relief,* she thought. *It's bad enough having to stand on my feet all day but, with a sore ankle, I know I wouldn't have made it.*

Ruth couldn't afford to take a day off. Mr. Baker was such an old grouch that it might cost her the job if she did. It was a bitter struggle for her now, trying to pay the rent on this horrible flat and taking care of her father, whose life was ebbing away day by day.

The doctor had recommended her father enter a nursing home where he would get the professional care and attention that he needed. When Ruth told her father what the doctor said, he cried like a baby. That had been more than two months ago. Since then he'd done nothing but whine and beg her not to send him away. She always had to reassure him that she wouldn't do that and would take care of him as long as he needed her. She never mentioned it again but he never let her forget her promise.

Her father was sitting at the table when she entered the kitchen.

"Oh, Dad," she said, "How long have you been up?"

"I don't know. It's so hot, Ruthie, I just couldn't stay in bed."

"Why didn't you wake me? It's after eight o'clock. If I'm late I could be fired!"

"I'm sorry, Ruthie. It's so hot. I just couldn't stay in bed. Don't be mad at me, Ruthie," he whined.

"Oh Pop, I'm not mad at you. It's just that, as long as you were up, you shouldn't have let me oversleep."

"You won't send me away, will you, Ruthie?"

"No, Pop, I won't send you away."

"It's too hot for coffee, but I'll make some if you want. Will you stay and have some coffee with me?" He forced a toothless grin. His course, grey hair stuck out all over. Messy from restless sleep.

"I'd like to, but I really can't. Like you said, it's too hot for coffee and..." She was about to remind him that she had to go to work, but it wouldn't have made any difference to him.

"I wish it wasn't so hot!" He put his head down on the table. "Why does it have to be so damned hot?"

Ruth shook her head and sighed. It was warm but it was worse for her father since he was plagued with constant fever. Touching his shoulder, she left the room and quietly closed the door behind her. She hurried down the stairs as fast as she could, almost falling. She grabbed onto the banister just in time or she might have ended up at the bottom of the stairs with a broken arm or worse. Once outside, she practically ran down the street to reach the bus stop, praying all the time that she wouldn't be late. *Maybe something will happen to prevent Mr. Baker from arriving on time.* She chuckled at the thought. *That's wishful thinking.* The bus was coming when she reached the stop. Heaving a sigh of relief at not having to stand all the way downtown, she sat in the one empty place on the long bench behind the driver.

Can't this bus go any faster? What am I doing here? She thought. *Why should I care about that old man? He never cared about me. It was only when he was alone and dying that he remembered that he even had a daughter. Damn! When will I learn to think of myself first?*

Even as she cursed her weakness, she knew she couldn't change.

Ruth was and always had been kind, a gentle and good person. She had remained that way despite her deprived childhood. Still unshaken in her determination to rise above a life of poverty, she told herself, again and again, to regard this time spent with her father as a temporary intrusion, an obligation that needed to be fulfilled.

Ruth's mother died when Ruth was five years old. The five years following her mother's death were one long, painful nightmare. Her father drank all the time. Ruth never saw him sober. If she had, he wouldn't have seemed like the same man.

She remembered accepting handouts from friends and neighbors, going from one family to another. She would show up at a friend's house around suppertime and ask if her friend could play. The answer was always no, of course, because it was time for dinner. Ruth would hang around for a while hoping they would invite her to eat with them, and most of the time they did. She never realized that everyone was on to her little game. No one had the heart to turn her away.

Finally, the neighbors got together and called the child welfare association. This was child neglect, they told them. At first, Ruth was terrified. Although she hated the life she was living, it was familiar and one to which she was accustomed. She remembered the ladies from the welfare office coming to look around the apartment and talking to her father. Evidently, they weren't satisfied with the way things were and condemned the place an unfit environment in which to raise a child. Ruth ended up in an orphanage. She was ten years old and terrified at being ripped from her familiar routine.

She felt so alone at first, but it wasn't long before she realized that being in the orphanage was the best thing that could have happened to her. She was well cared for and quickly made many friends. She had clean clothes and plenty of food. The nuns and the other ladies who worked in the home were very fond of her, as she was of them. They showed love and kindness to all the children while preparing them for a life on their own. They wanted all the children to be safe and happy. Ruth, with her endearing charms, developed a special place in their hearts. When Ruth turned eighteen, the sisters offered her a job in the home so she would have a place to stay while finishing her college education. They let her stay until she was twenty-two, until she'd saved enough money to start living independently.

Two weeks before Ruth was to leave, she got a call from a neighbor informing her of her father's illness. The neighbor said, "He keeps calling for you all the time and told me where to find you." Instinct told Ruth to run, run as fast as she could, to never see or care about her father again. But her heart and her conscience wouldn't let her do that, so she finally went to see him.

Ruth knocked on the first floor door of the building.

When the landlady opened the door, she asked, "Who are you? What do you want?"

"I'm Ruth Lawson. I've come to see my father."

"You're little Ruthie?" The lady said with wide-eyed surprise. "You sure grew up to be a pretty young lady."

Ruth didn't remember the landlady but it would become obvious that the neighbors remembered her.

"Your father is upstairs, Ruthie. He never goes anywhere. Do you want me to go up with you?"

"Yes, if you don't mind."

The landlady opened the door to the upstairs flat, stood aside and motioned for Ruth to go in. Even before Ruth stepped inside, she was assailed by the stench emanating from her father's apartment. A strong smell of urine and general decay caused her to take a step back.

Her father was sitting in a threadbare overstuffed chair, propped up by pillows. The odor of unwashed clothing competed with the fetid smell of the room. He had stopped shaving, washing and dental hygiene. The smell of stale cigarette smoke, spoiled milk and rotting food was overwhelming. The garbage had piled up everywhere. Paper plates and opened but empty food cans lay near his chair. The table by his side held a lamp and a large ashtray overflowing with cigarette butts and ashes. There was a small radio on the table. The only sound was the constant hiss of static coming from the radio, making the scene all the more surreal.

Most of the light in the room would come from a flickering floor lamp in the corner. It was a bright afternoon. Why hadn't he turned off the lamp?

"Hello, Father," Ruth said after surveying the situation.

The dying man raised his head. He opened his eyes and tried to focus on the person standing there. He didn't recognize his own flesh and blood. "Who is it?" the old man asked. "Who's there?"

"It's Ruth. You remember your daughter, don't you?"

The old man started to get out of the chair but fell back down as he gasped, "Oh my God! Are you Ruthie? Is my little Ruthie really here?"

"Yes, it's me. I'm here."

"You're going to stay, aren't you, Ruthie? You won't leave me?" He started to cough.

When she saw this man, whom she barely knew, in such a pitiful condition, she knew she couldn't leave him to die alone. She knew she had to stay and take care of him as long as she was needed.

"Take it easy, Dad." That word didn't come easily to her. As the coughing subsided, Ruth took a deep breath thought, *why am I even here?* "I'll stay," she finished.

The landlady was still standing there with a deep frown on her face, she said, "I'm not at all happy with this situation, Ruth. You're going to have to do something with the old man. If things aren't cleaned up here immediately, he'll have to go! I didn't realize things were this bad until now. You got your work cut out for you, dearie." She walked away, leaving the door wide open.

Ruth didn't know what to do first or where to start. She decided to do the most important thing first and that was to call a doctor to find out how badly off her father really was and what, if anything, could be done for him. She picked up most of the garbage before she made the call.

When the doctor arrived, Ruth watched him survey the room. Distaste was evident from his expression but he didn't say a word about the apartment's condition. His examination complete, Ruth had only to see the look on his face to have her suspicion confirmed; her father was dying.

"I'm sorry, Ms. Lawson. Your father is seriously ill. His lungs are failing. He's in the final stage of emphysema. His coughing spells will become more severe. He should be in a constant care facility, because recovery is not imminent. All you can do now is relieve most of his discomfort by giving him the medicine that I've prescribed." He handed her three prescriptions he'd written. "There's nothing else to be done for him now."

"I understand," Ruth said. "He's been drinking and smoking for years and never cared about the toll it was taking on his health."

"I wish there was more I could do," the doctor said with a sigh, "but you've waited far too long to call a doctor.'

"I've been away for quite some time, Doctor," she replied. "I didn't know he was so ill." *Why do I feel the need to make excuses?* she thought. *Why do I suddenly have this guilty feeling, even though I know there's no reason to feel this way? Maybe it's because the doctor is a stranger and has no way of knowing how selfish and irresponsible this man was, or what he put me through. I feel embarrassed for him now when I shouldn't.* "I don't even know if he has any way to pay for this," she finished.

"I see." The doctor closed his bag and turned to leave, then turned back. "Just so you know, he'll soon be too much for you to take care of alone. You do understand what I'm saying, don't you?"

"Yes, I understand. Thank you, Doctor."

The bus bumped and rattled toward the stop where Ruth would be getting off. She continued her ruminations about the situation. *It's been almost six months since the doctor made that visit. The situation hasn't changed and I've done my best to keep things going. I think the worst part about all this has been having to return to that horrible flat each night. It's taken so much effort to get it back into some semblance of order.* Ruth's heart pounded faster as the bus rounded the last corner. *Oh, God! I'm late!*

As usual, Mr. Baker was already there. Ruth had never known him to be even one minute late. She ran into the shop, closed the door behind her and tried to catch her breath. Mr. Baker was behind the counter, busily looking over some books.

"Well, Miss Lawson, you do realize it's ten minutes past nine, don't you?" he said without raising his head.

"I'm sorry, Mr. Baker, but you see I was in an accident last night and..."

"I'm not interested in excuses, Miss Lawson," he interrupted. "Your work begins at nine o'clock and you will either be here at that time or not at all."

"Yes, Mr. Baker."

"Then we understand each other?"

"Yes, Mr. Baker."

"Of course, I will have to deduct something from your wages."

"Of course, Mr. Baker."

"Miss Lawson, I'll be gone most of the day. There is a new shipment of books at the distributor's warehouse. I'm hoping that I can purchase some at bargain prices." He looked up from what he was doing and frowned more deeply. "Well, are you going to get to work or just stand there?"

"Oh no, Mr. Baker. I'll get right to work, and don't worry about the shop while you're gone. I'll take good care of things." Ruth hurried to the back room and hung her purse on the coat rack.

Mr. Baker was a strange looking man. He had a mass of snow-white hair but his bushy eyebrows were dark. Not a bit good looking, he was short and plump but, just around the middle. He had spindly legs and arms, but his belly protruded like a big balloon. Ruth had had the funniest thought when she first looked at his belly. She'd imagined the belt that held up his trousers slipping right off that big expanse and leaving him standing there in his underwear. Somehow, it never happened.

She never could get used to his small beady eyes. Ruth was never sure in what direction he was looking. He wore old-fashioned metal-rimmed glasses and he seemed to always look over, under or around them but never through them. At least it seemed that way to her.

"I'll be back before closing time, Miss Lawson," Mr. Baker called from the front door. She heard the bell jingle as he left the store and then all was silent. Ruth heaved a sigh.

That was a close one, she thought and smiled. *This is going to be one pleasant day without him peeking over my shoulder every minute.* She started organizing the books that had been left in disarray by the customers from the day before.

The day passed quickly. Without Mr. Baker there, Ruth had to eat her lunch on the run. Whenever there were no customers, she went to the back room and took a few bites of her sandwich that she'd hurriedly thrown together before leaving the house. She didn't mind though. Without Mr. Baker watching her every move, she felt no pressure.

When Ruth glanced up at the clock, she was surprised to see that it was only twenty minutes before closing time. While the last customers were leaving, she hurried to put the remaining books back in their places on the shelves and tables.

The bell jingled. She turned to see a tall, dark-haired young man enter the shop.

"May I help you?" she asked

"Perhaps you can, Miss Lawson. Or may I call you Ruth?"

"I beg your pardon." She looked puzzled. *Who is this person and how does he know my name?*

"Surely you haven't forgotten our accidental meeting last night?"

Ruth smiled shyly when she remembered last night. "Oh yes, you're Mr.... Mr...."

"Malcolm, Jon Malcolm."

"Yes! Mr. Malcolm, of course! I remember, now. I didn't recognize you."

"That's all right. I'm the same guy that ran you down just so I could get to meet you. But, more importantly, the reason I'm here, I had to find out if you were all right."

"I'm fine. You needn't have troubled yourself." *He's better looking than I remembered,* she thought, and found herself blushing.

"I had to know. So, when do you get through here?"

"I'm through at five. Why do you ask?"

"Five, that's fine, it's almost five now. I'll wait for you."

"Wait for me?"

"Yes, of course. You're having dinner with me tonight."

"Having dinner with you?"

"Do you hear an echo in this place?" Jon frowned as he looked around.

"Just what makes you think you can walk in here and demand that I have dinner with you? What makes you think I'd even want to?" She turned away from him, suddenly angry and a little humiliated.

"Oh, Ruth." Jon's voice was suddenly contrite. "I'm sorry! I thought I was being funny. I realize now that it was a bad joke. Will you forgive me?" He waited for her answer. "Ruth?"

She turned, smiled, and said, "All right, since you were so concerned that you came back to see that I was okay, I'll have dinner with you."

"I'm forgiven then?"

"Yes, you are." she laughed, wondering why she'd accepted. *What are you thinking? You don't even know this guy.*

"Then, let's start over. Miss Lawson will you honor me with your company at dinner this evening?" He flashed an irresistible smile.

"Well, I don't know." She hesitated now, going along with the game. "This is rather unusual. I don't really know you?"

"Why, Miss Lawson, didn't I get you home, safe and sound, after I ran you down?"

Ruth had to laugh then. "All right, you win. After all, it's probably safer riding with you than taking my chances as a pedestrian." They both laughed.

Suddenly, Ruth saw Mr. Baker coming across the street. In a panic, she said, "Pretend you are looking for a book. My boss is coming." She turned quickly and began arranging books again. The bell jingled and Mr. Baker entered the shop. He went directly to the back room. The minutes passed, and then it was five o'clock.

"You may leave now Miss Lawson," he called, "May I expect you to arrive at nine o'clock tomorrow?"

"Yes, Mr. Baker," she answered, stifling the sudden anger she felt because he called to her like she was a child being scolded, as she hurried to the back room for her purse. Baker had his back to her, looking over some papers. She said goodnight but he didn't answer. She left the shop, leaving Jon behind pretending to look for a book. Once outside, she began walking slowly, knowing that Jon would catch up to her. She liked the feel of his touch when he came up beside her and put her arm in his. They were at the end of the block.

"The car is just across the street, Ruth." He held her as they waited for a break in the traffic. When they reached the car, he opened the door for her then got in behind the wheel. They drove for quite a while without speaking. Ruth broke the silence.

"Where are you taking me?" she asked.

"You'll see. It's a wonderful place and the food is out of this world. We're almost there."

Finally, Jon turned into the entrance to a well lighted, swanky looking restaurant and stopped under the canopy. A man in uniform stepped forward. Jon helped Ruth out of the car. A valet got behind the wheel to park the car. Ruth looked around, turned to Jon and said, "I can't go in there!"

"Why not, for goodness sake? What's wrong?"

"I'm not properly dressed for this place."

"Don't be silly. There's nothing wrong with the way you look. Your blouse and skirt are perfectly suitable. People aren't going to be wearing gowns and tuxedos." He took her arm and ushered her inside.

Once inside, Ruth was overwhelmed. It was, indeed, a fancy place. There were white tablecloths, crystal chandeliers, and a candle on each table. The Maitre de' led them to a table on the terrace overlooking a beautiful little lake. Ruth was fascinated by the elegant ambiance and the quiet reserve of everyone she saw.

"What would you like?" Jon asked as he opened the menu.

Ruth was shocked when she saw the prices on the menu she was given and, feeling very ill at ease, said, "I'm not sure, Will you please order for me"

Jon smiled and replied, "Happy to. They prepare a very nice Chicken Marsala. I think you'll like it.

They ate mostly in silence. Ruth did enjoy her meal. Jon talked a little, trying to get Ruth to relax, but Ruth was so interested in everything around her she only managed an occasional comment or nod. She tried to act casual but knew it wasn't working. When the meal was over, Jon ordered after-dinner drinks for them.

"This is a lovely place, Mr. Malcolm. I can't remember when I've felt so relaxed and calm," she lied.

"I knew you'd like it and, if you notice, we fit in just fine." Jon leaned across the table and looked into her deep green eyes. "Do you realize that you're the most beautiful woman in the place?" he whispered.

Ruth blushed and lowered her eyes. "Please, Mr. Malcolm. You're embarrassing me."

Jon sat back again. "I'm sorry you don't think much of me, Miss Lawson."

Ruth frowned. "Whatever makes you say that?"

"Well, we're not strangers, are we?"

"No, I guess not."

"Might you consider me a friend, then?" Jon asked.

"I suppose I could."

"Well then, as long as we are friends, why don't you call me Jon and let's drop all this formality. You make me feel like my grandfather."

Ruth smiled, "You're right. From now on it's Jon and, please call me Ruth."

"There you have it," he said with a smile. "They go very well together, don't you think? Jon and Ruth."

"I think you're deliberately trying to embarrass me, now" she said and laughed. "But here's what I'd really like to know. How did you know where to find me?"

"All I did was ask everyone where the prettiest girl in town worked."

"Please, I'm serious. How did you know?"

He covered her hand with his. "All I have to do is make a call or two and I can find out whatever it is I want to know. You might as well know that when I set my mind on something, I usually get what I want." Their eyes met and held.

There was something about his demeanor that made Ruth feel somewhat uneasy. *What does he mean by that? This has got to stop now if he thinks I'm that kind of girl.* She smiled to hide her discomfort but tried to justify this dinner.

It doesn't matter. I doubt that he could ever be serious about someone like me. I'm someone from outside his world. I couldn't even dare think that he would? But those thoughts soon faded, and in their place, as she looked in his face, an immediate replacement. *Oh,* my *gosh! He's so good looking.*

Jon was looking at her face, but taking in everything about her. *She's gorgeous!* He thought. *I must have her! She's so sweet and lovely.* He could feel the pounding in his temples just thinking about her body and how she would feel in his arms.

"I must be getting home, now," she said. His staring had made her uncomfortable again. "My dad's not well and I don't want to leave him alone any longer than I have to."

"Oh, of course," he said, shaken out of his reverie. "We'll leave right away."

Ruth enjoyed the ride home. The air was calm and the stars were bright. Every so often, she turned slightly to glance at Jon, wondering what he was thinking.

Only when the car stopped moving did she become aware that they were back in her world looking at the old broken down building where she lived. It had nothing to set it apart, not even a light in the hallway tonight. Again, she felt embarrassed to have him see where she lived. She wanted to run. *How quickly the magic fades when reality steps in,* she thought.

"May I see you safely in, Ruth?"

"No!" she said too loudly. "I mean, it's late and my father is probably sleeping. I'll just say goodnight, now, and thank you for a lovely evening."

He put his hand on her arm and firmly held her there.

"You're not going to rush away from me tonight, at least not until you tell me when I can see you again."

"I... I really... I'm pretty busy now, taking care of my dad and all. Perhaps we'd better not..."

He reached across her and put his arm around her waist and pulled her to him. Her head fell back and he looked into her eyes, which were opened wide now. "I've got to see you again, Ruth," he whispered, as he began kissing her cheek and then her eyes and then the tip of her nose.

"No," she breathed, "I mustn't see you again."

"Yes, Ruth," he whispered, "Yes." His mouth was on hers and he held her so tightly she could hardly breathe. *No,* she thought *I can't do this. I have to stop him, but I can't.* Her response surprised even her, as her arms moved slowly around his neck. She hungrily kissed him back. Her body was weak and she felt herself trembling. His kiss was tender yet passionate. She felt the force of his body against hers and every muscle in his powerful arms. She was completely drawn to him. She'd never felt so out of control and yet so free.

Suddenly, two old men burst into laughter as they came staggering around the corner, arms around each other, they started singing as they stumbled down the street.

The moment shattered, Ruth pushed him away. "I have to go in now."

"Ruth, will I see you tomorrow?" he asked, in a husky voice.

"No!" she cried. "I can't see you ever again." She hurried out of the car and into the hallway. Jon didn't try to follow her.

Despite her intentions, she had no choice but to see him again. He waited outside the bookshop until she left work and wouldn't let her refuse. They met every night for weeks. Jon always had something planned for them to do; a movie, a play, a new restaurant... or just driving around and stopping for an ice cream cone to eat while they strolled along the beach. Their meetings always ended with tender, passionate kisses. The more they were together the more difficult it was to break away at the end of the evening. Ruth always regained control but, each night after they parted, she wondered what was holding her back. She knew she loved him now, and he seemed so understanding about her reticence to go further into intimacy. She was sure it meant that he loved her and wouldn't force her into anything for which she wasn't ready.

A month went by and it was August. Ruth was living on a cloud; she was in love! The days had never passed so quickly and life was beautiful. She was sure that Jon loved her, too. If he didn't, he wouldn't insist on seeing her so often. At first, she thought his interest was centered on one thing only but now she was certain that it was more than that. After all, they hadn't been intimate and, surely, no man would be so persistent about seeing a girl he couldn't have sex with if he didn't love her. At least that's what she'd learned in all the love stories she'd read. There must have been other women in his life and any one of them would probably do anything for him. After all, he was so handsome and, all that money!

Ruth had never thought of herself as beautiful or irresistible. *What man would want to hang around for so long unless his intentions were honorable? I'm sure that it won't be long before Jon will ask me to marry him.* She was also sure that it wouldn't be long before she gave in to her sexual desires. She wanted him as much as he wanted her.

She did think it a little unusual, however, that he never suggested she meet his family. For that matter, she'd never met anyone he knew. They always went to some very nice but out-of-the-way place, where the only people that seemed to know him were waiters and the like.

Oh, I'm just being silly, she thought, *I'm sure he wants to keep me all to himself. He's probably waiting until the right moment to surprise everyone when we become engaged. That must be it! I'm sure of it. Oh, how I wish he would hurry and ask me, though. Each time we're alone it's harder to control myself. I love him so much.* She smiled at her next thought. *It's been a long time since he's been so insistent in his lovemaking. He must be finally convinced that I'm not that kind of girl. Maybe tonight, maybe he'll ask me tonight.* Her heart sang, "He loves me. He loves me. He loves me."

CHAPTER 2

Miles away, in another world, Jon was daydreaming, too. He whistled a tune while he combed his hair. Taking his time to enjoy the reflection he saw in the mirror. It was very satisfactory. He saw broad shoulders that tapered down to slim hips. Dark wavy hair, big blue eyes, a straight proud nose, and a square set jaw.

I must be losing my touch, he thought. *It's been a month now, and still nothing. God, she's beautiful! It's got to be soon. Many more nights without her and I'll go stark raving mad! I knew it had to be slow, but how much can a guy take? A few more nights of playing it cool ought to do it though. I can't lose my head now. She's like a frightened little rabbit; you've got to approach them slowly; any fast moves and you'll scare them away. I know she cares for me, and I care for her, too, but... I can't let mother know about this. She'd have a fit.*

Very proud of himself, Jon thought he had all the answers. He left his room and skipped down the beautifully curved staircase. His mother, already seated at the table when he entered the dinning room, seemed troubled. Matthew, the butler, was ladling soup into a bowl in front of her.

"Must you always come rushing in at the last minute, Jonathan?" she asked, smiling coldly.

"Sorry, Mother," he said, and stopped to kiss her on the forehead before sitting in his chair.

"Stop that foolishness," she said, as she brushed his kiss away. "And, hereafter, kindly be in your seat before dinner is served."

"Yes, Mother."

"And don't wolf your food down again tonight. It would be nice if we could chat for a little while. You're always rushing away somewhere.

I don't know what's come over you lately." She smiled pleasantly. "By the way, have you seen Sally Thompson lately?"

Jon hesitated. "Why, yes, mother, of course I have."

"Then you must have had a good time at her lawn party last week? It seems you neglected to tell me about it."

"The lawn party? Yes, of course, the party. I'm sorry, Mother. I didn't think you'd be interested. It was just another party, same old crowd."

"It's too bad about Dennis Martin."

"Dennis Martin?"

"Yes! You were there when he fell on the tennis court and broke his arm, weren't you?"

"Why, yes. Yes, of course. It was rotten luck."

"Jonathan, there's no need to continue this subterfuge!" she exclaimed.

"I don't understand, Mother?"

"Sally called last evening to ask about you. You haven't been at the club or called her in weeks. She wondered if you were ill or something. She also said you haven't seen any of your other friends lately, either."

"It's just that I've been rather busy lately. I have..." He paused because he wanted to tell her about Ruth but, as usual, felt intimidated by her. "Other interests, you might say."

"It's obvious you don't wish to discuss it with me."

"Please, Mother, not now!"

"You know it's foolish to try to keep anything from me. I always find out, don't I? Whatever is taking up all your time, I'll know everything soon enough."

"I'm not very hungry, mother. Will you excuse me?" Jon rose from his chair.

"Jonathan, you will sit down and finish your dinner. If you wish to act like a child, you will be treated like one. I'll not have you stomping out of here and spoiling my dinner!"

"Yes, Mother." Jon sat down again. He picked at his food just to satisfy her. Except for a few more comments his mother made hoping to coax more information from him, they ate their meal in silence. At last she was finished and, once again, Jon asked to be excused.

"Jonathan, are you in some kind of trouble?" she asked. "I've been worried about you."

"No, Mother. There's nothing wrong. Really, I would tell you if there were."

"I hope so," she sighed. Her voice regained its sternness. "Very well then, you may leave."

Once outside the house, Jon relaxed. Soon, he was speeding down the darkened streets, feeling his old self again. Ruth was outside waiting for him when he stopped in front of her house. She smiled when she saw him and ran to the car. Jon smelled the clean, fresh, sweetness of her body as she sat down beside him.

"What is our destination tonight milady?" he asked.

"It's so warm tonight. I thought we might just drive around for a while, if you don't mind.

"Your wish is my command, my dear." He pressed down on the gas petal, and the big car moved away from the curb. They quickly left the neighborhood and turned onto the highway. Soon, they were driving along a wide, lonely stretch of beach. Jon parked the car in an open area next to the beach and they both got out. Walking along the water's edge, Ruth took his arm and said, "Wait Jon, I want to take off my shoes."

She held his arm and stopped to remove her shoes. "Take your shoes off, Jon," she prodded innocently.

"Anything to make my lady happy," he said. Reluctantly, Jon sat down in the sand and took off his shoes and stockings, something that he'd never done before.

The night was very clear. The moon was so big and bright that it seemed that one might reach out and touch it. There were huge rock formations strewn along the beach.

"It's so lovely and cool here by the water," she said. "I wish I never had to go back to that sweltering place of mine."

"I wish you didn't have to go back, too," he replied.

They walked along until they came to the next cluster of rocks. Grouped together in an unusual way, they formed a cave-like shelter. It was closed on three sides but open to the sky.

"Would you like to rest a while and enjoy the moment, Ruth?"

"All right," she said.

Jon slipped between the rocks, assisting Ruth after him. He took off his jacket and spread it on the ground. They shared it as they sat close together in the shelter of the rocks. Jon took out a cigarette. "Would you like one?" He asked.

"You know I don't smoke," she said, as she wriggled her toes in the sand. "It's easy to forget the terrible heat in town when you're sitting here by the water, isn't it, Jon?"

"Yes. I know what you mean."

"I wish I could just stay here forever. It's so quiet and beautiful."

"Then why don't we?"

"That would be wonderful." She laughed and lay back. The sky was dark but blazed with millions of stars.

"Ruth?"

"Yes, Jon."

"Do you care for me... even a little?"

"Yes, I do," she whispered. "More than you know."

"I was hoping you would say that." He sighed, as he flipped his cigarette out towards the water and bent to kiss her.

She turned her face away. *This is the perfect situation to lose control,* she thought. "Please don't," she said. "You know this is wrong. I don't want anything to spoil the way we feel about one another."

"Spoil it! Ruth, how could this spoil anything? I'll only love you more." His hand gently stroked her neck, and then ever so slowly moved it over her shoulder and slowly down her arm.

"Then you do love me?" she asked.

"Of course I do!" His hand was on her waist now and, as he moved it across her body, he was kissing her face all over.

"Why didn't you tell me this before?" she asked, trying to speak through his kisses.

"I don't know," he said. "Maybe I wanted to be sure you loved me too. Maybe I had to be sure you wanted me and not my money."

"Oh, how can you think that?" She was stunned.

"I'm sorry Ruth, but there are too many girls who will marry a man they don't give a damn about, just to get his money. When I marry, I want to be sure it's for who I am and nothing else."

"I suppose you have the right to feel the way you do. I never thought about things from your side. Oh! I hope you don't think that I..."

"Of course I don't, Ruth"

"I do love you Jon. Truly, I do."

"If I could only be sure," he whispered.

"Oh, dear, what can I do to make you believe me?

"Oh, Ruthie, Ruthie," he said, his voice suddenly hoarse with passion.

He kissed her hard on the mouth as his hand moved, tenderly, under her blouse and across her smooth, soft stomach. He cautiously moved to her small firm breast. Ruth didn't protest. She wrapped her arms around his neck and drew him to her. His hands fumbled with the buttons on her blouse. Ruth slid her fingers through his hair. She felt the dampness on his forehead.

"Tell me you love me, Jon. Tell me now!" she demanded.

"I love you, I love you. My beautiful Ruthie, I love you." His lips were all over her and came to rest on her breasts. She raised her body as he lifted her skirt and slid her panties down. His hand went between her legs as he forced them apart. Then, his body covered her. She felt no thrill, no sensation of arousal at this first intercourse, only the fullness of his penis as it forced its way into her vagina.

Jon was a wild man, beating into her with an intensity that frightened Ruth.

Suddenly, a wind came up from nowhere and swept the water high upon the beach. Lightning flashed across the sky as clouds passed in front of the moon. The night became black as pitch. Then, as suddenly as it began, the wind's fury ended. The night was quiet once again. Jon relaxed and Ruth felt his weight upon her. *He needed this,* she thought. *I made him wait too long. It's no wonder he's in such a hurry.*

His hunger fed, Jon withdrew and rolled over. When he did, Ruth felt wetness trickle from her body. He seemed very calm beside her now. *Is this the way making love is supposed to feel?* she thought? *It ended so soon!* She wondered why she didn't feel more than she did. *I know I love him! What's wrong with me?* Ruth's soft weeping broke the silence now.

"What have I done?" she sobbed. "What have I done?'

"Please, Ruth, don't cry? Was it as bad as all that?"

"Oh, no!" She couldn't tell him the truth. "I'm sorry. It's just that I feel so strange. I know I'll look the same tomorrow, but I won't feel the same. And everyone who looks at me will know what I've done. It's like... like my whole life... has changed."

"I'm not sure how making love can change your life." Jon said, as he put his hand on hers. "I know that life without sex is just a dull existence. I know you won't be sorry. Now you're really alive!" He laughed and squeezed her hand.

"Please don't make fun of me, Jon," she pleaded. "It's a new and strange sensation. Sort of... well... sad, and... and... ominous. Like the night turning black?"

"Please, Ruth, now you're being ridiculous." He smirked but his smile slowly faded to a frown. There *was* something strange about it all. Jon sensed it too. Somehow it was different this time. He had no feeling of satisfaction. He had been victorious! He should be proud, reveling in this conquest... but, he couldn't. He couldn't admit it to Ruth, but he did have a sense of guilt about what he'd just done. *What the hell's the matter with me?* he thought, as he ran his fingers through his hair, *It's the same. It's always the same!* He ruthlessly pushed those strange thoughts from his mind, stood up and brushed the sand from of his clothes.

"We better go now, Ruth. I know you don't want to be away from your father all night."

"You're right, of course," she said softly, as she struggled to stand, tears again welling in her eyes.

"You better button yourself up," he said coldly, as he turned, picked up his jacket and walked back towards the car.

Wondering what had happened to change Jon so quickly, she meekly obeyed. She tried to compose herself as she straightened her clothing. Her underpants were full of sand so she shook them twice and put them in her purse. Jon was getting away from her. "Wait." she called as she ran to catch up to him.

They were silent during the drive home. Finally, Ruth broke the silence and asked if he would stop the car for a moment. He tossed the cigarette he had been smoking out of the window and pulled the car over to the curb.

"I hope you don't think less of me now," she said, her voice faltering.

"Why should I think less of you, Ruth?"

"It's just that... well, I was wondering. Did I do the wrong thing, letting you make love to me? You suddenly seem so distant.

"How can something so wonderful be wrong?" he asked.

"Oh, I know I'm probably just being silly, but every girl has dreams of her marriage and the wedding night. Now..." Again, tears reached the surface. "It won't be the same."

"No. Now you won't be surprised." He grinned, intending on having her again, right where they were.

"Will you promise me something, darling?" she asked.

"Anything." He said leaning closer to her thinking about the taste of her body.

"Could we... I mean... well... Let's not do anything again until after we're married."

"Married!" Jon said with a surprised look on his face.

"We are going to get married, aren't we? I know you wouldn't have done this if you didn't love me." Ruth turned his face to hers and looked in his eyes.

"Of course, I love you! It's just that I hadn't thought about marriage, not now anyway. It may not be for some time. After all, with my education over, I need to prepare myself for business. We don't want to rush into anything, do we?"

"No, of course not." She was suddenly hurt.

"And darling," he whispered, "After tonight, it would be pure hell if I couldn't have you anymore. Every time I'm with you, I want you. Haven't I been patient? You kept me waiting a very long time, you know. I'm only a man, after all." He pulled her close to him and kissed her passionately. She struggled from his grasp and pushed him away. "Now what's the matter?" he said, obviously annoyed.

"Everything is happening so fast. I have to think."

"Think later darling, not now." He reached for her again.

"Please, Jon, if you don't mind, I want to walk the rest of the way home."

"That's pretty silly, isn't it? Why would you want to do that? You're still three blocks from home."

"Walking helps to calm me. I need to compose myself. I need to think about this... alone, please."

He shrugged, knowing that he had to play this woman differently from all the others. "All right, but I think it's a little ridiculous."

Ruth opened the door and got out. She shut the door again and stood for a moment by the open window.

"Will I see you tomorrow?" she asked.

"Yes, but if something should turn up, I'll call you at the shop."

"I love you," she whispered.

"See you soon Ruth," he called, as he put the car in drive. She stepped back and watched his taillights disappear down the street.

Slowly she turned and walked toward home. Her mind was in

turmoil. She was happy and frightened at the same time. She could feel her heart pounding.

I know he loves me, she thought. *I know he does! I wonder if it's like this with every girl the first time she does it. Not knowing whether you've done the right thing or not. But how could I refuse him when I love him so much? He must know that it's him I want and not his money.* Her doubtful thoughts soon began to change. *Poor darling, it must be terrible to be so unsure of people. I'm glad it happened! Now we're as close as two people can be! I'll be good for him. I know I will. He'll never be sorry. I won't let him be sorry! Our worlds will become one. I'll fit in, I know. And if I have to change to make him proud of me, I will! I only hope his mother won't object. But then, she must be a wonderful woman to have a son like Jon. I know she'll understand. Oh, please make her understand.*

CHAPTER 3

Ruth was a block from her place now, and she was feeling good again. She was remembering the smell of Jon's aftershave and the feel of his body on hers. The guilt had vanished.

Looking ahead down the street, Ruth saw a group of people standing on the corner at the end of the block. There was a lot of talking going on, but not so loud that they were causing a disturbance. At first, she paid no mind to it. They were always having some sort of party around here and, if it became too hot inside, they would move outdoors and continue the party out on the sidewalk. It was strange, though. They weren't making as much noise and laughing the way they usually did.

It looks like they are standing in front of my building? She thought. Then she saw the ambulance parked at the curb. Her heartbeat quickened. "Father!" she shouted, and ran the rest of the way down the block. The people saw her coming and opened the way for her. As she searched the faces of her neighbors, no one said anything. "Father?" she cried. "Is it my father?"

Mrs. Miller, from the first floor flat, walked to her side and put her hand on Ruth's arm. "I heard a thump on the floor a while ago and I knew you weren't home so I went upstairs to see what happened. You know your father doesn't make much noise when he's there alone. He just sits in that chair by the window."

"I know, I know. Tell me what happened!" Ruth insisted, nervously.

"Well, I went upstairs and I called to him but he didn't answer, and I knocked on the door but he still didn't answer. The door was ajar, so I went in. There he was, lying on the kitchen floor. Well, I didn't know what to do. I didn't want to touch him," she said with a pleading look in her eyes. "You understand, right, Ruthie?" Ruth nodded. "Well, anyway,

I went downstairs again and I called the operator and told her we gotta have a doctor here right away. The ambulance came pretty quick too! The men are up there with your pop now. You better go up there, Ruthie. I'm sorry, honey. We're all sorry." The others murmured something to the affirmative and lowered their heads. Ruth managed a thank you as she turned away and ran into the hall and up the stairs.

Now she knew why everyone was standing out in front. No one wanted to come near her flat because of her father's sickness. They were afraid. They weren't sure what he had. She understood and didn't blame them. It was then that it came to her, that all these people were really good people. In their hearts, they had compassion for others. Being poor didn't make them less valuable. They lacked the strength and determination to rise above their environment. She felt sorry for them. Like her father, they were weak and uneducated but simple, caring human beings.

Ruth stopped in the open doorway and watched as the two men in white jackets put a blanket over her father's face; he was dead. They lifted him onto a stretcher. When they looked up and saw her, one of them spoke. "Are you a relative, Miss?"

"That's my father."

"Sorry, Miss."

They lifted the stretcher and Ruth stepped out of the way as they carried him out. She slowly walked over to a kitchen chair and sat down. There was sympathy in her heart for the man who had suffered here; a man, who at fifty-five wasn't yet old enough to die, but so diseased that now he was dead. She couldn't cry. How could she cry for a man that she hardly knew, a man who had never shown her love? She felt ashamed because the tears wouldn't come, and yet, as she sat there, a feeling of relief, no... of freedom, surged through her. At last it was over. She was now free to pursue her own happiness and live the way she wanted to. At last, her life was her own. The obligation she felt she had to fulfill as a daughter was now over.

All the days that followed seemed like part of a dream. Everyone was sympathetic and, somehow, Ruth managed to say and do everything that was expected of her.

After the funeral, Ruth returned to her father's flat. Her initial reaction was to leave this place as soon as possible but, after thinking it through, she thought better of it. Where was she to go? This place was all she could afford on her salary. She was ashamed of having to live in this neighborhood but at least she didn't have to pretend with Jon. He already knew where she came from, and he still loved her. She decided then that she would remain here until she and Jon could marry. That very afternoon, she began the arduous take of scrubbing everything in the house from top to bottom. In no time at all, the house was more than presentable. She dropped into bed that night exhausted and happy, thinking that tomorrow she would buy some new curtains for the windows.

When she arrived at work the next morning, she was surprised to find a very sympathetic Mr. Baker.

"I'm sorry to hear about your father," he said. "If you need anything or if I can be of some help to you, all you have to do was ask."

She had called him the day after her father died and Mr. Baker told her to take as much time off as she needed. All day, whenever their eyes met, Ruth thought she saw a look of sadness on his face. Apparently, Baker had a more humane side that he'd kept well hidden.

Late in the afternoon, the telephone rang and Ruth answered. It was Jon.

"I'm sorry I couldn't call you sooner, Ruth," he apologized, "but I've been occupied with business affairs that I've been putting off."

"I understand, Jon. I was hoping you'd call, though. I have some bad news." Unexpectedly, a sob tore from her throat. "My father passed away."

"I'm sorry, sweetheart. I wish I could have been there for you. Is there anything I can do? May I see you tonight?"

"Yes, of course, Jon. Will you come upstairs when you get to my house?"

"Are you sure you want me to come up?"

"Yes."

"Will nine o'clock be all right? I don't think I can make it before then."

"That's fine! I'll be waiting for you. Good-bye."

Ruth was excited and happy that evening. She found herself humming as she took her bath and dressed. While she waited, she looked around the house and straightened things here and there. She was satisfied that the place looked clean and comfortable. It wasn't the beautiful place she wanted it to be but it was clean and presentable. The ratty, old chair her father had always sat in was now in the trash in the alley behind the building.

At five minutes after nine, she heard a car stop in front of the house. She ran to the window and looked out. Jon got out of the car and stood on the sidewalk looking up. When he saw her in the window, he walked to the front steps and into the hall. Ruth opened the door and waited for him at the top of the stairs. When he was inside, she closed the door and turned around. All at once, she was in his arms and he was kissing her passionately.

"Oh, Jon", she sighed. *How can this intense emotion be welling up inside me?* she thought. I *was the one who wanted him to promise not to make love to me again.*

"Ruth, Ruth," he whispered, "It's been so long."

"Only a little over a week, darling," she replied, and laughed with joy.

"It can't be! It seems like a year." He held her at arms length, as his eyes drank her in. "God, but you're beautiful," he whispered.

She lowered her eyes. "Please Jon; there you go embarrassing me again."

"You know, I think you really don't realize how lovely you are."

She turned away from him. "Could it be that you are just a little bit prejudice?" she smiled.

"Not about something so obvious," he said.

Ruth slipped her hands from his grasp and walked to the stove. She took the coffee pot from the stove, walked to the sink and filled it with water. "I'll make some coffee," she said.

Jon watched in silence as she prepared the coffee. She set the pot on the stove and was about to turn on the flame when Jon walked over to her and put his hands on her shoulders. He turned her around.

"I can have coffee any time. Right now, all I want is you!" He pulled her into his arms and peppered her with short kisses, while his hands moved over her body hungrily. Ruth was amazed to find that she was responding to his every caress. Her heart was pounding in her chest. She wanted him, too! There was no denying the trembling excitement that flowed from his fingertips into her body.

He whispered in her ear with a tremor in his voice that she knew would be present in her own should she speak. "Where do we go?" he asked.

Slowly, Ruth moved toward the bedroom. Jon was unwilling to let go of her. Ruth switched off the kitchen light as they moved around the table. He followed her into the bedroom.

The moonlight shone through the window, barely illuminating the room so that just the outline of the furniture could be seen. They stood facing each other at the side of the bed. As they slowly became accustomed to the darkened room, their eyes met and held. Jon began to unbutton his shirt, while Ruth unzipped her dress. She let it fall to the floor and stepped out of it. She waited and watched, as Jon removed the rest of his clothes. She had never seen a naked man before. *So that's what was inside of me,* she thought, *what a strange appendage. I'm not sure I like the looks of it. It doesn't seem to be comfortable sticking out like that.*

He was touching her again as his hands reached around her and unhooked her bra. He slid her panties down to her ankles, and after Ruth kicked off her shoes, helped her step out of them.

At last, they were standing there naked. Ruth looked at the body of the man she loved. His muscular frame made her want to run her hands over his entire body, to feel the touch of his bare skin. The moonlight caught parts of her body, with her long hair cascading over her breasts, their little pink nipples pointing up and out. She watched Jon's face as he looked at her, his breath came fast.

Ruth was the first to move. She stepped into him and her slim whiteness curved to follow the mold of his masculine frame. She raised her arms and cupped his face in her hands. She felt the stubble of a new beard as she moved her fingers down his face and onto his shoulders, then over his broad chest. His arms moved around her and crushed her to him, hurting her. He kissed her so hard her lips parted and she felt his tongue penetrate, and she responded. Their bodies were shaking as he picked her up and gently laid her on the bed.

Jon eased his body on top of hers. He began kissing her all over while her hands were busy exploring his nakedness. She felt the protrusion between her legs as he forced them apart. She didn't resist. Once more she became part of him. They were one! A moan escaped her lips as their bodies moved in unison. There was no pain, only the sweet instinctive discovery of passion. Their fever mounted until it was all consuming, and continued until a final release brought nature back to equanimity.

He fell away from her and lay on his back, breathing hard. She remained in her place, satisfied and unashamed. Jon turned then, gathered her into his arms, and held her gently. Ruth kissed his ear and whispered, "I love you, Jon."

His hands moved slowly over her body, fondling her breasts. He kissed her mouth, gently at first, then hungrily. He kissed her breasts, her stomach, her thighs. Needing to come together once again, he was on top of her.

It was a long time later when they separated, weak and exhausted. Their bodies were wet with perspiration and, for a while, it felt cool, as they lie very still and quiet.

"Jon," she whispered, in the darkness.

"Yes, Ruth."

"I'm glad you didn't keep that promise I asked you to make."

"Did you really think I could?"

"No!" she said. "I wouldn't have been strong enough to keep that promise myself."

"You're mine now, Ruth. Always remember that I had you first!"

"And last, my darling," she sighed, as she snuggled against his chest. He held her close. Now, she felt safe and protected. She loved and was loved in return. Her eyes were drowsy. She looked up at Jon and saw that his eyes were closed. She moved a little in his arms and marveled at the exciting sweetness that comes when two bodies are pressed close together. She smiled and let her eyelids close. In a moment, she was asleep.

Several hours later, half-awake, Ruth reached out for him. Her arm moved across the bed. There was no one there beside her. She opened her eyes and raised her head. The first faint rays of morning light were far off on the edge of the window sill. She heard a click as the door closed quietly. He was gone. With a sigh, she snuggled back and gathered the pillow into her arms pretending it was him as her eyes closed again in sleep.

In the weeks that followed, Ruth was happier than she had ever been in her life. Every day was beautiful, but seemingly endless, as her thoughts kept drifting away to the coming night when she would be with the man she loved and their passion would once again be sated. The neighbors were aware of her affair. On occasion, she would meet

Mrs. Miller in the hall or out in front of the building. Mrs. Miller, being the busybody that she was, would ask, "Hi, Ruthie. Are you expecting a visitor again?" Ruth would just shrug and keep walking. She felt a twinge of shame at times but it passed quickly. She knew that she and Jon were meant for each other and when the time was right, they would be married. What difference did it make what others thought, now?

One afternoon, while Ruth was sorting and shelving books, it suddenly occurred to her that it had been a while since she'd had her period. It was something she'd never had to think about before. *I can't be pregnant,* she thought, *Jon always uses protection when we make love.* Then she recalled that first night on the beach. The first time they'd had intercourse, Jon hadn't used anything. There had been the wetness.

She stopped what she was doing and stared into space. A baby! Having a baby was something that should be planned, not this way. Jon would have to be told. Jon! How will he take the news? With all his obligations, this wouldn't be happy news. She thought about all the ways she could break it to him. Talking to herself, she rehearsed what she would say.

"Jon, I'll say, I'm going to have your baby. Jon, I'm going to have our baby."

Saying it out loud made it real and soon, it didn't seem so wrong. *It really won't change anything. Our plans will just have to be expedited.* She felt the current of excitement welling up in her. It really was quite marvelous to be carrying the child of the man she loved.

When Jon arrived that evening, she tried desperately to conceal her excitement. Several times she started to tell him, but the moment wasn't right. She silently kept repeating to herself; *please make him be happy too.* Finally, when it was very late and they were cradled in each other's arms, and his strong body was relaxed, she felt it was the right moment to talk about it.

"Darling," she whispered

"Yes," he murmured.

"I have something to tell you."

"What is it?" he said, sleepily.

"It's about us."

"What about us?'

"Do you think we can be married right away?"

"Ruth, honey, I explained all that to you before," he said, impatiently.

"I know, but things have changed now and it wouldn't be fair."

"What do you mean, fair, fair to whom?"

"Fair to our child, Jon."

"Fair to our..." his eyes opened wide when he heard those words. He raised his head to look at her face. "Fair to our child?" he repeated.

"Yes," she said, smiling, "I'm carrying your baby, Jon."

Jon sat up and drew up his legs. He put his arms around his legs and rested his head on his knees.

Ruth sat up and put her hand on his back. "What is it, Jon?" She was almost in tears. "Aren't you pleased? I know it's overwhelming at first. That's the way I felt when I realized what had happened, but, darling, it really is wonderful. We love each other and there's no reason why we can't be married now. Please, dear, tell me it's going to be all right."

"It's all right, Ruth. It was stupid of me to have let this happen. I should have known better. It was that night on the beach wasn't it?"

"You're disappointed, aren't you, Jon," she said sadly.

"No, of course not." He was unconvincing. Ruth was silent.

"Well, why shouldn't I be disappointed?" he said defensively, as he threw his legs over the side of the bed and got up. He began to dress slowly and deliberately. "Why don't you say something?" he demanded.

Ruth remained silent. Pulling up her knees, she drew the sheet to her chin. When Jon finished dressing, Ruth got out of bed and put on her robe. He came up behind her and put his hands on her shoulders. She turned to face him, her head bowed. He put his hand under her chin and lifted her face to his.

"Forgive me, Ruth. I didn't mean to sound so harsh."

"I understand your anxiety and concern darling," she whispered, "It's just that I didn't expect your reaction. I thought you would be as pleased as I am."

"Ruth, I'm trying to be calm and reasonable." He turned away from her and sat on the edge of the bed. "But you don't understand. It's my mother I'm thinking about. I hate like hell to pull a trick like this on her."

Ruth went to his side and put her hand on his arm. "Perhaps your mother will be hurt at first, but she'll get over it. I know she'll understand."

"You don't know my mother!" he exclaimed, as he stood up and walked to the kitchen. He switched on the light, walked over to the stove, and turned the gas on under the coffeepot. He knew it was the morning's coffee, but he didn't care. He sat down at the table and put his face in his hands. Ruth came out of the bedroom, went to the cabinet, and took down two cups. She set the cups on the table and sat down across from him.

"Jon, it's always frightening when things like this happen, something that wasn't planned. But really, dear, our situation isn't unique. People have experienced this before and they managed to go on."

"Not the Malcolm's," he said flatly.

She got up, took the milk out of the refrigerator, poured their coffee and sat down again. They were both silent for a long time, sipping coffee, lost in their thoughts. Finally, Jon spoke. "Don't worry, Ruth. I'll try to fix things with Mother. We'll work something out."

"I'm not worried, dear. I know you'll take care of things."

He stood up. "I'd better go now. It's pretty late, or should I say early?" He forced a smile.

"You're right, it is very early! Not much point in going to bed." She laughed but it was forced and insincere.

He said good night and gave her a quick kiss on the cheek, then started for the door.

"Jon," she said. He stopped with his hand on the knob and turned to her. "I love you," she said softly. He grinned, gave her a wink, and left, closing the door quietly. In a few moments, Ruth heard the car start and he drove off.

CHAPTER 4

It was late afternoon when Jon awoke. He put on casual clothes and went downstairs. After having lunch out on the terrace, he spent the rest of the day just sitting around thinking. He was relieved that his mother had gone out for the day, not being in the mood for one of her lectures. He tried walking around the grounds for a while, but that didn't help. The dogs started barking as he came close to the kennel but he ignored them. He went back to the house and started to drink.

He was all mixed up, unable to work things out in his mind. He despised himself for letting the situation upset him so, and yet, he couldn't control his emotions. There was no doubt as to what had to be done, but for the first time in his life, he felt the pangs of guilt and remorse. He berated himself for being so stupid as to let this happen.

Telling his mother would be difficult. He knew what her reaction would be. He was afraid to face her. Being incapable of asserting himself against his mother's dominating influence made him angry. He hated his own weakness. Still, the worst part was that he knew he couldn't change. How could he have let his life become so complicated? He knew why! "Because Ruth is so beautiful and the purest thing that I've ever known," he said out loud. The liquor wasn't helping. After several drinks, his thoughts were still racing. He wandered into the parlor and sat on the couch.

When he stood up he swayed a little, and then suddenly, swiped his hand across the coffee table and sent his glass flying across the room. Stumbling upstairs to his room, he threw himself down on the bed and lay there staring up at the ceiling. He must have slept for a while because his mother knocking on the door startled him.

"Jonathan, she called, "are you coming down to dinner?"

"Yes, Mother," he said as he jumped out of bed and rubbed his eyes. He went to the bathroom to splash some cold water on his face before he went downstairs.

They ate in silence until Jon said, "Mother, I wish Dad were here."

"So do I, dear. It's not an easy thing having to make all the decisions. I miss having your father here to share the responsibilities. I thought I would be able to depend more on you now but it seems you're still not ready to take on the responsibility as the man of the house."

Jon hesitated. "There's something I have to tell you, mother."

"What is it, dear?"

"Well, it's about this girl I've been seeing."

"What about this girl? Is she someone I should meet? Is she new in town?"

"No. Not exactly, that is. She... Well..."

"Oh Jon, please don't stammer. If you have something to say, then say it for goodness sake."

"She told me last night that she's going to have a baby."

"I see."

"You're not surprised?"

"Should I be? The way you carry on with the girls in this town is no surprise to anyone. You're a handsome boy and you know it. I'm sure you use that to your advantage. I should be ashamed, but you're my son after all and I love you. Just how long did you think you could carry on this clandestine affair while I remained ignorant?"

"Not long at all, obviously."

"Well, how much is it going to cost me this time?" she demanded.

"I'm not sure that's the answer this time, Mother."

"What do you mean?"

"She...that is... Ruth... well, she's nothing like the others. She's not that kind of girl." Jon stood up and began pacing.

"What do you mean, she's not that kind of girl," Mrs. Malcolm said, angrily, "She's pregnant, isn't she?"

"But Mother," he stopped and put his hands on the table. "She *is* different. I know she's a good girl. That is, she was until I met her." He started pacing around again.

Mrs. Malcolm seemed unmoved by her son's confession. She sat with her usual stoic countenance, picking at her food while watching Jon pace back and forth. Finally, after an awkward silence, she said, "Oh,

I'm certain she is, especially with that background. I must tell you I had my attorney do some research on this girl. Oh, don't look so surprised! I knew you were involved with someone or something for quite a while now. I was just waiting for you to come to your senses."

"I should have known you'd have your nose in it."

"She was raised without the guidance of a mother, influenced by an alcoholic father, then off to an orphanage to be raised with all those other unfortunates, only to return to her old environment, penniless and uneducated. You see the apple doesn't fall far from the tree. She certainly has improved herself," she said sarcastically.

"You can't blame a person for the mistakes their parents make, Mother, just as you can't blame parents for the mistakes their children make. Furthermore, Ruth was brought up very well, and she's not an illiterate person. The only reason she came back was to take care of her dying father. Maybe she was crazy for doing it, but that's the kind of a person she is."

"Do I sense something a little more significant in this relationship? I certainly hope not. I don't recall your being so defensive in the past."

"I have to take my share of responsibility. There was always reason for doubt with the others. I could never be sure, but I'm sure this time, Mother. I know the child she carries is mine. She was a virgin until..."

"Don't tell me you expect to receive my blessing along with my consent to marry this girl?"

"I know better!"

"Tell me, Jon. Are you in love with this girl?"

"I didn't think I was but I'm not sure."

"And you still don't!"

"I don't know."

"I said you still don't," she insisted. Jon didn't answer. "Don't you see, Jon, dear?" Her voice became sophisticatedly tender. "She has played on your sympathies."

"I know you'd like to believe that, but I've never met anyone more sincere," he said defensively.

"My dear, when one is playing for high stakes, you would be surprised at the sincerity that one can acquire."

"How well I know," he murmured.

"You do realize, my dear that marriage to this girl is definitely out of the question. After your father and your grandfather before him worked so hard to put us in the position we are in today, it would be a travesty to bring a nobody into the family. Why, what would everyone think? Besides, Jon, you know you're not ready for marriage. You're young and headstrong, with the impatience of youth. If you rush into this thing, you'll regret it for the rest of your life. When this is over, you will be able to joke about it with your friends. If you marry this girl, it'll be whispered about in secret. We'll be the talk of the town. How will I face everyone?"

"Oh course, how would you face everyone?"

She hesitated and her voice became soft again. "I don't want to hurt you, darling, but you realize it's for your own good that I say these things to you".

Jon, condescendingly, hanging his head, replied "I realize it's my welfare you're interested in, Mother."

"I knew you would understand, and in the future, you'll be convinced that you acted wisely. I love you, Jon. You're all that I have in this world that means anything to me." Mrs. Malcolm heaved a sigh of relief and rose from the table. "It seems I've lost the desire to eat any more," she said. "Shall we have some coffee in the parlor, dear?"

"As you wish, Mother."

Mrs. Malcolm rang for Matthew and ordered their coffee.

"Well, dear," she said, after the coffee had been brought in, "I'm glad we have this thing settled." She handed Jon his coffee and then filled her own cup. "Now, then, the only thing left to do is to talk to the girl and find out how much she will take."

"How will you arrange it?" Jon said nervously. "I don't want to be the one to tell her."

"I'll take care of everything, dear. All you have to do is invite her here tomorrow evening. Tell her I'd like to meet her. I'll handle it from there. You can be sure, my dear, that when she hears the generous offer I'm prepared to make, she won't hesitate to accept it."

"I hope you're right, Mother. I still have my doubts"

"Of course, I'm right. Years from now, you'll thank me for interceding."

When Jon arrived at Ruth's place early the next evening, he told her that they would be going to his home that evening. "I've explained everything to my mother and she wants to meet you."

"Jon," Ruth answered with obvious excitement in her voice, "even though that's what I've been waiting for, I'm not ready to face your mother just yet. I need a little time to think about what to say and do. It's such short notice," she pleaded. "Does it have to be tonight?"

"My mother is waiting," Jon explained, "and since your meeting is inevitable, it might as well be now." Ruth couldn't dissuade him, so she reluctantly agreed to go.

"Let me freshen up," she said. "Should I change, dress up a little?"

"You look fine, Ruth, but let's hurry. I don't want to keep Mother waiting."

During the drive to Jon's home, Ruth deluged him with questions.

"How did your mother take the news? Does she seem to understand? Will there be anyone else there?"

Jon gave evasive and ambiguous answers, finally saying, "It'll be fine. Don't worry."

As they stood in the large foyer, Ruth was awed by the beautiful, spacious home. She gawked at the huge crystal chandelier above the handsome, curved staircase. Jon took her arm and led her through several rooms and out onto the terrace. Ruth kept turning her head, mesmerized by the handsome décor and expensive furniture, trying to take in everything as she passed.

"Mother thought you'd be more comfortable out on the terrace. She assured me that the informal setting would put you at ease. It's a clear, cool night with a refreshing breeze." After Ruth was seated on the expensive couch, he said, "Can I get you something to drink, Ruth?

"No, thank you, Jon. I'm too nervous right now."

"Make yourself comfortable and I'll tell Mother we're here. I won't be a minute."

"Jon, please don't leave me alone with her."

"Don't worry," he said, and went inside.

It wasn't long before Mrs. Malcolm appeared in the doorway. Ruth began to rise from her chair when she entered.

"Please, don't get up, my dear," she said. Ruth sat down again. Mrs. Malcolm walked to the chair opposite Ruth and sat down. For a few seconds she just looked at Ruth without saying anything.

Ruth thought, *'hello,' or, 'happy to meet you.' would have been nice. I'll bet she's making mental notes on everything about me that doesn't measure up to her standards.*

"Would you care for a drink, Miss Lawson?" Mrs. Malcolm asked

"No thank you, Ma'am."

"Something cool, perhaps?"

"Nothing, thank you."

The woman sitting across from Ruth was very impressive. Ruth estimated her height to be about five foot three, and she carried herself straight. A buxom woman, she wore a white, lace-covered cotton gown that flowed when she walked. On her wrist she wore a diamond-emerald bracelet, with matching earrings, and two large diamonds on perfectly manicured hands. Her hair, more gray than brown, was neatly coifed on top of her head. Her face was almost expressionless except for the hint of a smile, which played on her thin lips. Her eyes were cold and penetrating. Her austere, commanding nature was evident. Ruth felt very uneasy. The hope of Jon's mother being a pleasant gracious woman was suddenly shattered as she faced this woman.

"Well, my dear, shall we get right to the point?" Mrs. Malcolm asked.

"The point?" Ruth was puzzled.

"Yes, Jon has told me everything."

Ruth looked around for Jon, but he had not returned. *Jon, where are you?* "You have been seeing my son for quite some time now."

"I love Jon, Mrs. Malcolm."

"Yes, I'm sure you do. However, you do realize that you and Jon are... well... What can I say? You're socially incompatible."

"I am aware that I've been less fortunate than Jon," Ruth replied. "I'm not wealthy and have had a less than normal childhood but one has no power in the accident of birth."

"That's quite true, my dear, but you must understand that we have a station to maintain in this town and your marriage to Jon would be, to say the least, improper in our position."

"But I love Jon, Mrs. Malcolm, and he loves me," Ruth insisted.

"Are you quite sure of that, my dear?'

"Of course, I'm sure!" She hesitated; the question had been so unexpected. "Jon wouldn't have told me if it weren't true."

"Really, Miss Lawson. You can't be that naïve, can you? You do understand that most young men experience a period in their lives where they indulge in innocent promiscuity. If you prefer a more common expression, they sow wild oats'."

"Are you trying to make me believe that I've been nothing more than a passing experience to Jon?" Ruth was shocked and horrified. How could this woman be so composed, so insensitive!

"I'm very sorry, my dear".

Ruth rose from her chair. "I don't believe you," she said. "You're just saying this because you think I'm not good enough for Jon. You don't want us to get married, so you're trying to hurt me by telling me all these lies. Well, I refuse to believe you. I'll have to hear it from Jon and I know I never will! Especially, not now!"

"You mean now that you're going to have a child?"

Ruth just stared at her.

"Yes," Mrs. Malcolm said, very calmly, "I know that you also profess it to be Jon's child."

Ruth sank down in her chair. "How dare you?" Ruth felt like she'd been slapped in the face!

"Oh, come now, Miss Lawson, did you really think I would have no knowledge of all this? Do you think this is the first situation of this kind that I've had to deal with?" The woman chuckled humorlessly. "No, my dear, this isn't the first indiscretion I've had to untangle for my son."

"How can you be so cruel?" Ruth cried.

"On the contrary, I love my son very much and I'm only interested in his happiness. If I allowed this marriage to take place I would be shirking my duty as a mother. I cannot condone exogamy. Nor will I see Jon forced into a union with someone he does not love simply because there is a child involved."

"But he does love me! Why don't you ask him to come here? Let *him* tell you how he feels."

"My dear, Jon has told me exactly how he feels. I was hoping to spare you the pain of hearing it from him."

Ruth stood up again. "If what you say is true, Mrs. Malcolm, then nothing will be spared me."

"Now, now, Miss Lawson, we don't need melodrama. You naturally are frantic about this whole thing but I'm sure it'll ease your heartache to know that I'm prepared to be very generous in the financial settlement I'm about to offer you." Ruth glared at her all the while she spoke. "Before we continue, tell me just how much you have in mind?" Mrs. Malcolm asked.

Ruth was furious. "I don't want your money, you vicious, evil old woman! You think I had this... this blackmail planned from the start, don't you? Well, I didn't! How your shallow mind could conceive that someone would bring a child into this world for profit is beyond my comprehension. Only a wicked mind would be so cynical and calculating."

"I'm sure you would know more about that than I do," Mrs. Malcolm replied calmly.

Ruth heaved a sigh of exasperation. "And I had you pictured so differently." Then, looking right in her face, she said, "All I can think of to say to you now is, as you sow, you will surely reap!" Ruth turned and started to leave, fighting to hold back her tears.

"Please wait, Ms. Lawson! I'll have my driver take you home."

Ruth was too shaken to even hear the woman. She wanted to get away as fast as she could. There was only a moment's hesitation before Mrs. Malcolm spoke again.

"I'll be waiting for your call. We'll talk again."

Jon was standing in the shadows just outside the door. Ruth saw him and went to him, putting her arms around him. His arms just hung by his side.

"Jon, did you hear your mother's horrible accusations?" she cried

"Yes."

"Tell me all those things she said aren't true, that I mean more to you than she realizes. Tell her you love me." She was crying now, pleading with him for reassurance. He couldn't look her in the eye. "Darling," she pleaded, "tell her you love me! Tell her!" Her voice sounded almost hysterical. "Jon, you know it's your baby I carry. It's been you from the start, only you darling. You know that." She waited. "Why don't you say something?" She saw the confused look on his face.

Jon looked into her pleading eyes and saw the tears rolling down her cheeks. "Ruth," he said softly, putting his hands on her arms. Then, he saw his mother watching through the doorway, her eyes cold and threatening. He quickly dropped his arms, raised his head and looked away.

"I'm so sorry, Ruth," he whispered. Beads of sweat appeared on his forehead.

Ruth took a step back and could only stand there, staring at him. She could hardly believe what she had heard. His uncaring attitude crushed her spirit. If he'd slapped her face, she couldn't have been more surprised. Yet, standing there looking at him, she wanted to rush back into the sanctuary of his arms. She needed to feel the protection she had always felt in his arms.

Why is this happening to me? she thought *"This has to be a horrible dream,"* she then said it. "This can't really be happening to me." She looked at Mrs. Malcolm then turned and looked back at Jon. His lips parted as if he was about to say something, but he didn't. Ruth walked, as if in a trance, to the front door. The house didn't look the same any more. The furniture had lost its charm and the rooms had suddenly turned cold. She thought she heard Jon call to her and then his mother's voice telling him to be quiet.

Ruth staggered down the long driveway. Blinded by tears, she kept losing her footing on the gravel drive. Stumbling along, she came to the main highway that would take her back to town. She wasn't crying now but was still in a daze and hurting so badly that she wondered why the tears had stopped.

She was aware enough to avoid the ditch on the side of the road as she walked, although she had to stay close to avoid being hit by the passing traffic. Several cars slowed down, their drivers asking if she needed a ride. She ignored them, afraid of what she would be letting herself in for, and just kept walking. As luck would have it, a taxi came along. Ruth waved to the driver and he stopped. "Please, can you give me a ride?" she called.

"I have a fare waiting for me, lady," he told her. He looked at her disheveled appearance; her red eyes and tear stained face and didn't have the heart to leave her there. "I can drive you into town," he said, "but you'll have to take public transportation from there."

Ruth's feet hurt so badly now, she could hardly walk. "Thank you so much." Once inside the cab, she began to cry again. The kindness of this person was almost too much to bear. It was something that she needed but couldn't seem to handle.

CHAPTER 5

There were many times in the months that followed when Ruth wished she could die, but the new life growing within her was reason enough to want to live. While every day was more unbearable than the last, the nights were agonizingly lonely. To live with this guilt and shame was torture enough but the worst part was being alone. There was no one to whom she could turn. There was no one to talk to and nowhere to run. She knew that she had sinned and she would have to suffer because of it. That she had lost the respect of some of her neighbors was evident in their faces whenever they passed. They would turn their heads to avoid looking at her. It was more than she could stand.

Christmas came and went without a trace of having been there, no cards, no calls, nothing but loneliness. It was painful to see happy people come into the shop to buy books for their loved ones.

One cold January evening, as Ruth prepared for bed, it became clear to her that she had to go away, not only from this neighborhood but this town. There was nothing left for her here. Each night, as she climbed into bed, it was impossible not to think of Jon and the love that they'd shared in this room. That was over. Now she had the child to consider. She wouldn't allow her baby to share its mother's disgrace. Ruth decided she would go to a big city, perhaps, Chicago. Why she picked Chicago, she didn't know. Maybe it was from an old article in a newspaper about a group of people starting a collection to keep an old lady from losing her house that warmed Ruth? People must be very kind to one another there. Ruth would have no friends there to point fingers at her situation. Ruth didn't know what she would do when she got there. All she could think of was that she could lose herself in a big city where no one knew her and no one would ever find her.

It was too late now to consider her pride. When Saturday morning came, she called Mrs. Malcolm. She listened as the phone rang. Once, twice, three times. In a way, she hoped Jon would answer the phone. How she longed to hear his voice again, but what would she say? What would he say? It didn't matter; the voice at the other end of the line wasn't his.

"Hello," Mrs. Malcolm said

"This is Ruth Lawson, Mrs. Malcolm."

"How are you, dear?" the woman's voice was cold. Maybe she thought she sounded friendly.

"Things aren't going too well for me now."

"I'm sorry to hear that dear."

Ruth came right to the point. "If you still want to help me through this pregnancy, I would be very grateful."

"I will do what I can, dear." Ruth thought she sounded smug. Mrs. Malcolm continued, "A check will be delivered to you in the morning."

"I sincerely thank you, Mrs. Malcolm. Good-bye."

The very next day a messenger came to the house and Ruth signed for an envelope. When the messenger left, Ruth opened the envelope. It surprised Ruth to see that Mrs. Malcolm had given her cash. She couldn't believe her eyes when she counted out five thousand dollars. She was stunned! This was so much more than she expected. "Five hundred dollars would have been enough for a train ticket with enough to spare until a job could be found. Ruth instantly felt indignant. "That nasty woman is treating me like a whore and paying me for services rendered."

She crumpled the money in her fist and threw the bills hard against the wall and began pacing. When she walked into the bedroom, she could almost smell Jon's cologne all around her. Her awareness of being alone was so overwhelming that she threw herself on the bed and burst into tears. "Jon, why did you lie?" She cried until she fell into an exhausted sleep.

Morning found Ruth still sprawled across the bed. It was the cold that woke her. She rolled herself up in the covers and tried to come awake. Looking out of the window, she saw that it was snowing. The huge flakes floated down ever so gently, some of them melting as they touched the windowpane.

How confident they are in their journey from heaven to earth, she thought. *They know where they came from and where they are going. I wish I knew what fate has in store for me. Will I ever be happy again?*

She finally dragged herself out of bed and walked to the kitchen. Her eyes fell on the money strewn all over the floor. All through her toast and coffee, she stared at the money; she was still bristling with hostility. Finally, she sat up straight and heaved a sigh. Her mind was clearer now. She stood up and chided herself as she walked around the table.

"Of course you're being paid off, you fool!" She was talking to herself. "Who do you think you are? You're in no position to be proud. Take the money and be quiet. It's just a drop in the bucket to her, anyway."

She dropped to her knees and gathered up the crumpled bills. Returning to her chair, she straightened each one and put most of the money back in the envelope, keeping only five hundred dollars. Tears filled her eyes again so she couldn't see clearly. Putting her head down on her arms, her body racked with sobs as she released the last bit of frustration and rejection.

"This is it", she said and started packing her clothes. "I'll leave and this will all be behind me. I've got two people to take care of now."

That evening, when the taxi came to take her to the train station, Ruth closed the door behind her, not bothering to lock it, and walked away. Without a word to anyone, she left her flat for the last time.

Ruth had the driver stop at the Malcolm residence on the way to the station. She hurried out of the taxi, ran up the steps to the house, dropped the envelope in the mailbox, and hurried back to the cab.

An hour later she sat on one of the long wooden benches in the train station waiting for the ten o'clock train. Her suitcase held a few changes of clothing and a picture of her and Jon, taken by a photographer as they'd walked along the beach one day.

Ruth looked at her watch. It was only eight forty-five. She walked over to the newsstand and bought a magazine for thirty-five cents. As she turned the pages, it came to her that perhaps one day she would wish desperately to have those thirty-five cents back. She began to smile. It was such a tragic thought that it made her laugh and at the same time brought tears to her eyes. *Oh God,* she thought, *could anything be worse? Here I am five months pregnant, no husband, no family, and no place to go. How could anything be worse?* Her thoughts returned to Mrs. Malcolm. *Why did I return most of the money? My foolish pride, naturally. I was a fool to return it. Well, it's too late now. My decision is irrevocable.* She knew the real reason for returning the money. That tiny spark of bitterness and pride she couldn't eject from her heart kept her from keeping it all.

She hoped that, perhaps a long time from now, they would remember all the hurt they'd caused. Maybe, they would be sorry for treating her so shabbily. Maybe, they would wish to make it up to her and Jon's child; hopefully, then they would reap what they had sown.

All at once, she began to shiver. It wasn't from the cold but rather it was like the strange sensation she had felt that very first time with Jon on the beach. *What is this strange awareness? Is it a foreboding? No! A warning! But of what? The night plays strange tricks on one's mind. It's best to be calm. For all you know, the worst is yet to come.* "Oh, no," she said quietly.

With a start, she returned to the present and the words and pictures in the magazine. She glanced around to see if anyone had heard her. There were four people sitting far enough away that they couldn't hear her. The girl behind the counter was looking the other way as she straightened the magazine rack. The ticket agent didn't even raise his head. Ruth continued to turn pages, trying to keep her mind on the pictures in the magazine and what she was struggling to read. She thought of her job and Mr. Baker. She never called to say she was quitting and that she was going to leave town. He never knew she was pregnant. He probably would have looked down on her like the rest of the people do when a girl gets pregnant and she's not married. She knew he would find someone to replace her. Jobs weren't that easy to find.

From out of the night, there came a long low whistle. Ruth looked at her watch. It was nine fifty-five and the train was pulling into the station. Ruth buttoned her coat, pulled her scarf tightly about her neck, and walked out onto the platform. The train was straining to brake. Even after it had stopped, it seemed anxious to continue its long, endless journey. A light snow that was falling steadily left the trees and rooftops glistening in the moonlight. For a moment, Ruth hesitated as her eyes traced the familiar surroundings. Somewhere out there, beyond the great expanse of city lights, lay Brandon Hill, Brandon Hill and Jon. The conductor shouted, "All board," and Ruth hurried to the steps of the train. The train huffed its way out of the station. As quickly as it had arrived, it was as hurriedly departing.

Once inside, Ruth found a seat and settled down for the long ride ahead. Before the night was over, however, Ruth found herself wishing she had bought a Pullman sleeper. With each clickety clack of the wheels she became more uncomfortable. At this hour, the car wasn't too crowded so the passengers were able to stretch themselves across the seats in a vain effort to catch a little sleep. Ruth guessed that she must be on a milk train because it ground to a stop at each small station. Not a single sleeper's head bobbed up, half awake with curiosity about why the train had stopped yet again.

The train was moving again. A shabby little old lady stood in the doorway. She looked around at all the passengers until her eyes rested on Ruth. She smiled crookedly as she walked over to the seat on which Ruth was sitting and sat down beside her. She carried a worn out, brown, paper, shopping bag, which she shoved between her legs. Ruth tried to remain detached and turned to look out the window. The snow blew heavily against the windows. Outside, the dark countryside flew by. Ruth could see nothing but her own reflection in the glass.

"Are you traveling alone, honey?" The old lady asked, trying to make conversation.

Ruth turned her head and smiled at the old lady. "Yes I am," she said.

Ruth caught a faint odor about the old lady, which made her shift a little closer to the window. She could see the many worn spots in the lady's old black coat, which was covered with lint and fuzz. When she smiled back, she revealed a mouthful of half-rotten teeth, with one missing in the front.

"Are you going far, honey?"

"Chicago," Ruth replied.

"Oh, my, you have a long way to go, don't you?"

"I guess so."

"Are you just gonna visit, or do your folks live there, dearie?"

"My family lives there," Ruth lied. The old lady annoyed Ruth enough to wish she would move to one of the other seats.

"That's nice," said the old lady. "Looks like you're gonna give'em a little surprise, like there's three of us in this seat, right?" With that, she put her hand on Ruth's stomach. Ruth cringed and turned her body as she pushed the old lady's hand off.

"Please, don't do that."

"I'm sorry, honey, but I think babies are so precious. I don't have any kids of my own. I'm all alone in the world you know. I don't have anyone who cares about me. I try hard to keep going but you know nobody gives a damn about an old lady. I have to take any kind of work I can get and even that isn't easy to find."

The old lady rattled on and on about every problem she'd ever had and Ruth could only respond with a nod of her head or a polite yes or mm umm. It didn't seem to matter if anyone was listening or not. The old lady just kept talking.

"I'm feeling a little sleepy now," Ruth finally broke in.

"Well, you just go right ahead and sleep, honey. Don't let me keep you awake. When I meet a nice person like yourself, I kinda get carried away with my talkin'. I'll shut up now so's you can sleep a while."

"It would certainly be nice to stretch out a bit." Ruth continued. Hoping the old lady would get the hint and move.

"It sure is kinda cramped in these seats, ain't it? Well, you just rest your head on my shoulder, if you like. I won't mind at all."

"Oh, no! That's kind of you but I'm as comfortable as I'll ever be in these seats."

The old lady stopped talking. Ruth faced the window and put her head on her arm. She closed her eyes and resigned herself to the fact that the old lady would probably remain in her seat for the duration of her journey. Ruth hoped it would be a short one. It never occurred to Ruth to tell the lady to move to another seat. Most of the seats had people who were stretched out taking up the whole seat.

I'm sure I would feel better if I could get away from this smelly old lady.

The old lady tapped Ruth's shoulder "Are you more comfortable now dear?"

"Yes, thank you." *Don't talk to her. She might never leave.*

Ruth opened her eyes briefly to see the old lady reach down and remove a dirty ball of yarn and two knitting needles from the paper bag. Ruth promptly turned her head in disgust, rested her head on her arm and closed her eyes again.

It was some time before the jostling train woke her. As the train screeched to a halt, Ruth opened her eyes. For a moment, she remained still in that fleeting state of contentment between sleep and wakefulness. When she tried to move, she groaned with pain. Her body was stiff from the cramped position she had been in for so long. Looking around, she saw that she was alone in the seat.

Thank goodness that old lady is gone, she thought. She sat up and stretched, moving her head from side to side. Her shoulder was sore too. It was almost dawn as the first rays of light were breaking over the horizon. The little station looked deserted. Outside, she heard someone yell, "See you next trip, Joe," as the train began to move again. Ruth automatically felt for her purse, which she had held in her lap. It wasn't there. She looked down at the floor. Halfway under the seat, lay her purse. As she picked it up most of its contents fell out. Ruth picked up everything and put it back in her purse.

Suddenly, she wondered why it was open. She would never leave her purse open. Frantically, she began to search through her purse to see if everything was there. *Oh no! The inner change purse was missing!*

Ruth searched through the purse again. She turned it over and dumped its contents out onto the seat. It wasn't there. She looked under the seat again, this time on her hands and knees. "Oh my God", she said, and remembered the old lady.

What was I thinking of to allow her to sit next to me? She must have taken my purse. Ruth, are you ever going to learn that you can't trust everyone?

Just then, the conductor entered the car. Ruth jumped up and hurried to him.

"Did you see an old lady get off here?" she shouted.

"Why, no Miss. No one got off here."

"Are you sure?" she cried.

"Yes ma'am, I'm sure. Is something wrong?"

"Have we made any stops between this one and Mayfield?"

"Yes, Miss, we've been making stops all night."

"Oh no, it just can't be."

"But it is, Miss. We always make those stops."

"Oh, I'm sorry, I didn't mean that."

"Did you fall asleep and miss your station?"

"No sir." Tears began to well up in her eyes. "An old lady boarded the train at the stop after Mayfield. She sat next to me and just now, when I woke up, I discovered that all my money is gone."

"By gosh, lady, I'm awful sorry to hear that. I hate to admit it but that sort of thing has been done before. You know you should hide your money or other valuables somewhere secure when you're traveling. You never know what kind of people you're liable to run into when you travel alone."

"I know now, sir." Ruth wiped her eyes. There were several people still in the car but, with heads down; they ignored what was taking place. Was it to lessen Ruth's embarrassment, or because no one wanted to get involved.

"Have you got any relatives you could wire for more money, or are you on your way home?"

"I'll be all right Sir. I'm on my way home," she lied again.

"If I can be of some help to you, miss..."

"No, no thank you. You're very kind but I'll be all right."

Ruth turned and started back to her seat. Suddenly, the train picked up speed and began to rock back and forth. This made Ruth lose her balance so she quickly grabbed the back of the nearest seat. Holding on to each one she passed, she slowly, made her way back to her place.

She stared out the window for a long time, her mind numb to all emotion or feeling. Maybe later, when she had time to think about her predicament, she would be able to feel something, but at this moment, she couldn't feel anything. *Get some backbone, Ruth. Stop this childish crying all the time. It solves nothing.*

Slowly, her brain began to function again as she watched the bleak, snow-covered scenery passing by.

All that had happened in the last few months came back to her. Hadn't it been only yesterday that she'd left her protected, happy life with the sisters?

How was it possible that so much could happen to change my life so drastically in so short a time? She thought.

As the fields and towns flew by, she watched a new day being born right before her eyes. There was no yesterday and there might not be tomorrow. There was only now! The birth of a new day was struggling to live, just as her child would soon be struggling to be born.

Her child, her child and Jon's! A feeling of despondency flooded through her with the realization that her child would never know his father.

Jon, oh Jon, did you struggle to be born, you poor pitiful creature, or did your mother order you out? Did she demand, with her hubristic breeding, that you obey? Did she promise she would protect you from all evil women who profess to carry a child of love within their inferior bodies? Poor Jon, how could you not know that I loved you so?

"May heaven help me to raise my son with sound judgment, that he may grow strong in mind as well as in body?" she whispered to the windowpane. *My son,* she thought. It seemed to just pop into her mind. "My son," she whispered. She smiled and thought, *it comes so naturally to my lips. Wait a minute. It could be a girl. Yes.* She smiled. *It could be my daughter.* The train clicked on. Soon her journey would be over. No! Her journey into the mysterious unknown was just about to begin.

CHAPTER 6

It didn't take long for Jon Malcolm to at least seem to return to his routine. In a few short weeks, he was in full swing again. Dates, parties, drinking, and seductions were again a familiar pastime. Only now, he seemed to be moving at a more furious pace. If he had an occasional qualm regarding his coerced treatment of Ruth, it was soon forgotten, or perhaps, camouflaged with another martini and another girl? All this kept Mrs. Malcolm in a constant state of frustration and anxiety. She knew she was losing her hold on him. Jon had become increasingly more distant and uncontrollable.

It was late Saturday or, to be more precise, early Sunday, when Jon returned from another night on the town. Without deviating from the usual, he sped into the icy driveway and, after nearly hitting a tree, screeched the black Cadillac to a halt. He slowly opened the door and practically fell out of the car. He was feeling exceptionally brave in his drunken stupor, so, like many other times before, instead of going into the house, he decided to visit the dogs. Leaving the car door open, he staggered and stumbled across the back lawn in the direction of the kennels. Once there, he would enjoy the near sadistic pleasure of tormenting the animals.

Because of his frequent drunken visits, the dogs had become vicious beasts when Jon was around and the mere smell or sight of Jon would send them into a fury.

Jon's father had been a lover of animals but Jon had never shared that love. In the early days of Jon's youth, his father had several thoroughbred horses stabled in back. Mr. Malcolm had tried to instill some enthusiasm for them in Jon by encouraging interaction with the animals. He hoped that learning to care for and animal would initiate understanding, thereby love. Nothing worked so Mr. Malcolm stopped trying.

Later, because of changing times and the fact that Mr. Malcolm had begun to travel frequently, the horses were sold. They were replaced with champion Dobermans, which required less care and smaller quarters.

Mrs. Malcolm had never shared her husband's enthusiasm for animals, so after Mr. Malcolm's death she sold all but two of the dogs. These two Dobermans were kept only for show and to prove to the people in their circle that she respected her husband's memory by keeping them. Another reason they were allowed to stay was because they were very good watchdogs, which helped to mitigate the distaste Mrs. Malcolm had for them.

Jon had never liked the dogs. His mother's distaste for animals had been passed on to him in the form of hate and fear. He took pleasure in teasing them. Consequently, when the mood suited him, he would sneak out to the kennels and tease them. The dogs' trainer, Jim Mc Murray, was the only one who could control the dogs now. They loved him and obeyed him, but only so long as Jon stayed away and the scent of him never reached the animals.

Before the high wire fence surrounding the kennels came completely into view, Jon could hear the animals begin to snarl and growl. When he reached the fence, the dogs were already throwing themselves against the fence, showing their teeth and leaping frantically trying to surmount it. Jon stood there laughing and looked around for something he could use to tease them. There was snow on the ground, so he made snowballs and threw them at the dogs. Spotting a fallen tree branch, he picked it up and poked at them through the wire. Of course, the branch had to be long enough so Jon didn't have to stand too close. The more frenzied they became, the more Jon laughed. He was brave only as long as there was a fence between him and the beasts.

It wasn't long before Jon became bored with the whole thing. The game lost its excitement and proved to be too strenuous for him in his condition. His stomach was upset now. He threw down the branch and started for the house, throwing up on the way.

He went around the house back to the front door. He fumbled with his keys, finally, getting the door open he staggered upstairs to his room. Not caring that he'd left the car door open.

The screeching of brakes had awakened Mrs. Malcolm. She sat up in bed and listened. When all became quiet, she thought Jon had come in and was on his way to bed. She was about to lie back down when she heard the dogs begin to bark. At first, she thought it might have been a burglar? Almost immediately, she was sure that Jon had again gone to the kennels to bedevil the dogs. When the dogs didn't stop barking, she got out of bed, put on her robe and slippers and started down the stairs. She was determined to demand that Jon stop what he was doing.

She didn't know that Jon was in his room now but, the dogs had not calmed down as yet. She walked through the kitchen to the rear of the house and opened the back door. A cold wind rushed in at her, so she quickly closed the door. She knew going out in only her robe would be very unwise so she started back through the house to get a coat. On her way back through the kitchen, she passed the closet where the door stood ajar. One of Jon's winter jackets was hanging on a hook inside the closet door. She took the jacket down and placed it around her shoulders. Clutching the coat close about her, she went back to the door and out into the night.

"Jon!" she called, "Jon, come into the house this instant!" She stood for a moment waiting for his reply but heard only the barking of the dogs. They were still upset over Jon's visit but were beginning to calm down.

He can't hear me above this wind and the dogs, she thought, and proceeded towards the kennels. The dogs again went crazy and started throwing themselves against the fence. As they kept hitting the section where the gate was attached, the old latch began to give way. Mrs. Malcolm came through the hedges just as the lock broke loose. The dogs, as if bewildered by their sudden freedom, stopped barking and stood still for a few seconds. They then bolted towards the hated scent of the jacket that stood before them.

Mrs. Malcolm screamed in terror, as they leapt upon her, knocking her to the ground. She screamed in pain as their fangs dug into her legs and her body. She flailed her arms wildly in a vain attempt to shield her face from the iron jaws and slashing white teeth. One of the dogs went for her neck, its fangs penetrating and ripping the flesh. Blood began to run and the screaming ended but the dogs continued to claw and tear chunks of flesh from the now dead woman. Finally, their energy spent, and their mouths dripping with the blood of their enemy, they quietly crept back to the safety of their kennel.

Jon's loud snoring echoed through the quiet house. He hadn't heard any of the ruckus that he'd initiated.

CHAPTER 7

The train passed through the poorest section of each town as the tracks ran parallel to the highway. There were bare fields, an occasional shopping area and apartment buildings. There were miles of dense trees and, every so often, the trees opened up to reveal small towns, gone as quickly as they'd appeared.

Now the view from the window showed a herd of cows in a fenced pasture. The train passed a refinery that was lit up like a Christmas tree. Then it passed a huge electrical plant, whose tall chimneys belched a steady cloud of black smoke. It passed a grain elevator and, next to it, a boarded-up gas station. It sped through a field of above-ground pipes and huge round tanks of pressurized natural gas. The train continued through a wonderland of industrial waste on the Illinois/Indiana state line. It rocked and shimmied through China town making slow progress through city intersections.

The train was full now. The holiday season was in full swing. College students, parents with kids and older people were on their way to celebrate with family and friends.

The train approached Canal Street. As he walked through the cars, the conductor shouted, "Next stop, Union Station,"

The train bumped through a switch onto another track and crept through the tunnels of Union Station until it came to a halt. The passengers were standing in the aisle with their bulky luggage, poking and pushing each other in an anxious attempt to exit the train as quickly as possible. Ruth decided to remain safely in her seat until she could alight with ease.

When she stepped off the train, Ruth was amazed by the size of the station. It was bigger than the park in Mayfield. She had never seen so many people gathered together in one place and had no idea which way to go. Soon, she was caught up in the throng of moving people. She had no time to ponder how to get out of the train station. Both the train and the station had been overheated. The station smelled of beef, newsprint, beer and the lurking smells of unclean bodies and perfumed lotions. The vending machine spillovers of peanuts and popcorn crunched underfoot. She clutched her handbag closer to her and tightened her grip on the suitcase that held all her worldly belongings. She was headed toward the nearest exit, whether she wanted to go that way or not. When she stepped outside, the sharp wind blew away every trace of the smells.

Once outside, she gawked like a schoolgirl at the busy intersection. All of the activity was mesmerizing. Somebody spoke as the crowd passed her by. "A front's coming through, I just know it." A little farther on someone said, "I hear this is going to be an unseasonably mild winter."

Ruth chose a direction and began walking slowly down the street. Looking everywhere, she couldn't stop gawking, trying to see everything. The unfamiliar surroundings were fascinating but a little frightening. She spent her first hour in a big city just following the crowd.

There was a little snack shop at the end of the block called Barney's Biting Beauties. It had been a long time since Ruth had eaten and the neon hamburger sign blinking in the window looked very appetizing to her. She went inside and sat down in a booth at the far end of the diner. It wasn't a busy hour. There were only five other people in the place, a young couple in a booth and paying attention only to each other, two men that were having a heated discussion, and an older woman at the counter. A short plump waitress with bleached blond hair walked over to her.

"What'll ya have?" Blondie asked

"I'll have coffee and a hamburger, please."

"With or without onions?"

"Oh, without, I guess."

"Will there be anything else?'

"No, thank you," Ruth said, glad that the waitress wasn't ready for conversation.

It felt good to sit down in a warm place. Her feet were cold. Much of the snow had turned to slush on the sidewalks. While she waited for her food, Ruth wondered how far she'd walked. It had seemed like many blocks. When her food arrived, Ruth ate gustily. When she finished, she continued to sit and sip her coffee. She was calm but tired. Time seemed to move slowly. She had nothing to do and nowhere to go. Like entering a long dark tunnel, depression and loneliness closed in about her.

The lunch hour had arrived and, before long, almost every seat in the place was occupied. Ruth felt conspicuous sitting so long and taking up a booth when the place was filling with others waiting to eat. She knew it was time to leave, especially when the man sitting at the register -- she assumed that he was the owner -- began giving her agitated looks. She reached into her pocket and took out some money, thankful that when she bought her ticket she had shoved all the bills and change into her pocket instead of into her purse as she usually did.

Once outside, she stood for a moment. Not knowing what to do, she continued to walk in the direction she had been going. Her feet were beginning to hurt so she knew she had to have been walking for quite a while. It was getting colder and evening was coming on quickly as the winter days were short. Ruth began thinking about where she was going to sleep. She had passed hotels earlier, but they looked expensive. As she walked, she worried that her decision to leave Mayfield, without a thought about where she was going and what she would do, had been a little hasty. The first thing she had to do was find a place to stay, then, she would begin her search for a job.

At the next corner a drugstore's light spilled onto the sidewalk. Outside the drugstore was a newspaper stand. The man was closing and pulling his stock inside the little Kiosk. Ruth hurried to buy a paper and went into the drugstore. She sat on a stool at the soda fountain and ordered a hot chocolate. The young man behind the counter was very cordial. Ruth asked him, "Do you know where I can get a room for the night that isn't expensive."

"There's a hotel about three blocks away miss, but I don't know how much the rooms cost."

"Thank you," she said and opened the paper. Slowly, her finger moved down the column in the want ad section hoping to find something that she was qualified to apply for. She was certain there wouldn't be that many positions open to her once they saw she was pregnant. Most employers would be skeptical even after she explained that she would have to continue to work after the baby was born. Thinking ahead brought another problem to mind. What would she do with the baby after it was born? Who would take care of it while she worked?

Once again, that hopeless feeling enveloped her. It was terrifying to be alone. *What in the world will I do?* she thought. *If only that old lady hadn't taken my money!* Her eyes were misty as she tried to make out the words on the paper, then she saw the notice.

GIRLS!

COME TO US WITH YOUR PROBLEM! EXPERT CARE PROVIDED! ALL EXPENSES PAID! CALL ANYTIME.

RO 4-1324 ASK FOR MRS. TRAVIS

It was only a cluster of words but to Ruth it meant salvation and hope. *Oh, if only this ad means what I think it means,* Ruth thought. She took a dollar from her pocket, walked over to the lady at the register and paid for her hot chocolate.

"Where's your telephone?" she asked.

"Next to the pharmacy in the back," the cashier said, gesturing in that direction.

Ruth hurried to the phone booth, closed the door and sat down. She put a nickel in the slot and dialed the number. She could hear it ringing once, twice, three times. Finally, a woman's voice answered. "Hello?" To Ruth it sounded like an angel speaking.

"Hello. My name is Ruth Lawson and I'm calling in response to a notice you have in the newspaper."

"Yes, my dear. Are you calling because you're in trouble?"

"Well, yes, I am."

"Can you tell me how many months you are at this time?"

"Well, it's just about five months now."

"I see. Do you have any friends or relatives that might be able to help you with this matter?"

"No, I don't have anyone. I just arrived here this afternoon and I don't know a soul in this city." Ruth's hands began shaking a little.

"Do you have a place to stay tonight?" the woman asked.

"No I don't, but I could rent a hotel room. I have enough money for one night, possibly two."

"It sounds to me like you need help in a hurry, my dear."

"Yes, I'm afraid I do."

"Let me see. Where are you now?"

"I'm calling from a Rexall drugstore but I don't know the name of the street it's on."

"Well, we're just finishing dinner. I'll have to get preparations started for your arrival. Do you think you can hold out for about an hour or so?"

"I don't seem to have any choice!"

"Fine. I'll have my driver pick you up but, as I said, it'll be a little while before he can get there. Now, go outside and look at the street signs then come back and tell me what corner you're on."

Ruth set the receiver down and hurried outside. The temperature seemed to have dropped below freezing. It was snowing lightly now and the wind blew the powdery flakes into her face. She looked at the street signs and rushed back to the telephone. "I'm on the corner of Canal and Monroe streets." She told the angel on the other end.

"My driver will be in a brown and white station wagon, so you watch for him. Tell me what you're wearing so he'll have some way to recognize you?"

"Well, my coat is black, I have a white scarf that I'll let drape on the outside of my coat and, of course, I'll have my suitcase."

"That's perfect. I'm sure you won't miss each other. Now, don't you worry, my dear. Everything will turn out for the best. You'll see."

They said goodbye. Ruth hung up the phone and heaved a sighed of relief. Her heart was much lighter now and a hopeful smile graced her lips. With a new-found spring in her step, her head held high, she walked back to her seat at the soda fountain. Looking around with a new attitude, the store seemed different to her now. The bright lights and colorful signs gave her a warm feeling. She'd found someone who cared and that made everything easier to bear. The ice cream signs above the soda fountain were provocatively appealing. Ruth smiled and motioned to the young man behind the counter.

"I'll have a cherry phosphate. No… make that a black cow, please.

Ruth stood outside, waiting for that brown and white station wagon to appear. Her feet were very cold and it was still snowing. The flakes were bigger now. She didn't mind though. She was waiting for a miracle.

Finally, a brown and white station wagon was on the other side of the street, delayed by a red light. She walked to the curb. When the light turned green, the wagon made a u-turn and pulled along side the curb in front of her. The man in the car leaned over and rolled down the window on the passenger side.

"Are you Miss Lawson?" he shouted.

"Yes I am. Did Mrs. Travis send you?"

"Yes." The man got out of the car and walked to Ruth's side. He took her suitcase, put it in the back of the wagon and opened the passenger's door. "Please get in."

The car was warm. Ruth moved her feet closer to the heater blowing warm air on the floor. It had seemed like hours before this man had arrived but she knew it had only been about forty-five minutes. She tried to relax but being alone with a stranger in a new city going to an unfamiliar place made it a little difficult. *Calm down,* she told herself. *Everything is going to be fine now.*

The man behind the wheel was very tall. His head was about an inch from the car's roof. He had on a long black coat and wore a black cap. Ruth could only see his profile. He had a large nose, protruding chin and black eyebrows. Keeping his head straight, his eyes never left the road. He didn't speak during the entire ride. Ruth made a casual remark about the weather but received no response and was quiet after that.

As they drove through the city, Ruth found the brightly lighted shops and theaters absolutely fascinating. Soon they were on the outskirts and the only thing to hold her attention now, was snow covered fields gleaming in the moonlight. Ruth very much wanted to ask some questions but she didn't think this man would answer, so she remained silent.

The long ride ended when the car slowed and pulled into a dimly lighted driveway. There was one light on a pole at the entrance to the house. Ruth could see the outline of a large house surrounded by huge leafless trees. The lights were on in the downstairs windows throwing an inviting glow out into the still night. The driver followed the circular driveway to the front door, parked and got out of the car. He hurried around to open the door for Ruth. She took another look at him when the door opened and the light went on. He was very tall but seemed to be slightly stooped. He walked with a pronounced limp that Ruth hadn't noticed before. It was obvious that his physical impairment in no way hampered his efficiency. He kept his head down and waited as Ruth got out of the car. The front door opened and a short, plump woman walked out onto the porch.

"Come in. Come in, my dear," she called.

The woman had a welcoming smile on her round face. Her hair was white and combed smoothly into a neat little bun at the back of her head. The sides covered her ears and a perfect wave fell over her forehead. Her eyes seemed to have a merry twinkle, completing a face that was the picture of warmth and understanding. It was the face of "home."

Ruth walked up onto the porch. Mrs. Travis took Ruth's arm and led her into a comfortable, old-fashioned parlor with overstuffed chairs and a peaceful fire flickering in the fireplace. The driver appeared in the doorway carrying Ruth's suitcase. He didn't say a word, just waited.

"Take her bags to room four, Stanley, and bring us some tea before you put the car away." She turned again to Ruth and pointed to one of the big chairs. "Please, take off your coat and sit down dear," she said as she eased herself into the chair across from Ruth.

"My name is Martha Travis," she began. "And your name is Ruth?"

"Lawson, Ruth Lawson. I can't tell you how much I appreciate what you're doing for me. You'll never know how glad I am to have found you."

"I think I do. I know what it's like to be in your situation. This is my home and I've opened the doors to girls in trouble, like you, who need someone to help them through this delicate time. There are four girls staying here now. Two of them are expecting to deliver this month." Martha's expression changed subtly as she continued. "Receiving help for the girls now is of the utmost importance but, as you can see, I'm not a wealthy woman. When you are well and able to work again, we will expect to be reimbursed for the doctor's fees and also for your care while waiting. Be assured that the fee will be nominal. However, you do realize the professionals working with me need to be paid up front. We have a physician who takes care of my girls exclusively. He is a very competent doctor, as you will soon know, and his fee is much less than what you would expect."

Stanley came in with the tea. "Bring the tray over here and put it on the coffee table, Stanley." Stanley set the tray down and waited. "Thank you. That will be all." He left the room.

The tea was sweet and satisfying. As Ruth sat there feeling the warmth of the fire and looking at a friendly face, she was very much at ease with the thought that everything would be all right from now on.

"Mrs. Travis?"

"Yes, my dear," she smiled.

"I don't know how to thank you but I promise that, when this is over, I'll repay you for all your kindness and for whatever expenses I accrue during my stay here. For the help you're giving me now, I will never forget you!"

"Now, now, my dear, save your gratitude. After all, you're really paying your own way. We know how important it is to retain one's independence." The woman's face again changed. "I must also tell you that we have another service here that brings happiness to others. We are registered with the county as an approved adoption agency. Some of the girls are unable to keep their babies for personal reasons. In that case, we find suitable, loving couples who desperately want children but can't have them. If you should decide to give up your child, the adopting parents will pay all expenses."

Ruth frowned and squirmed a little in her chair. The idea that she might have to give up her baby because she couldn't afford to keep it had never entered her mind.

"Give up my child?" Ruth said in an anxious tone.

"Apparently, the thought is new to you, Ruth. Don't burden yourself with worry now. There's plenty of time to make plans for the child's and your future. Remember that the child's welfare should always come first. Whatever happens will be your decision but let me say that you would do well to give this careful consideration. To begin with, you have no family to depend on, no income, no prospects and, most of all, no husband." Ruth winced from embarrassment.

"You're no different than all the rest of the girls who come here," she continued, "but I'll be very frank in telling you that the smart ones give up their child. Not because they don't care, mind you, but because they do care! They know the child will grow up in a home where there is love from two people, a mother and a father. There will be financial security with freedom from ridicule and a greater chance for happiness. Now, in comparison, I ask, what have you to offer this child?"

Ruth couldn't answer right away. What this woman said was true. She had never looked at things quite that objectively. "But give up my child?" she said. Her brow creased in a deep frown. "I don't know if I can do that."

"I'm sorry, dear," Mrs. Travis said, "I didn't mean to upset you. I just wanted to point out the facts. As I said, you have time to think this over.

There's no need to make that decision right now." Mrs. Travis rose from her chair, walked to Ruth's side, and put her hand on Ruth's shoulder.

"We won't talk any more, dear. You've had a busy day and you must be tired. Come. Let me show you to your room. This is your home, now, and I want you to enjoy it. First, though, I'll show you where our guests meet for meals before we go upstairs."

Ruth followed her back through the foyer into the large dining room.

"This is where our happy family meets when Edie rings the come-and-get-it bell. Edith Turner's been with us a long time and I know you'll enjoy the meals she prepares."

Back in the foyer, Mrs. Travis pointed to the corridor alongside the staircase and said,

"This hall leads to the kitchen and beyond that is the room where you'll be having your baby. No one is allowed in that room unless Dr. Roman is here. He keeps it antiseptically clean. You'll meet him soon. He comes once a month to give the girls their exam and check their progress. I know you'll like him"

She started up the stairs and Ruth followed. The upstairs consisted of a long hall with seven doors, three on each side and one at the far end.

"As you can see, we have six rooms," Mrs. Travis said over her shoulder as they moved down the hall. "Four of them are occupied. The door at the end is the bathroom. You'll have to share it with the other girls. They usually retire to their rooms early, so you'll meet them in the morning." She stopped at the end of the hall. "This is your room; a very good location, I might add, being right next to the bathroom."

Ruth followed her into the room, as Mrs. Travis flicked on the wall switch to the overhead light. It was a small room with a single bed and a dresser. A large wardrobe stood in one corner. The nightstand held an ashtray and a small lamp. It seemed cozy enough. Mrs. Travis crossed her arms as she stood in the doorway waiting, while Ruth looked around. "I hope you'll be comfortable here," Travis said.

"I'm sure I will be," Ruth said, trying to show that she was pleased "It's a nice room."

"Is there anything else I can do for you before I say goodnight?"

"No, thank you, Mrs. Travis, I think I'll go right to bed. I really am quite tired."

"Of course you are. You get a good night's sleep and don't you worry about anything."

"You're very kind," Ruth said.

"Goodnight, my dear." Mrs. Travis turned and left the room.

Ruth sighed and looked about the room. *Well,* she thought, *here I am. This is home for the next four months.*

Quietly, she began to unpack her things but, very soon, exhaustion overcame her. The ordeal of the last few hours had taken its toll. *I'll worry about unpacking tomorrow.* Turning off the light, she undressed by the light of the moon shining brightly through the window. As she lay relaxed between the covers, Ruth made an effort to think about her new home and what Mrs. Travis had said. She kept rubbing her feet together trying to warm them with friction. Sleep was all she wanted and, in a moment, her eyes closed.

CHAPTER 8

Voices crept into her consciousness. Sleepily, Ruth sighed and stretched. Her eyes flew open when she remembered where she was. Sitting up in bed, she looked around the room. *I thought it had only one window.* It was a bright room. One window looked out over the front of the house and the driveway, the other over an endless stretch of landscape. Steam hissed from the radiator under the window by her bed. She heard voices in the hall.

"Come on, Rose," she heard someone say. "You've been in there for half an hour! Hurry up, will ya!"

"Aw, hold your horses," another muffled voice answered.

Ruth lay there listening to the friendly bickering. When all became quiet, she got out of bed and began to dress. When she opened her bedroom door, she could see that the bathroom door was ajar, so she hurried through it. She splashed some cool water on her face then started down the stairs. She could hear the girls talking in the dining room. They stopped talking and turned to look as she entered the room.

"Hello," Ruth said timidly.

A red head at the far end of the table raised her spoon in the air and said, "Ah-ha, another little mother in the making. Welcome to God's little acre."

"Oh, dry up, you creep," said a brown-haired girl at the other end of the table.

"Yeah, don't pay any attention to that one," the bleached blond girl on the right said, as she pointed her thumb in the redhead's direction "Come and join us. My name is Myrna."

Myrna was nice looking; not really attractive, but was very pleasant.

She had blue eyes and long blond hair. She was very heavy with child. Not very smart, but liked to talk.

"I hope you didn't take offense, kid," the redhead said. "I'm Rose."

Before Ruth could reply, the brown-haired girl said, "Na, Rose didn't mean nothin' by it. We're just getting a little stir crazy in this joint. I'm Sheila. Welcome."

Sheila was a friendly person. She was a pretty girl with short brown hair. She had big, brown eyes and pale complexion.

Ruth sat down next to the small, quiet girl who sat on the left. As she did, the sweet-looking honey blond turned to her and said softly, "My name is Carol."

Ruth looked at everyone and said, "I'm pleased to meet all of you. My name is Ruth."

A tall, large-boned woman with heavy hips came in. She had short kinky hair, small mean eyes, and thin lips; a big woman and solid all through. She carried a bowl of oatmeal and a glass of orange juice. As she set the dishes down in front of Ruth, she spoke harshly. "Since this is your first day, I'll excuse you, but breakfast is at 8:00 o'clock sharp and anyone who ain't here, don't eat!"

"Aw, listen to swivel hips," said Rose. She turned to the other. "You'd think she was doin' charity work, the way she gives orders."

"Yeah," Myrna chimed in, "old liver lips, lover boy Harvey musta give her a hard time last night."

"Listen, shut-ins," Turner snapped, "the hard time I had last night, you haven't had in months."

"Quit rubbin' it in," Sheila snickered, "this female garden center is bad enough without you rubbin' it in. We don't want to hear about your sex life."

"I like to see you squirm," Turner said, smirking. "Besides, that's what you dopes get for getting' yourselves knocked up!"

"Oh, yeah," said Myrna, "Well, that was no tumor *you* was sproutin' a couple o' years ago. So, you should talk!"

"You know that wasn't my fault." Turner laughed, as she left the room. "I was raped!"

"Yeah, yeah, we know," Rose said, and chuckled.

Rose was an attractive girl with long red hair. She was the smartest of the three but did not know how to use her intelligence to better herself. She wore a stern expression most of the time and was always very serious.

"Yeah, yeah," Sheila mimicked.

Rose spoke softly then, as she directed her question to Ruth. "So how'd you find out about this place, Ruth?"

"I saw an ad in the newspaper."

"That's how we found the place," said Myrna. "That was a while ago though, I've been here before. Mrs. Travis has been in business for a long time."

"This is my second time here," Sheila chimed in, resting her chin on her hand and looking at Ruth.

"Okay, Sheila, that's nothing to brag about," Rose scolded.

"You know how to play pinochle?" Myrna asked.

"No, I don't," Ruth replied.

"Jesus, that's too bad," Myrna groaned.

"Shit," said Rose, slapping the table with her hands "Looks like we'll have to stick to poker."

"I'd like to learn if you'd be willing to teach me," Ruth said.

"You're on!" Rose said, a little too loudly. "I'll do anything to change the monotony around this dump."

"How far gone are you, Ruth?" Myrna asked, as she brushed some hair out of her face.

"Five months."

"Gee, you've got a long way to go yet. I'm seven months, but I'm small the doctor said. Small babies run in my family. You're giving the kid up, right?"

"I... I haven't made up my mind about that yet," Ruth faltered. Being uncertain about how truthful she should be with this group. "How about you, Myrna?"

"My boyfriend hates kids," Myrna whined. "He said either I give up the kid or he's givin' me up. Jeez," she whimpered, "What can I do?"

"I don't know what you see in that bastard," Rose chided, with a sneer. "You could be independent if you'd listen to me."

"But I love him," Myrna squealed.

"Love... crap." Rose shrugged.

"How about you Rose? Do you want a boy or a girl?" Ruth asked.

"Gee, I never thought about it." Rose frowned. "It don't make no difference to me."

"Does that mean you're giving up your baby, too?" Ruth asked.

"Yeah, I guess it does. This kid will be better off without me. I can't make it a good home."

"I want to keep my baby," Sheila popped up, "but my parents won't let me."

Turner's husky form entered the room again. She set a dish of pills on the table and turned to leave.

"Don't forget your vitamins, little mothers," she called back. "We want healthy little bastards, you know."

Rose and Myrna gestured and murmured obscenities at Turner's back. The dish was passed around and each girl took her vitamin pill. Carol, the round faced, soft spoken tiny person with dark blond hair who sat silently though the entire meal, handed the dish to Ruth. Their eyes met and Ruth smiled into her sweet young face. Carol returned the smile. Ruth was pleased and touched by this person who sent a sudden kindred feeling of warmth and friendship through her.

"Have you been here long?" Ruth asked her.

"Just two weeks," answered Carol in her sweet little voice.

"When are you expecting your baby?"

"I have two months to go."

"Are you planning to give up your baby, too?"

"Oh, I'm keeping my baby!" Carol said, without hesitation, like she thought everybody knew.

When everyone had finished their breakfast, one by one, they rose to leave the table.

"Jesus, this kid is heavy," Rose groaned, as she pulled herself up. "I'd like to shove it back up the head that put it there."

"Ha, that would take some research, girl," Myrna quipped, as she stood up and patted her stomach tenderly. "You know," she said with a quizzical look on her face, "it's really somethin' though. I mean, isn't it somethin' to feel someone movin' around inside of you?"

"It makes my stomach upset," Rose said.

"I wonder if the kid will look like Walter; like maybe his eyes or somethin'," Myrna mused, dreamily.

"Who knows what a baby is gonna look like." Rose shrugged and laughed loudly then said, "Mine could look like the League of Nations."

Ruth could see then how long the wait was going to be, in this place with nothing to do.

Sheila and Rose went off to Rose's room to play cards. Rose asked, "Ruth, you care to join us?"

Ruth said, "I've got letters to write. Sorry."

Myrna said, "I'm going to write a letter to Walter

Ruth learned later that Myrna wrote a letter to Walter every day, although no letter ever came for Myrna. Ruth found out later that the girls were kept incognito. Their letters were destroyed instead of being mailed.

Carol and Ruth went upstairs. Carol went directly to her room, which was next to Ruth's.

Ruth sat down on the bed. She was trying to get her mind to focus on something but she couldn't concentrate. Her mind kept drawing blanks. She looked around the room for something to do. She could straighten out her clothes. She had just tossed them into the dresser drawers earlier. She could clean the room. Mrs. Travis said the girls had to clean their own rooms. She could clean it now even though it didn't look dirty. She lay back on the bed. *My bed isn't made,* she thought. *That's what I'll do, I'll make my bed.* She closed her eyes.

A gentle tapping woke Ruth. "Come in," she called sleepily.

The door opened slowly and in walked Carol.

"I thought you may have taken a little nap and I didn't want you to miss your lunch," she said. "I hope you don't mind."

"Mind?" Ruth said, as she rose from the bed, "I'm very grateful."

Lunch was a repetition of breakfast with the same nonsensical conversation. Dinner brought more of the same. And so it went day after endless day. However, mealtime was eagerly anticipated since it broke the monotony of each long day.

Mrs. Travis appeared from time to time giving lectures on health and cleanliness with stern but motherly projection. She didn't want her girls to have any alcohol and, if they smoked, she suggested they have only three cigarettes a day, one after each meal, but in their own rooms. She kept reminding the girls that the unborn child was entitled to a healthy start. Of course, most of the time, the girls did what they wanted to, as long as they kept Mrs. Travis from finding out.

One evening Mrs. Travis asked Ruth to meet her in the parlor. "I thought I'd inquire about the baby. Have you decided what you're going to do about the child?"

"I *have* decided," Ruth replied, "and my decision to keep my baby hasn't changed. I know it won't be easy, but other women have done it and I know I can too."

Mrs. Travis raised her eyebrows. "Ruth, you have no idea of the trouble you'll have. A single unwed woman with a child can't get a job. No one will hire her because of the time she'll have to take off to care for a sick baby. You really need to reconsider, if only for the sake of your baby."

Ruth listened without responding as Mrs. Travis continued to try to convince Ruth that she ought to change her mind about keeping the child, but inside she kept screaming, "Shut up!"

After half an hour, Mrs. Travis realized that Ruth wasn't going to change her mind. "There's no more to be said, then. I urge you to think very hard about this Ruth."

Ruth never did learn how to play pinochle and despite their professed need for deliverance from routine, Myrna and Rose preferred each other's company. Both women lost in their own dubious world of familiarity. They were both prostitutes and didn't seem to want to better themselves.

The days seemed to move slower. Ruth would sit by her window occasionally. From there she watched the beige station wagon coming and going. Stanley was always there, moving about dutifully and silently, pulling that bad leg after him which seemed to struggle to keep pace.. Ruth felt uneasy each time he was around. She didn't know why but he just gave her the creeps.

One evening, she heard laughter coming from Rose's room. The door was ajar, so she gave it a couple of taps.

"Friend or foe?" called a husky voice that sounded like Rose.

"Friend," called Ruth. "May I come in?"

"Enter at your own risk," was followed by laughter.

Ruth went in. There was Rose, Myrna, and Sheila sitting on Rose's bed passing around a bottle of whiskey. They were obviously very inebriated.

"Well, well, if it ain't Ruthie, Come on, join the party," Rose said, her voice slurred from the alcohol. "Sheila, give 'er her the bottle."

"No thanks," Ruth said, as she put up her hand. "I heard you laughing and wondered what was going on."

"Just a little diversion, sweetie," said Myrna. "You can have a couple of free swigs this time honey but, next time, if you wanna party, you gotta take your turn with Stanley."

"Stanley? I don't understand."

"Yeah, Stanley. He's our delivery boy, our lifesaver. Give a little head, get a big bottle."

Everybody laughed, except Ruth. She felt nothing but shock. These weren't her kind of people. She turned and quickly left the room, closing the door behind her. The other three laughed. After that incident, Ruth kept her distance from the three girls but remained cordial so there would be no cause for animosity.

The bookshelf in the parlor was a refuge for her. She loved to read and she encouraged Carol to join her. Although Carol wasn't the most stimulating of conversationalists, she had a calming effect on Ruth. The process of gaining Carol's confidence was slow but steady.

Eventually, Carol talked freely to Ruth. During their many conversations they found they were alike in many ways. Each said how fortunate she felt at having found the other under such desperate circumstances and each knew their friendship was going to last. They took pleasure in making plans to live together. Since Carol was keeping her baby they could help each other.

The doctor came at regular intervals to check the girls' progress. One afternoon, Myrna knocked on Ruth's door to tell her that the doctor was there and it was her turn to go downstairs for her exam. Myrna took her downstairs to a room that Ruth had forgotten was there. Somewhat isolated behind the kitchen, it looked as if it had been added on after the house had been built.

Ruth slowly opened the door. The doctor sat at a desk in one corner of the room. Without looking up from his writing, he called, "Come right in."

Ruth entered the room and quietly closed the door behind her. Without turning around, the doctor pointed to a chair next to the desk. "Sit here, please?"

Ruth walked over and sat down. A few more cursory notes and the doctor turned to her.

"My name is Doctor Roman," he began. "I'm a obstetrician and will be here to deliver your baby." He glanced around the room as he spoke. "As you can see, we are well equipped here. We have everything one would find in a hospital. The room is antiseptically clean and I'm prepared to handle any complications that might arise during childbirth. I've delivered hundreds of babies, so you're in competent hands. Please know that we're interested in yours and the baby's welfare."

Ruth studied him while he spoke. He appeared to be in his late fifties and looked very professional in his blue suit and red bow tie. He had a full head of gray hair with a slightly receding hairline. He didn't have a mustache but his dense, gray goatee covered his chin completely. He wore thick wire-rimmed glasses and Ruth thought his eyes looked friendly. He was obviously overweight.

The doctor continued, "The reason we're here and not in the hospital is because the fee for this room is much less than a delivery room there. Mrs. Travis and I have your safety and interests at heart; therefore, we try to keep the costs to a minimum. I also have an excellent nurse who assists me during delivery." He smiled at Ruth and his voice softened. "If you have any questions, please don't hesitate to ask. I want you to be completely at ease. If you can relax and trust me, it'll be easier for both of us." He waited for a response.

Ruth looked around. Everything was orderly and spotlessly clean. The room even smelled like a hospital. There were objects on the countertop that one might expect; cotton, tongue depressors, bandages, scissors, and a box of sterile gloves. The cabinets held authentic looking medicine bottles and instruments, and a neat stack of clean white linen. A blood pressure unit and a scale stood in one corner. The examining table stood in the middle of the room under a huge ceiling light. Along with all the familiar things, there was enough unfamiliar equipment to make it look as complete as Ruth imagined any hospital delivery room to be. "I can't think of anything to ask at the moment," Ruth said.

The doctor took Ruth's medical history, then went to one of the cabinets and took out a sheet. He asked Ruth to step behind the screen that stood at one end of the room, remove her clothing, and get onto the table. He left the room and Ruth unfolded the sheet. It was so worn and thin, she could almost see through it. Ruth did what the doctor had asked. The doctor knocked on the door and came in. He put his stethoscope around his neck then told Ruth to put her feet in the stirrups at the foot of the table. He picked up the speculum from the sterilizer and walked back to Ruth. His exam was thorough but very embarrassing for Ruth. He prodded her stomach to find out how the baby was facing and examined her breasts for any irregular tissue changes. "I'm pleased that you're in such a healthy condition. Giving birth should be no problem," Ruth was glad to have the exam over and to hear the doctor praise her condition.

CHAPTER 9

As the old saying goes, March came in like a lion, wanting to be noticed. It was cold and rained a lot. On several occasions, some persistent snow flakes returned. One Saturday evening, the ladies were just finishing their dinner. It had been a comparatively quiet meal until Myrna suddenly dropped her fork and stood up,

"Hey," she said, with a shocked expression on her face, "I just felt a pain."

"What kind of pain?" Rose asked.

"I don't know a sharp pain in my stomach. Oh," she said and sat down, "There it is again."

"Jesus," Sheila said, "You're not due till next month."

"Something must be wrong," Myrna said, overreacting as she usually did. "You better get Mrs. Travis."

Everyone jumped up and called to Mrs. Travis to hurry. Turner came rushing in.

"It's Myrna," they said in unison.

Turner went to Myrna's side and helped her out of the chair.

"Come on," she said, "let's go to your room. You can lie down until we get the doctor."

Somehow Turner seemed gentle and calm, quite unlike her usual self. "These things usually take a while so no need to get excited."

Mrs. Travis came in from the kitchen, saw what was happening and said "I'll make the phone call."

They all waited around the table, sometimes sitting, sometimes pacing, for what seemed like an eternity. It was only about forty-five minutes. All the while, they could hear Myrna yelling and groaning upstairs. Nobody spoke. They just waited, looking at each other now and then. Finally, they heard the car on the stony driveway as it approached the house. The doctor came in and hurried past the dining room and up the stairs. A short, dark-haired nurse wearing white oxfords followed him.

"Thank goodness the doctor is here!" Carol said, as they all released a sigh of relief.

Soon, Turner and the doctor came down, holding Myrna up between them. The girls watched as Myrna was helped to the room behind the kitchen. The nurse followed close behind. Myrna was about to have her baby.

Any doubts or apprehension Ruth had harbored in the past were quickly dispelled when she saw how competent and efficient the staff was as they went into action. *My baby will be born there, too,* she thought, and felt suddenly joyful.

There was nothing left to do but wait. They sat around the fireplace in the parlor, talking occasionally in whispered tones. Rose and Sheila made a wager.

Sheila said, "I bet she has a boy"

Rose said, "Five bucks says it's a girl."

"Yer on!" Sheila exclaimed.

Sheila was the first to get out of her chair. "I don't know about the rest of you," she moaned, "but I can't keep my eyes open. I'm going to bed."

"Me, too," sighed Rose. "There's no sense in all of us losing sleep over the kid."

"We might as well go too," Ruth said to Carol.

"We'll find out in the morning," Carol said, "I hope everything will be all right."

Single file, they trudged up the stairs and went to bed.

The girls all woke about the same time. It was early but they had gone to bed with Myrna on their minds. Ruth opened her door and stood in the hall. Carol came out, then Rose and Sheila.

"Did any of you hear anything?" asked Ruth.

They shook their heads. Sheila walked to Myrna's room and slowly opened the door.

"She's here, kids," she whispered. "She's in bed."

"Come on in," said a faint voice from the bed.

Slowly, they tiptoed in and stood around the bed. Myrna looked so pale lying there. She looked from one to the other and smiled weakly.

"How'd it go, kid?" asked Rose.

"It hurts, Rose," she whispered. "It really hurts. You know, I didn't think it was gonna hurt that much. The doctor said because the baby was early, it wasn't turned right. He was comin' out ass first, so the Doc had to turn him around. Christ, you know that could have killed me!"

"Did you say he, Myrna?" asked Rose. "Was it a boy?"

"Yeah," smiled Myrna, "it's a boy."

"Well, Hoo-ray," said Rose sarcastically, grinning at Sheila. "You owe me five bucks, bitch."

"Aw, kiss my ass!" Sheila snapped almost angrily. "You'll get your dough."

"Did you see the baby?" Ruth asked

"Yea, I saw him. Not for long though. He sure didn't look like no baby I expected to see. He was red all over and his face was kinda wrinkled. Boy, when he opened his mouth, he sure let out some holler. That kid's gonna have a pair of lungs all right. Just like his father's." Myrna looked wistfully at the ceiling then and spoke as if she was thinking out loud. "His hair looked pretty dark, but of course, it was wet. There was a lot of it though, just like Walter's." She turned to Rose and frowned. "You know, Rose," she said, "I never did get to see his eyes."

Rose patted her arm with reassuring gentleness.

"That's okay, kid. You know its better this way. A fast, clean break, that's the way it's gotta be."

"Yeah," said Myrna, feigning a smile and blinking hard to suppress the tears welling up in her eyes, "its better this way."

Ruth touched the foot under the covers. "We better go now, Myrna, and let you get the rest you need."

The others agreed. They went to their rooms to get dressed for breakfast. It was nearly 8:00 o'clock.

When they were all seated at the table, Ruth said, "I think that Myrna acted like she wanted to keep her baby. "

"She only thinks so now," Sheila said with a snicker, "but she'll forget all about it as soon as she's back in Walter's arms."

"Yeah," said Rose, "that pimp can make her do anything. Besides," she added in her husky voice, "I think Mrs. Travis would kill her before she'd give her kid back."

That statement took Ruth by surprise. She smiled faintly and said, "You're kidding of course. Mrs. Travis would..."

"Shh!" interrupted Sheila, gesturing frantically, "You want Travis to hear you?"

"Listen kid," Rose leaned closer, "You don't think Travis is in this racket because she feels sorry for jerks like us who get knocked up and need a hand out, do you?"

"Racket?" Ruth frowned. "What do you mean, racket?"

"Yeah, sister, racket," said Rose, "That's why you kinda threw me when you said you were gonna keep your kid. That goes for little lockjaw over there, too." she tilted her head towards Carol. "She wants to do the same. I never knew Travis to do no charity work. The only girls that come to this place don't walk out of here with their package re-located in their arms."

"But this isn't charity," Ruth explained. "Mrs. Travis is charging us a fee for the services. She has to be repaid in full within so many months following our departure; I've already signed an agreement."

"You did?" Rose was surprised. "Well, how much did she say it would cost you?"

"Well, she couldn't quote an exact amount. She said it depended on how long we stayed here and if there are any birth complications. It could go as high as a thousand dollars."

"A thousand bucks, huh!" Rose said "Do you know how much she gets for these kids? Three thousand would be the minimum. I'll bet five thousand is closer to average. She don't give a damn about you. All she wants is your baby, preferably a healthy one."

"I don't believe you," said Ruth. "Mrs. Travis is so kind. At least she seems sincere."

Rose shrugged. "Look, honey, I don't know the ins and outs of this business. All I know is no one takes their kid home after they have it here. Maybe business has been poor; maybe I was wrong about her. Anyway, it's none of my business. It's your headache not mine." She turned to leave, then quickly turned back and put her hand on Ruth's arm. "Hey, listen kid," she gently warned. "Don't you go talkin' to Travis about what I been telling you. You keep your mouth shut or I might get my ass kicked out of here."

"I won't say a word to anyone, Rose. Besides, I still think you may have misjudged her."

"Yeah, sure. What the hell do I know?"

The table seemed empty without Myrna. She was a simple-minded chatterbox but now everyone missed her warm, friendly chatter. They could hear Turner's voice in the kitchen, remonstrating with some delivery person. Soon, she came to the table with a tray full of bacon and eggs. The food looked and smelled delicious and everyone made a comment about it.

"Watch those calories girls, you're getting a little fat around the middle," Turner laughed.

"I bet you say that to all the dames," Rose said, smirking.

"Watch those calories girls," Sheila mimicked. "You're getting a little fat around the middle."

"Yeah," chided Rose, "why don't you get your agent to write you some new material."

"Sure," said Turner, "I'll have it ready for you next time."

They joined in with protestations. "Not for me," Rose yelled.

"Don't hold your breath," Sheila said.

"Turner," Carol called, as Turner was about to leave the room. "Did you see the baby?"

"No," Turner answered, matter-of-factly. "They don't let me hang around in there. Anyway, they always hustle the kid out of here in a hurry."

Myrna stayed for another week, only because her delivery had been so difficult. There were hugs and kisses and lots of well wishes the day she left.

Three weeks later, Rose had her baby and, a week after that, Sheila had hers.

It was the first week in April. The weather had turned warmer but it rained almost every day. The house was quiet now that the others had gone and no new girls had arrived. Carol and Ruth sat alone at the dinner table. Carol thought she was overdue for the baby but she felt fine. She said she would go to the Child Welfare offices after the baby was born. They would help her find a place to stay and help her find a job and a sitter for the baby.

Carol spoke with such excitement. "I'll send you my address when I get one so you'll know where to find me after you have your baby. I feel so positive about our plans to live together. Wouldn't it be great if I could work days and you nights or vice-versa? We wouldn't need a sitter. That would save money."

Ruth said she thought that was a great idea but all the while they were talking she was thinking of the loneliness she was sure to feel after Carol left.

It was a little after midnight a couple of nights later when Ruth was awakened from a sound sleep by a disturbance in the hall. She slipped out of bed and tried to listen at the door.

A man's voice was asking, "What are we going to do about this one?"

A woman answered, "I'll handle it. Quit worrying." It was Mrs. Travis' voice.

She heard someone moaning and crying. The sounds faded down the hall. Ruth opened the door and looked out. There was Stanley and Mrs. Travis, just rounding the corner at the top of the stairs, holding Carol up between them. Ruth hurried after them.

"Is Carol having labor pains?" Not waiting for an answer. "Carol, it's me, Ruth. I'm here."

Mrs. Travis turned her head. "Go back to bed, Ruth, there's nothing you can do. Carol's in good hands. The doctor has been called, and he'll be here shortly."

Ruth stopped and watched them as they turned at the bottom of the stairs towards the delivery room. Carol's muffled cries brought tears to Ruth's eyes. She couldn't sleep now! She went back to her room for her robe, and then slowly crept down the stairs to the parlor. She would wait there, in the dark. It wasn't long till she heard a car pull into the drive. Dr. Roman rushed in alone and closed the door hard behind him. He went straight to the back room.

Ruth sat for what seemed like hours. Indeed, it was more than three hours. Every now and then she would venture from her chair in the dark corner of the room and walk to the hall to listen. She could hear muffled voices. The doctor was giving orders to Mrs. Travis. Then she heard Mrs. Travis' voice. Ruth jumped when she heard Carol scream. Then all was silent. A few minutes later, she heard the baby cry and she heaved a sigh. It was over. Now she could go to bed knowing Carol and her baby were all right.

She hurried up the stairs and into her room before anyone saw her. She heard someone come out of the room downstairs just as she quietly closed her door. She was about to climb into bed when she heard the front door slam. Going to the window, she saw the doctor rush to his car with what looked like a bundle of blankets cradled in his arms. Something didn't seem right, but what? She climbed into bed and pondered the situation until she fell asleep.

It was after 10 A.M. when Ruth awoke. She'd missed breakfast but didn't care. Her first thought was of Carol. She put on her robe and slippers and went next door to Carol's room. She opened the door slowly and peeked in.

"Carol," she called softly, "Are you awake? May I come in?"

Carol had been slow to come out of the heavy dose of anesthesia she'd been given and it still affected her. Her voice had a quiver when she spoke. "Come in, Ruth," she whispered.

Ruth closed the door and sat down on the bed next to Carol.

"How do you feel, Carol? You must have been in a lot of pain. I heard you cry out."

"I'm still groggy, Ruth. The doctor waited too long to give me anesthetic. I felt the worst pain in my life, and then they put me out. I don't even know what I had. Do you know? Was it a boy or a girl?"

"I don't know. I saw them when they were taking you downstairs last night. I wanted to follow but Mrs. Travis told me to go back to my room. I pretended to go back to my room, but when they disappeared at the bottom of the stairs, I crept down and hid in the parlor all night. I didn't leave until I heard the baby cry, then I figured everything was all right and I went back upstairs. I'll get dressed and go down and talk to Mrs. Travis now if you want me to. I'll tell her you're awake and they can bring the baby up."

"Thank you, Ruth. I can't wait to hold him...or her."

Ruth went back to her room, quickly dressed and went downstairs. Turner was fussing with some dishes on the table. "Do you know where Mrs. Travis is?" Ruth asked.

"I expect she's in the delivery room cleaning and sanitizing."

Ruth went to the back room. She rapped on the door, but not waiting for an invitation to enter, walked right in. Mrs. Travis was in the process of cleaning the room.

"Good morning."

Mrs. Travis stopped what she was doing. She looked surprised when she turned and saw Ruth in the doorway.

"What are you doing here, Ruth? Don't come in. This room has to be sanitized at all times."

"I know that but I wanted to ask you about the baby."

Mrs. Travis seemed flustered by Ruth's intrusion. "What about the baby?"

"Well, I was just in to see Carol and she's waiting for you to bring the baby to her. She doesn't even know if it is a boy or a girl. What did she have, Mrs. Travis?"

"I'll talk to Carol as soon as I've finished in here. Please leave now, so I can get things done."

"But, what about the baby?' What did she have?"

"I told you to leave, Ruth. I'll be up to see Carol as soon as I'm through here."

Mrs. Travis walked to the door and closed it, shutting Ruth out. Ruth stood outside, staring at the closed door.

Something's wrong, she thought. *Why won't Mrs. Travis talk about the baby? Why won't she say what it is?* Ruth turned and went back upstairs to Carol's room.

"I saw Mrs. Travis, Carol. She was cleaning the delivery room and wouldn't talk to me. She said she'll be up to see you as soon as she finished."

"Well, did she say if it was a boy or girl?"

"I told you, she wouldn't talk to me. She even closed the door in my face."

"Oh, well," Carol's eyes were still half closed. "I guess it won't be much longer."

"I'll stay here with you till she comes. I think I'm as anxious as you are to see the baby."

Ruth sat down in the chair next to the bed while Carol lay in her sleepy state, both quietly waiting. Ruth's eyelids were getting heavy when the door suddenly opened and Mrs. Travis walked in. Ruth stood up and blinked several times. Without hesitation, Mrs. Travis said, "Ruth, this is a private matter. Please leave."

"I told Carol I would stay with her till the baby came." Ruth hesitated. "Where is the baby, Mrs. Travis?" Carol was wide-awake now and got up on one elbow.

"I want to see my baby. Where is my baby?" Carol asked.

Mrs. Travis held the door open and once again she said to Ruth, "I told you to leave the room please! What I have to say is between Carol and me."

No one ever argued when that stern command was given. Ruth sidestepped past Mrs. Travis and left the room. The door closed behind her. Ruth lingered in the hall and pressed her ear against the door hoping to hear what Mrs. Travis had to say to Carol. She could hear Mrs. Travis speaking but couldn't make out what she was saying. All was quiet for a few seconds then Ruth jumped back as Carol let out a blood-curdling scream.

"Oh, no!" she heard Carol scream. "Oh, no!" Then she heard Carol begin to cry hysterically.

Ruth opened the door and rushed in. "What's the matter?" she demanded.

"Ruth!" Carol said, almost yelling. "She said my baby's dead! It can't be! I want my baby!" The poor girl only whimpered the last words.

Hurrying to the bed, Ruth gathered Carol in her arms. "Oh, my God!" Ruth felt her tears starting as Carol clung desperately to her. "Carol, I'm so sorry."

Neither of them noticed Mrs. Travis edge slowly toward the door and leave the room.

One can only cry so long before the body can no longer take the racking sobs, then the tears stop. Ruth stopped crying but continued to hold Carol until, with one last choking sob, Carol fell back on the pillow and lay there staring at the ceiling.

Stroking Carol's head as she lay in trance-like state, Ruth could easily put herself in Carol's place as she thought about the child she was carrying. She pushed those thoughts from her mind as she tried to concentrate on how she was going to help Carol get through this. Ruth stood up and slowly moved around the room, bending from side to side trying to unlock her body from the awkward position it had been in while holding Carol. Something seemed amiss here but what it was she couldn't seem to pinpoint.

"Ruth?" Carol's voice brought her back to the present. Ruth went to the bed and sat down next to Carol again. "How can it be that my baby is dead? I heard it cry! At least, I thought I did. I want my baby, Ruth. I want to see him or her…I have to see what he looks like, I have to touch him. Go tell Mrs. Travis, please!"

Ruth could feel the tears begin to surface again as she looked at the pain in Carol's face. "Okay, Carol." She bent to kiss the forehead of the grief- stricken girl and left the room.

Ruth found Mrs. Travis in the kitchen talking to Turner. Turner's head was bent over the sink with the water running, while Mrs. Travis stood beside her, speaking quietly. Ruth rapped on the open door. They both turned their heads to see who it was. Turner went right back to what she was doing. Mrs. Travis faced Ruth with that familiar annoyed look on her face. "What is it now, Ruth?"

"Carol wants to know about the baby. She wants to see it...and touch it...even though it's dead! Surely you can understand that. The poor girl is devastated. She needs to see her child!"

"The baby is gone! The doctor took it away immediately. We don't keep stillborn babies around. We used to let girls that lost their babies see them but that just caused depression. The doctor takes care of everything. I might add, we expunge all charges when this happens. There is also the matter of burial expense, which we take care of. Tell Carol we know what's best for her. Now, if you don't mind, I'm busy here." She turned back to Turner and resumed talking in quiet tones.

Ruth stood for a moment looking at the two of them. *How cruel! How insensitive,* she thought. *Sheila and Rose were right about Mrs. Travis. This is just a business to her, no heart in it at all.* She turned and slowly started back upstairs.

Carol was sitting up with a look of anticipation on her face when Ruth walked in. Ruth was slow in closing the door and, with her head down, even slower walking to the side of the bed.

Carol had a touch of hysteria in her voice when she asked, "When can I see my baby? Ruth?"

"I'm sorry, Carol. The doctor took the baby away right after it was born. Mrs. Travis said they do that with all of the stillborns to make it easier on the mothers."

"Easier? Easier! After carrying that baby for nine months only to have it eradicated like some wart I had growing on me! They call that easier? They expect me to just forget it? That's insane!"

Rolling over, she buried her head in the pillow and began sobbing convulsively again. Ruth could only sit there patting Carol's back while tears ran quietly down Ruth's face.

It was three days before Carol would speak again. She did get out of bed but only to go to the bathroom. She didn't shower or get dressed. When she wasn't lying in bed and staring at the ceiling, she sat in the chair staring out of the window.

It was also a desolate time for Ruth. She was so lonely. Each time she and Mrs. Travis passed in the hall, neither spoke. Ruth would stare, with contempt in her eyes, while Mrs. Travis would turn her head to avoid eye contact. She never came to Carol's room to see how she was doing. No one came, for that matter.

Ruth thought it best to leave Carol alone with her grief, so she didn't intrude. However, Ruth brought a tray of food to Carol each mealtime, but returned later to find nothing had been touched. She missed Carol the most at mealtime. It was lonely sitting at the table alone! Turner had little to say, perfunctory questions at most, and would set Ruth's plate on the table along with the food, then disappear back to the kitchen.

On the evening of the third day, Ruth entered Carol's room with the dinner tray. Carol was sitting up and turned her head when she heard the door open. She had a weak smile on her face.

"Carol," Ruth said, "You've come back to me! Thank God!"

"I wish I could die, but I can't," Carol said mournfully.

"Please don't talk like that. I don't want to lose you. I've missed you so much! Will you please eat something? You need to get your strength back. There's a cup of chicken noodle soup here. That's just what you need."

Ruth set the tray down on Carol's lap. She gave Carol the spoon but Carol was shaking too much to feed herself, so Ruth took the spoon and fed Carol slowly. After several spoonfuls, Carol waved the spoon away. Ruth knew that, having gone without food for so long, Carol couldn't consume any more.

Slowly, Carol's strength began to return to her. Ruth would help her walk around the room, even though her legs were wobbly, until she was strong enough to take a shower and dress herself. It took a lot of urging, but finally, one evening, Carol agreed to have dinner in the dining room.

As they descended the stairs, Carol said she didn't think she could face anyone, especially Mrs. Travis.

"Mrs. Travis never comes into the dining room," Ruth said. "She might pass through but she never stays. You won't have to talk to anyone. I just want you there. It's been so lonely without you."

"I'm sorry, Ruth. I guess you've been pretty upset through all this."

"It was awful watching you suffer and not being able to do anything to help."

There was one place setting on the table. Ruth had Carol sit in the chair in front of the place setting and sat down next to her. When Turner entered the room, she was surprised to see Carol.

"Well, how nice to see you up and around again," Turner said, not sarcastically.

She gave Carol a sweet smile, which was not in Turner's nature, to show she really meant what she said. She set a dish of mashed potatoes down and left the room. When she returned, she had a place setting for Ruth, a platter of pork chops, and a bowl of peas. Looking at Carol, she said, "You look well-rested. I hope you enjoy your dinner." She was in and out with other things, but that was the end of any conversation. Carol never responded.

Carol's appetite had improved to the point where she ate with a little more enthusiasm. For a while they both ate in silence, then Carol spoke.

"You know, Ruth, I'll have to be leaving very soon. Now that I'm out of bed, they'll make me go. It's for the best anyway. I can't stand being here any more."

"I know. That's all I've had on my mind. What about our plans to live together?"

"I don't want to hurt you, Ruth, but I know I couldn't look at your baby every day without thinking of mine. Please don't hate me."

"I could never hate you, and I do understand, but can we at least keep in touch?"

"You'll be here for a while longer, so when I get home, if my parents take me back, I'll send you my address right away. Otherwise, I don't know where I'll be. You see they wanted me to get an abortion or give my baby up for adoption. But I couldn't do either. Now there's nothing to quarrel about. They didn't like the guy I was in love with. They said he was no good. I said they were wrong but when I told him I was pregnant, he left town. I still couldn't do what they wanted so I left on my own. I was going to make it alone." She hesitated, "Just me and my baby."

"Carol, that's why all those girls were here, if we could compare stories there would be little difference, why is it always the woman that has to pay for the mistake? We didn't get this way alone!"

They finished their meal in silence, each again lost in her own thoughts. Ruth didn't say it, but she knew she would never see Carol again.

Two days later, Ruth watched as Carol packed her meager belongings. They didn't speak as Ruth followed her down the stairs to the front door.

"I'm so glad we met," Ruth whispered as she gave Carol a tenacious hug.

Carol whispered, "Me, too." Both tried desperately to hold back tears. Ruth held the door open and watched Carol get into the cab that would take them out of each other's lives forever. Carol waved as the taxi pulled out of the driveway. Ruth waved back then stepped inside and leaned against the closed door. The tears finally came.

Ruth took to spending more time in her room. It seemed less lonely than sitting at the huge dining room table all by herself. Besides, the stairs were becoming more exhausting.

When she didn't show for dinner the next evening, Turner knocked on her door. Ruth explained, "The stairs are tiring and I don't have much of an appetite anyway." Ruth was quite surprised when Turner said she would bring up the dinner tray, but that's all. Had Turner developed empathy?

Ruth had spent many hours writing letters to Jon. There were two letters written to the sisters. She knew they must have been waiting to hear from her. She felt bad that she hadn't written sooner. When there was something positive to say, she would write again, maybe even send them some pictures.

Late one evening, Ruth had trouble sleeping so she went downstairs to get a magazine from the parlor. When she reached the bottom of the stairs, she heard voices coming from the back room. She stopped to listen. One voice belonged to Mrs. Travis. The other was Doctor Roman. The doctor was saying, "How do we handle this one?"

"We'll have to be doubly careful this time," Mrs. Travis answered, "We almost lost the last one because you waited too long to give the anesthetic."

"It won't happen again, I assure you."

"Do you think it might be wise to induce labor?" Mrs. Travis asked. "I mean, not too soon, of course, but I would like to have it over before I get another girl. It's much easier when no one is here to ask questions."

"When is she due?" the doctor asked.

"You should know that," Mrs. Travis said, a little sarcastically. "You're the doctor and you examined her."

"Of course!" Roman seemed suddenly embarrassed. "She should be due in about two weeks."

"Good! Why don't we wait another week just to be on the safe side and, if nothing happens by then, you'll just happen to come by for an extra exam..."

"Sounds good to me. I've got to go now. I have to be at the hospital at six a.m."

"You can let yourself out," Mrs. Travis said, "but close the door quietly. You're not supposed to be here, you know."

Ruth hurried to the parlor and hid behind the door, pressing her body against the wall. She took deep breaths and held them as long as she could, letting the air out slowly, hoping she didn't make a sound. The doctor opened the front door very quietly and left. Ruth couldn't move. She knew she would be heard trying to go back upstairs. Her legs were getting weak but she dare not make a sound. Finally, she heard Mrs. Travis shuffling about. She waited until Mrs. Travis turned off the lights and went to her room. After a few more minutes Ruth slowly and quietly made her way back up the stairs to her room, her legs trembling from the effort.

With the realization of what this place was really like, she began to shake with terror. Things were becoming suddenly clear to her. She sat down in the chair by the window and stared out at the bare trees.

"Holy Mother of God!" she said aloud, "They're making plans to take my baby just as they've taken all the others. Oh, poor Carol! They lied to you! They stole your baby! I know I heard the baby cry that night. You weren't mistaken when you said that you heard it cry."

Ruth's thoughts went back to that night when she watched the doctor leave with an arm full of blankets. *I didn't know what was happening then but now I do. They had the whole thing planned. I remember thinking, when we were told the baby had died, that the doctor must have been taking the poor, dead infant away, but the baby was alive! The baby lived! Now, sweet Carol, you'll never know your baby is alive somewhere. What am I going to do? I can't let them take my baby!*

She thought about calling the police but remembered that every call was monitored. She knew she couldn't leave the house. Mrs. Travis wouldn't allow it in her condition. There wasn't much time left and no one to whom she could turn. Ruth stayed awake half the night. She tossed from side to side intermittently thinking and dozing, her predicament weighing heavily on her mind.

She didn't make it down for breakfast in the morning but that didn't evoke suspicion. Throughout the day she watched everyone with apprehension, hoping they couldn't recognize the terror she was feeling and trying hard not to show. That she'd discovered their plans. She watched Stanley come and go from her window. The man who limped and never said much still gave her the willies.

It was getting near dinnertime and still Ruth had no idea of how to escape. She only knew that she had to save herself and her baby. She jumped when she heard footsteps in the hall outside her room. Then she realized it was Turner with her dinner. Turner knocked gently and Ruth said, "Come in."

"How are you feeling this evening, Ruth?"

"I'm as well as can be expected, I guess."

"I'll be away for a couple of days or so. My brother was in an accident and they say it's serious. Since there's only you here, Mrs. Travis will be makin' the meals while I'm gone, so don't expect too much. I told her I've been bringin' your dinner up to you and she gave me a dirty look, so you may have to trudge down the stairs or starve."

"I really am sorry about your brother but thank you for thinking of me. I'm sure I'll manage."

Turner didn't say anything, just set the tray down and left the room.

The wheels began to turn in Ruth's head. With Turner gone, that meant one less person would be around to monitor her every move. She picked at her dinner. It might have been a tasty meal but she hadn't even notice what she'd eaten. Ideas of how to escape from this place went round and round in her head. Now it was a race against time. It had to be before Turner got back. She spent another night tossing and turning with only a couple hours of sleep.

The next morning, Ruth was up before anyone else. She took her heavy coat and quietly went downstairs. Stopping often to listen, she went into the parlor and hid her coat behind the sofa. She took a magazine from the pile on the coffee table and sat there pretending to read until she heard Mrs. Travis moving about. She coughed a couple of times, wanting to be heard. Mrs. Travis came hurrying in from the kitchen.

"Ruth, what are you doing here? You're never up this early."

"Good morning, Mrs. Travis. It's strange but I feel almost energetic and I think I have my appetite back. It feels so good to get out of that room, too. You know, I read somewhere that sometimes when something happens, like a sudden deviation from the expected, it turns out to be a precursor. Do you think it means the baby is making plans to fool us and will be coming sooner than we expected?"

There was a moment's hesitation, then, Mrs. Travis got a crooked smile on her face.

"You know, Ruth, you could be right. Why don't you just relax here while I fix you some breakfast? I won't be long."

"That would be so nice. Thank you very much."

"That's why I'm here, dear," she said, as she turned to leave. "That's why we're all here, to make your stay a pleasant one."

It wasn't long before Mrs. Travis called her to a breakfast of scrambled eggs with crispy bacon, a piece of wheat toast and a glass of orange juice. Everything looked delicious. Mrs. Travis did a good job despite Turner's warning. Ruth managed to get half of the food down even though it was a chore to eat when her stomach kept churning from nervous agitation. When Mrs. Travis returned, she said, "Is something wrong, Ruth? You haven't eaten all your breakfast."

"Everything is delicious but it'll take some time to bring my stomach back to its capacity. I hope you're not offended that I couldn't finish everything?"

"Oh, of course not. You're still feeling all right, aren't you?"

"I feel wonderful."

"Well, you just stay that way, my dear. Now, I'll be getting about my business."

Ruth wasn't wonderful. She was terrified. She got up from the table and went back to the parlor and sat down.

"I'll try to have lunch ready on time," Mrs. Travis called out as she began clearing the dishes from the table.

"Please don't hurry on my account," Ruth called back, "I'll be spending more time in here. It feels good to relax and catch up on the reading I've been neglecting."

"You just make yourself at home, dear."

Ruth couldn't help but lean over and look behind the couch to see if her coat was still there. She sat back quickly. *Of course it's still there, you ninny. You just put it there.* Still, she was relieved. She picked up a magazine and actually read through it this time.

Someone was shaking her. Ruth opened her eyes to find Mrs. Travis bending over her gently shaking her shoulder.

"Oh, my goodness, I must have dozed off," Ruth said as she sleepily came awake.

"You certainly did, honey. You were sleeping so soundly that I hated to wake you but lunch is ready."

"Thank you. Looks like you've succeeded in making me feel at home," Ruth called as Mrs. Travis left the room.

Ruth bent to pick up the magazine that had slid from her lap as she slept. She rose with exertion, stretched to awaken her body and then walked to the dining room. Mrs. Travis had prepared a grilled cheese sandwich, with sliced peaches and tea. Ruth ate the dish of peaches and half the sandwich. When Mrs. Travis returned, Ruth excused herself saying that since she felt so energetic she was going to tidy up her room and then take a relaxing shower before dinner.

Ruth didn't tidy up her room. She walked to her chair by the window and just sat there staring out for a long time. How and when she would leave was still a mystery to her. When she finally rose, she walked around the room, mentally choosing what she would take if she could take it. There was nothing. Opening a dresser drawer, she took out the letters she had written but never sent. Returning to the chair by the window, Ruth re-read every letter and methodically ripped them into little pieces. She had poured her soul into those letters and, since they'd never have been mailed by Mrs. Travis, and read by all the staff, destroying them was the only way to keep her thoughts private.

She spent a long time in the shower with the warm water cascading gently down her body. As the water caressed her, the memory of Jon and his embrace blocked out thoughts of the present, flooding her body with long repressed sensations. Realizing she was taking too long, she turned off the water, grabbed a towel and struggled to shake him out of her senses as well as struggled to get out of the tub. She went through her clothes, choosing a wool pair of slacks and a light sweater to wear under her blouse in case the weather became too cold. She wished she could take an umbrella because during April rain was always imminent.

She spent some time fixing her hair and putting on a little makeup. When it was time to go to dinner, Ruth put on the sweater, put her blouse on over it, and then buttoned the blouse up to her neck to hide it. She took one last look in the mirror to see that her clothes didn't look too bulky. Satisfied that they didn't, she went downstairs, hoping it would be for the last time.

Ruth went into the parlor, took a quick peek behind the couch, then sat down and began thumbing through a magazine. About ten minutes later, Mrs. Travis entered the dining room carrying a tureen and called, "Come and get it." She left the room again and a few moments later returned with some bread and a pot of tea.

"I'm in here, Mrs. Travis."

"Oh, my dear, you startled me," she said, as she came to stand in the doorway. "I was wondering if you were still upstairs waiting for me to fetch you. Dinner is ready if you are," she said, turning to leave.

"I'm ready, and thank you again for your trouble," Ruth called as she rose and started for the table.

The tureen held some delicious looking beef stew. Ruth put a ladle full on her plate and took a taste. It *was* delicious! She ate what she could, which was all but a couple of spoonfuls, and lingered at the table sipping her tea. When Mrs. Travis came in to clear the table, Ruth told her how good the stew was.

"I have to confess," Mrs. Travis answered, "I had Turner make some one-dish meals and put them in the freezer."

Ruth had to laugh. Mrs. Travis did, too. It was an unexpected light moment. Mrs. Travis continued to clear the table while Ruth finished her tea.

When the table was clean, Mrs. Travis asked, "Do you want more tea, dear?"

"No, thank you. Would it be all right if I stayed downstairs? I'd like to finish looking through the magazines I started?"

"Well, of course you can, Ruth. If you need anything, I'll be in the kitchen."

Time seemed to drag. Ruth had no idea how long she had been sitting there. She was certain she'd looked through every magazine. Her eyes were beginning to cross from the strain. The sweater under her blouse made her so warm that she was getting drowsy. Hopefully, she hadn't made all these preparations for nothing. She stood up and groaned quietly as each muscle was reluctantly coaxed back into its normal resiliency. *What time is it,* Ruth wondered, *and when is she going to go to bed? I don't know how much longer I can stand waiting here.*

She heard someone coming and quickly sat down. Mrs. Travis was making her rounds and turning off lights. When she saw Ruth still sitting there, she exclaimed, "For goodness sake, Ruth, what are you still doing up? It's well after ten o'clock."

Is that all it is, Ruth thought.

"I went upstairs for a while but couldn't sleep so I came down again," she lied. "Would it be all right if I stayed here until I get sleepy? I don't want to keep you up, though. I can turn the hall lights off when I leave."

"I don't like to leave my girls until their safe and sound in their rooms."

"You're always thinking of our safety and that's what makes you so special," Ruth replied, almost cooing. "I promise that, if I feel the least bit of discomfort, I'll wake everyone in the house with my cries for help."

"Well, all right then, but don't stay up too late. You know where my room is if you need me."

"I don't think I will, but I won't hesitate to call if I do. You have a good night's sleep now."

Ruth waited ever so long. Now and then, she would shake her head and slap herself in the face a few times trying to stay awake. When she thought it was safe to move, she walked quietly to the dining room to look at the clock on the wall. It was one o'clock. She felt sure that everyone was sound asleep by now and that it was safe to make her move.

She walked back to the parlor to retrieved her coat from behind the sofa and put it on. She walked quietly to the front door. Slowly, she unlocked the deadbolt above the doorknob, then, turning the knob until she felt it click, she opened the door. Suddenly a shrill bleep, bleep, bleep caused her to hesitate and tremble with fright. Like a flash, her thoughts went from, *should I close the door?* Or *should I keep going?* "Damn it!" she said, "I've got to keep going." She walked off the porch and trotted awkwardly down the driveway toward the highway. Turning around once, she saw the downstairs lights go on. Someone turned off the alarm. It wasn't easy to continue running with the weight of the baby she carried. When she reached the main road, she hesitated. *Which way?* She remembered making a right turn into the driveway when they arrived. *They might expect me to go back the same way,* she thought. *I'll go the other way.* She turned right onto the road and kept running.

What had at first been a misty evening when the sun went down had become a foggy night. The moon afforded little light, which made the road's edge barely discernable. Her eyes focused on the white line in the center of the road. The fog was a hindrance as much as a help.

Several times she stumbled and almost fell. She heard the sound of a car behind her screeching onto the highway. Quickly, she darted into the bushes at the side of the road. Crouching down, she waited. The sound of the motor was growing fainter. The car was going the other way, just as she hoped it would.

Ruth heaved a sigh and struggled to her feet. Pushing through the branches and back onto the road she resumed walking. The lateness of hour found very few cars on the road but each time she heard one approaching, she would dart into the shrubbery. Where there were no trees or bushes, she would lie down in the ditch beside the road until the car passed. It was too dark to recognize an approaching vehicle as friendly until it was upon her. By then it would be too late if it was Stanley and Mrs. Travis. She had to let them all pass.

Ruth's strength was ebbing. The child was heavy and the road in front of her seemed to stretch out endlessly. She had no idea how far she had come or where she was going, but each time she thought about the house from which she'd escaped and the horror that awaited her there, it helped her gain renewed energy to carry on. She had to keep reminding herself that two lives depended on her fortitude.

She heard a car approaching. When she turned to look, she saw flashlights searching the sides of the road. There was nowhere to go along this stretch of the road but the ditch. She slid down into the gully and lay on her side. The car was moving slowly. She knew it was them! "Oh, please," she whispered, "please don't let them see me!" There were several fallen branches near by. She reached for them and pulled them on top of her. She waited breathlessly as the car came slowly towards her. They were shining flashlights all around. The light went across her body as the car moved past her. When the car stopped a few feet in front of her, she almost panicked but relaxed when it moved on.

She lay there for several minutes, hoping they would think she got a ride from someone and abandon their search. Soon, a car approached from the opposite direction and passed her. She recognized the station wagon. It was them returning to the house. When their taillights vanished in the distance, Ruth struggled from beneath the branches that pulled at her coat, now filthy from crawling in the dirt at the bottom of the ditch. She crawled up the embankment and back onto the road, breathing heavily but crying with relief.

Ruth stumbled along until she felt she had reached her breaking point. She sat down to catch her breath. Her throat felt like she'd swallowed sand. She needed water desperately. A twinge of pain doubled her over. "Oh, no," she groaned. "Not now, not here. Please, not yet."

She forced herself to stand. It took a few more steps but, then she reached the bend in the road, and there, around the curve, she saw a light in the distance. Whatever was there, it was a safe haven. She started laughing and couldn't stop as she gratefully headed toward the light. When she was close enough to recognize the structure, she saw that it was a church. Bent over in pain, she reached the building and almost made it to the door, when she felt herself losing consciousness. She collapsed on the top step. A long time later and in a dazed state, she felt herself being lifted and placed on a bed. She thought she heard a siren but it sounded far away.

CHAPTER 10

When she regained consciousness, she saw two men bending over her. "Where am I?" she asked, struggling to sit up.

"Try to relax, Ma'am," one of the attendants said, as he pressed her shoulders, gently forcing her to lie back down. "You're in an ambulance on your way to the County hospital on Harrison Street. Father McDonald found you on the steps of his church when he opened the door just before locking up. Can you tell us what happened? You're pretty scratched up."

"Don't let them find me." Ruth was shaking and in a state of panic as she tried to get up again, "Don't let them find me," was all she kept saying.

"You're safe here, Ma'am," he told her as he eased her back down. "You'll be in the hospital in a few minutes. They'll take care of you."

"My baby! Is my baby all right?"

"Everything seems to be okay. Are you having labor pains?

Ruth paused to listen to her body, "Not now, but I did when I was walking."

"Where were you walking?"

"I was on the road for a long time, trying to escape from that place."

"What place?" he asked her, trying to keep her calm with conversation until they reached the hospital.

"They were going to take my baby!" Ruth sobbed, near hysteria now.

"Who was going to take your baby?" From past experience, the attendant was beginning to expect a mental breakdown at this point. He exchanged looks with his partner that meant restraints might be needed.

That look registered with Ruth. It had a cooling effect which brought her back to her senses and made her realize how out of control she must appear to be. She didn't say another word, even though the attendant kept asking her questions.

When they reached the hospital, Ruth was wheeled into the emergency room where she was transferred to a bed. The ambulance attendants told the attending physician where she'd been picked up and gave an account of her hysterical allegations. Then they left. The doctor quieted Ruth by assuring her that she was safe now and in capable hands.

"I'm Dr. Parker," he said, as he walked to the side of the bed and put his hand on Ruth's arm. "What's your name?"

"Ruth," she answered. She was beginning to quiet down and feel less anxious now.

"Ruth," he repeated. "Do you have a last name, Ruth?" he asked, with a reassuring smile.

"Lawson," she said, in a now composed voice. "Ruth Lawson."

Even in her condition, she couldn't help thinking that Dr. Parker was very good looking.

In her disheveled condition, Ruth wasn't very glamorous but her captivating charm still shone through. Dr. Parker saw the beauty in this woman, with her beautiful, long red hair spilling across the pillow and her pleading green eyes staring up at him. Somehow, the dirt on her face made her even more appealing.

Dr. Parker began the initial examination by checking all vital signs. Clearing his throat, he asked, "Do you want to tell me what happened to you, Ruth?"

Ruth wanted to tell him. She wanted to tell anybody who would listen and not think her crazy. The doctor seemed genuinely interested. In a trembling voice, she told him about Mrs. Travis' place and the discovery of how they were planning to steal her baby. "So I ran away." Intermittently wiping the tears with a shaking hand, she told him about Carol, too.

When I arrived, there were four other girls there. Three of them were… prostitutes but one of them said she would be keeping her baby. They… Mrs. Travis, that is, said the baby had been stillborn. I heard the baby cry, and I saw Dr. Roman carry it out to his car and drive away."

The doctor listened without making comment. Ordinarily, there wouldn't have been time for all this conversation but it was late and there was only one other person in the emergency room being attended to by another physician.

Helping her to sit up, Parker said, "I can't find anything immediately wrong, but I'm going to have you admitted for observation. Is there someone you want to call to let them know you're here; your husband, perhaps."

Ruth lowered her eyes. "I don't have a husband," she said. "I don't have anyone."

"Who will be picking you up when you're discharged?"

"I told you, I don't have anyone."

"Well, where do you live?" The doctor was very curious about this young woman.

"I don't live anywhere." Ruth was getting aggravated. "If you'd listened to my story, you wouldn't be asking me all these questions. Don't you believe what I told you?"

"I do believe you. I'm just trying to make some sense of it all. I need to know how we can help you."

"I don't have anything but the clothes on my back," she said, and with a shrug of embarrassment, added, "such as they are."

"Okay," he said, "let's get you taken care of and we'll sort out the rest, later. Are you able to walk?"

Twisting her body closer to the edge of the bed, she said, "I think I can still walk." When she tried to stand, she winced and sucked in a breath as her feet touched the floor. She swayed a little and the doctor took her arm, put his other arm around her waist and helped her into a wheel chair.

Touching this woman gave him a rush he wasn't expecting. Never before had he felt the need for an excuse to leave a patient. *What's happening here,* he wondered?

"There are other patients waiting for my attention," he said, "but someone will be with you very soon. Be patient, Ruth. I'll be around to talk to you later." As he walked away, he couldn't comprehend the emotional attraction he was experiencing; he felt a connection to this woman. *Why am I feeling this way?* He thought. *This woman has nothing. She has no family, no husband. Where does she come from? Does she live on the streets? She could even be a prostitute.* Still, the rest of his time on duty, he couldn't get her off his mind and the night seemed to drag by.

It wasn't long before a nurse, in a stiff white uniform and a cap set firmly on her head, came in.

"Hello," she said. "My name is Phyllis." She quickly got behind the chair and wheeled Ruth down a corridor to another room. Once inside, Ruth counted eight women who sat on the benches that lined the wall. The nurse helped Ruth out of the chair and onto a bench. Phyllis seemed very efficient, albeit, perfunctory.

"I'll be right back," she told Ruth, as she wheeled the chair back in the direction from which they came. About ten minutes passed when Phyllis returned. She handed Ruth a form and a ticket.

"You need to fill this out," she said, "and the ticket is your number in line. Please listen for your number to be called so you won't keep anyone waiting." Before Ruth could answer, she walked away again. The form held the usual questions; name, age, etc., and most important, medical information. Between filling in the answers, Ruth looked around at the other women. Five of them were black, two were Hispanic and one was white. They were all pregnant. She realized then that she had been taken to the maternity section of the hospital. Three of the women were busy filling out the same form as her. This was the County Hospital, after all, and that's where all the indigent people had to go. Since she just arrived, the other women were either looking her over or focusing on things around the room and trying to conceal their pain, which, by their expressions, wasn't working.

Ruth had just finished filling out the papers when the nurse returned. She took the form and told Ruth to follow her. Ruth tried to keep up as she limped after the nurse on painful feet. The nurse would turn and wait and look at her impatiently.

Ruth was led down another short hall to a room that held a shower stall. The shower stall was smaller than a broom closet. It had widely spaced wooden floor boards. The nurse told Ruth to remove her clothes and take a shower. Ruth started to undress as the nurse walked out of the room. When she was naked, she squeezed into the shower and turned on the water. Being so heavy with child, it was difficult to move around in the tiny space. She loved the feel of the warm water though, soothing her body after what she had put it through. She began to wash with the harsh, yellow, antiseptic soap that she found on the shelf. It was smelly and gritty but better than nothing.

Ruth finished showering just as the nurse entered the room with some clothes. She handed Ruth the folded bundle she carried and told her to put them on.

There was a short grey hospital gown with a long robe that went over it. There were long, gray stockings that wouldn't stay up because they had no garters. The nurse waited while Ruth dressed, then asked her to sit down in the one of the chairs by a vanity mirror and shelf. She fastened an identification band around Ruth's wrist. Then, she took a towel from the shelf and laid it across Ruth's shoulders. She put on rubber gloves, opened one of the jars that were on the shelf then, picked up a comb and started to part Ruth's hair. She applied some foul-smelling jell into Ruth's hair with her fingers. Ruth turned quickly to face her.

"What are you putting in my hair, Phyllis?" she asked with surprise.

"This has to be done, ma'am. Too many women come in here with lice. Now, you're probably going to tell me you don't have lice. Well, maybe you don't. It doesn't matter. I still have to do this. It's standard procedure."

Ruth had to bear the indignation. When the nurse was through, she wrapped the towel around Ruth's head and went to the small sink and washed her hands.

"We're through now," she said. Then she walked Ruth out into the hall and helped her into another wheelchair. Phyllis pushed her to the elevator. The doors opened and the elevator took them up to the fifth floor. She was wheeled across the hall into a large dormitory-like room. Women who were waiting to have their babies or who had already delivered occupied the beds. The room seemed very noisy for a hospital ward. Some of the women were walking around the room. Others paced by their bed. Still, others lay down in their beds, moaning as they tossed and turned. Many of them were crying. The quiet ones, or those who were trying to sleep, were those who'd already delivered. Three of the women were breast-feeding. She tried to keep from staring but Ruth couldn't take her eyes from this marvelously feminine act.

Phyllis wheeled Ruth to one of the empty beds and told her to rest there and wait for her number to be called. "A doctor will see you soon," Phyllis said, and left again.

The cots looked semi-clean. Ruth thought, *this is one area that could use a little more sanitation. If you don't come in with lice, you're sure to leave with them.*

It seemed like every twenty to thirty minutes; a nurse would come in and call out a number, then leave the room with the woman whose number she'd called. Soon, the woman would return alone.

The woman in the bed next to Ruth was called. About twenty minutes later, she returned. Ruth spoke to her.

"Can you tell me what happens next, here?" she asked.

The woman's face looked drained. Ruth guessed her age to be late thirties. "When they call your number," she said, "you have to see a doctor for an exam, and then you're back here to wait till your baby comes. When your pains are ten minutes apart, they won't bother you any more. They won't take you to be delivered till your pains are three minutes apart or less." She turned away, signifying the end of the conversation.

Soon, a nurse appeared in the doorway and called Ruth's number. Ruth struggled to stand and when the nurse saw her, beckoned her to follow. Ruth was taken to another near-by room, similar to the emergency room but much smaller. There were six cubicles separated by curtains. The nurse's station was in the middle of the room. Ruth was led to an unoccupied cubicle and a nurse closed the curtains around them.

"You'll have to remove the long robe, get onto the examining table and raise the back of your gown from under you," the attending nurse said. She helped Ruth put her feet in the stirrups then placed the long gown over her. "The doctor will be here shortly," she said, and left.

The doctor did arrive shortly. He took a pair of rubber gloves from the box on the table and put them on. After looking at the chart the nurse had placed in the room, he came to Ruth.

"Hello. I'm Dr. Martin. You say your baby is due in about a week? Why are you here now, Mrs. Lawson?"

Ruth didn't correct him, letting him assume that she was married. It made her feel proud and proper.

"I thought I was having labor pains earlier, but I don't feel anything now."

"Well then, as long as you're here, why don't we just see if everything is all right?"

Ruth hated these internal exams, as she knew all women did. However, it had to be done for her sake as well as the baby's. The doctor was gentle and it didn't take long before he finished.

Pulling Ruth's cover down, he said, "You look just fine, Ruth." He took off his gloves and tossed them into the waste can. "The baby's head is in the birthing position so you may not have to wait a week. You could go into labor any time now"

"It can't come too soon to suit me," Ruth said as she removed her feet from the stirrups and sat on the edge of the table.

A nurse took Ruth back to the large dormitory-like room where other women waited. Ruth saw an unoccupied bed in a corner against the wall and asked if she could have that one. It gave her the feeling of a little more privacy. The nurse had no problem with that. The bed wasn't bad. The sheets were fresh and there was a clean pillowcase on the pillow.

Am I going to scream and cry when I'm having labor pains, she thought, as she lay back on the pillow? *Maybe, but who cares, I'll never see any of these people again.* She closed her eyes and lapsed into a calm slumber.

CHAPTER 11

Ruth was awakened by the gentle touch of a hand on her shoulder. Stirring, she tried to come awake, then turned over quickly when she remembered the night before. Her eyes filled with terror. Instinctively, like a frightened child, she clutched the cover and pulled it up to her chin.

"It's all right Ruth. Everything is all right," he said, touching her shoulder once more. "I'm sorry. I didn't mean to startle you."

Ruth looked into the face of Doctor Parker.

"Oh, Doctor Parker," she said, as she heaved a sigh of relief. "You startled me."

"I'm sorry," he said again. "How are you feeling?" He wasn't wearing his doctor's smock but a dark blue suit, white shirt and blue striped tie.

"I think I'm okay." Her mind was still a little groggy. "What time is it?"

"It's six o'clock."

"You mean I've slept through the night?"

"Yes. You seem more rested and calm now. I hated to disturb you but I had to tell you that I couldn't get your story and our conversation out of my mind. If everything you've told me is true, and believe me, I don't doubt that it is, I'd like to help you expose this ring of baby thieves, if you'll let me."

"You mean you really believe me?" Still holding the cover close to her chin, she tried to shift to a sitting position.

Doctor Parker sat down at the foot of the bed. "What you told me needs to be reported to the authorities," he said.

Ruth bowed her head and closed her eyes. *Can it be that this person, someone I don't even know and who doesn't know me, is someone I can trust and who believes me?*

"Another thing, and please tell me if I'm overstepping propriety," he continued, "since you're without family or friends to be with at this time, I'd like to offer you a place to stay till you're able to find other accommodations."

Ruth raised her head and, and with a blank expression on her face, looked into his eyes. *What do I say now,* she thought? *Is this the beginning of another situation over which I'll have no control, or is this a real act of kindness? What do I say?*

"Please don't misunderstand." He saw her reluctance. "You'll be helping me as well. I'm in need of someone to keep house for me and, in return, you'll have a place to stay. Naturally, there'll also be a small salary." He waited while Ruth continued to stare. "You don't have to answer now. Just think about it." He smiled tenderly as he rose, turned and walked away.

Ruth just sat there, wide-eyed, watching him disappear. This person, who was able to see the desperation in her almost chaotic existence, was offering her a chance to make a new beginning, opening a door to stability and independence. She wasn't sure whether she wanted to laugh or cry but the giddy feeling that began to rise in her chest was likely to turn into hysterical laughter if she let it.

The nurses' aides began parading through with breakfast trays. When Ruth's tray was placed on the bedside table, she asked, "When can I take a shower?"

"Anytime you feel able to do so," the young girl replied.

Ruth took a couple bites of her breakfast of scrambled eggs, two slices of bacon and a piece of toast. It had been a while since she'd eaten, so the food went down easily and with enthusiasm. She cleaned her plate. *Now for my shower,* she thought. She hobbled to the shower room and entered one of the stalls. When the water temperature was right, she began to hum as the hot water pelted her head sending the smelly goop from her hair slithering between her breasts. This time she didn't think of Jon. Her thoughts were of the handsome doctor. Nothing could quench this feeling of elation, not even the horrible, hard, yellow, slow to lather soap that she used to pat all over her body.

Her excitement was short lived when she felt an unexpected pain shoot through her abdomen. "Oh," she blurted and wrapped her arms around herself. When another one came, she knew it was time. Somebody was getting ready to meet her face to face. She stepped out of the shower stall, slipped into her robe, and hunching over, walked back to her bed. The nurse saw her coming and helped her into bed.

"Looks like you're going to be a mama soon," she said, as she covered Ruth. "You see that clock on the wall?" she asked. Ruth nodded. "Well, you have to start timing your pains and when they get to be ten minutes apart, you call for me if I'm not here." Ruth nodded again, waiting for the next pain to come surging.

Again and again her labor pains preceded a ragged moan. It was clear that she couldn't pretend to handle the pain as a scream escaped her lips. She became a body of unmanageable misery. Her thoughts flashed back to her first reaction when she saw the other women in labor and how they carried on. She'd thought they were being a little melodramatic. *Please forgive me,* she thought, as she really tried to be quiet. The other women in the room didn't pay any attention to her. Either they were appreciating what she was going through because they had already gone through it, or were preoccupied with their own painful condition.

Her hair, which had dried somewhat, was now damp with perspiration. When she thought she could no longer stand it, she looked at the clock. Eight minutes apart. "Nurse!" she yelled. "Nurse?"

The nurse was quickly beside her.

"Okay, Ruth, let's get you into the prep room," she said with a smile. "We have to shave you and give you an enema. It won't be long now."

Easy for you to say, Ruth thought.

"Come on, Ruth, small breaths now," the nurse encouraged, as she wiped Ruth's brow. Ruth soon lay on the delivery bed where another nurse stood at the foot of the bed with the doctor. Ruth was in another world. All she could think about was the pain that was racking her body

"One more push, Ruth," Doctor Martin said, "I can see the head. Your baby is in a hurry to come into this world. Don't stop now."

Ruth let out a wail as she gave one longer, hard push.

"That's it! Here it comes. The baby is here! Good job, Ruth!" She heard the baby cry. "You have a handsome baby boy!" the doctor said brightly.

Ruth's head fell back. She was exhausted. *It's over,* she thought. *Thank God!*

The team was quick to examine the baby, register the time, date, weight.

It was all routine procedures.

"The baby is fine," the nurse told Ruth. "You have a beautiful, healthy, seven pound, six ounce, baby boy." As Ruth watched them go through their routine with the baby, tears slowly rolled down her cheeks. It was truly over.

"There's nothing to cry about now, Mom." The nurse patted Ruth's arm.

Ruth was moved to her previously occupied bed. The sheets had been changed. When she lay back, she could smell bleach in the pillowcase. That was reassuring. What made her suddenly think about that horrible evening with Jon's mother at a time like this she didn't know, but the anger and humiliation she felt then didn't seem to matter now? The pain that horrid woman had caused her had been washed away. She thought of Jon, too, and felt sorry for him. He would never see the beautiful creation they had made.

It was about forty-five minutes later when a nurse came in with a baby. As she approached, Ruth smiled. She knew it was her baby the nurse was carrying and threw back the covers.

"Here's your baby, Mom, and I think he's hungry," the nurse said as she placed the baby in Ruth's arms. "Call me when he's through nursing."

"Oh, let me have my boy," Ruth said cheerfully, as she reached for him. There was a voice in her head saying, *you're holding your son and he'll never be taken away*. She stroked his head and kept giving him kisses. The scent of this beautiful creation was a bouquet she would never forget. When she opened his tiny hand, he held tight to her finger.

Unfolding his blanket, she examined him. What little hair he had was dark. *Like Jon's,* she thought. His tiny feet were so smooth and his little toes were tightly curled. Ruth lifted his little leg and kissed the bottom of his foot. He began to kick and protest. His wrinkled brow and pursed lips left no doubt that his meal was late and it was making him anxious. He started to cry.

"Yes, my darling," she cooed. "Mommy won't keep you waiting."

Even though it was slightly painful when the baby began to suckle, Ruth was overwhelmed with emotion as she lived this fragile moment for the first time. The nurse had told her that it might be uncomfortable for a while. She kept stroking the top of his head. The voice in her head again said, *you really are holding your baby in your arms.*

Ruth felt surprisingly good after having given birth. Maybe it was the knowledge that she was safe now that brought on this untroubled spirit and made her so cheerful.

It was long after dinner of the same day but the trays hadn't been picked up yet. Ruth was sitting on the side of the bed sipping the last of her tea when Dr. Parker walked in. He smiled at her.

"How are you feeling, Ruth?"

"Hi! How nice of you to come, doctor. I feel very well, thank you." She felt like an old friend had just dropped in, someone with whom she could share her happiness. She really looked at the doctor now that her mind was clear.

Doctor Parker was in his middle thirties. He was six foot one, had broad shoulders, a clear complexion and sea blue eyes. He had light brown hair that was slicked back except for a stubborn lock of hair that fell on the left side of his forehead. His head was well shaped with a straight nose and a square jaw. He had a strong voice but his eyes held a compassionate expression and there was an air of confidence about him. He looked very professional and extremely handsome.

What a good-looking guy, Ruth thought again. "Did you see the baby?" she asked excitedly. "He's beautiful! Seven pounds, six ounces." She stopped then, feeling a little embarrassed by her exuberance. "I'm sorry. Why am I asking you this? Why would that mean anything to you?

"As a matter of fact, I did see him. He's a good-looking boy. You should be very proud. But that's not the only reason for my visit. You're probably going to be discharged in a couple of days, and I was wondering if you'd given my proposal any thought."

"As a matter of fact, I have," Ruth said. She inhaled deeply and sat up a little straighter, with an expectant look on her face. "I was hoping you hadn't changed your mind. I have no place to go and your offer to give me a job and a place to stay is like a gift from heaven. I promise we won't be a bother. I'll make sure the baby doesn't disturb you or get in your way," she rattled on.

"I'm not worried," he broke in with a chuckle, and gave her another big smile. "Besides, the house is like a tomb and a little activity will be a welcome change for me." He put his hand on hers then quickly pulled it back. "I'll check with Dr. Martin to find out what time you're to be discharged," he said as he turned to leave. Stopping for a moment, he turned around and said, "I think this'll be a very amicable arrangement for both of us." With that, he left the room.

Ruth suddenly wished she had a mirror. What must she look like? He was so handsome in his blue suit, white shirt and tie. She smoothed back her hair and ran her hands down the front of her body.

The nurse came in with the baby and nothing else mattered.

Doctor Parker arranged for Ruth to stay in the hospital for three more days. He wanted her to have plenty of time to recover before assuming responsibility for his house

CHAPTER 12

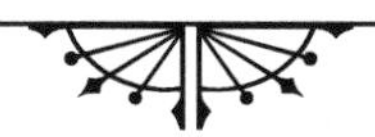

Ruth dressed in the clothes she'd worn when she arrived at the hospital. As shabby as they had been, they'd been laundered and hung in her closet. The nurses were very kind to her as she prepared to leave. They gave her some baby clothes that had been donated to the hospital and told her that, if she needed more, she could come back anytime. Ruth couldn't thank them enough.

Following procedure, when the time came for Ruth to leave the hospital, the nurse helped her into a wheelchair and put the baby in her arms. She was wheeled to an elevator that took them to the main floor. Ruth experienced a moment of panic when she didn't see Dr. Parker but, as she watched, a car pulled up in front of the main entrance. There he was behind the wheel. *Like an angel of mercy,* she thought. *Like the father I never had.*

Once outside, the nurse took the baby from Ruth, while Dr. Parker helped her into the car. Then the nurse handed Ruth the baby and closed the car door.

"Are you comfortable?" Parker asked, before pulling away.

"Yes, thank you."

Ruth's thoughts went back to the night she met Jon, when he drove her home in his fancy car. Even though this wasn't as luxurious as Jon's car had been and the man beside her wasn't wearing a five hundred dollar suit, she was having the same uneasy feelings of not belonging, of not fitting in. Surprisingly, though, she was feeling the same attraction to the man behind the wheel. She was overcome with mixed emotions. She'd been so sure there would never be another man in her life that could make her feel the way she'd felt about Jon. She told herself that she'd never trust another man or love again. Yet, here she was putting herself and her baby in the hands of a man she didn't know.

The streets and the houses flew past. She had no idea where he was taking her. As if he was reading her mind, he began to tell her some things about himself.

"My name is Eugene Harrison Parker. My friends call me Gene. My home is in Oak Park," he said. "I bought it for two reasons. First, it's not far from the hospital. Second, the neighborhood is nice and quiet. It's not a new house but there's plenty of room." He hesitated for a moment as if waiting for some response from Ruth, but none came.

Ruth was only half listening at this point as the baby in her arms was beginning to squirm. *Please make this be the right thing for us. He should be trustworthy, being a doctor and all. He seems sincere. I can always change my mind, but I have no place to go.*

Gene turned into the driveway, but didn't drive straight to the garage at the back of the house. He turned off the engine and walked around to open Ruth's door.

"Do you want me to hold the baby?" he asked.

"No, thank you. I can make it."

The doctor took the bag of baby clothes from the back seat and started to take Ruth's arm. She stopped to take a good look at the house.

"Your house is charming."

Gene thanked her and, once again, offered his arm as they started up the front steps of the two-story house. It had a huge wrap-around front porch. The house was old but beautiful. Brick and white wooden pillars supported the porch roof and railings. The house was painted mauve and grey and had a picture window. She voiced a fleeting thought, "This porch would be a perfect place for a swing, Doctor" Perhaps; it was because everything looked so peaceful.

"I thought we'd decided that you'd call me Gene, now that I'm no longer your doctor. But you're right. The porch needs a swing. I'll see to it."

The small bush in the front yard held pretty pink buds while the miniature lilac bush next to the steps was beginning to share its fragrance.

Gene opened the front door and they stepped into a very small vestibule. The door on the right opened to the living room that faced the front of the house. It was sparsely furnished. When the house had first been built, the room was the parlor, where guest were entertained. A dark brown couch sat against the straight wall and an over-stuffed chair with plaid upholstery was placed at an angle by the windows. Two small end tables with matching lamps sat at each end of the sofa, with a cocktail table in front of it.

It was almost painful to see the sparse furnishings here when compared to Jon's beautiful home that she'd once imagined would someday be hers.

"Why don't you lay the baby on the couch and I'll let me take your coat?"

Ruth laid the baby on the couch, shrugged off her coat and Gene hung it in the hall closet.

"As you can see, the place isn't very fancy but it's clean and comfortable. I'll be away a great deal of the time, so I want you to feel free to go anywhere in the house. Think of this as your home. Let me show you the rest of the place. Don't worry about the baby." He chuckled. The baby was asleep. "I don't think he's going anywhere."

The dining room was almost part of the living room because the only separation was a large archway. The room had a china cabinet built into the wall. Ruth thought that was nice but it had no china in it. An oval table with six chairs stood in the center of the otherwise bare room. An ornate chandelier hung over the table. They moved to the kitchen. It wasn't very big but the cozy bay window area held a small table and four chairs.

"As far as food is concerned," Gene explained, "you'll have to tell me what you need. You won't find much in the cabinets at the moment. I've been eating out a lot. Do you know how to drive, Ruth?"

"Yes, I do. Why?"

"Well, I was thinking that I'd have to take you shopping, but since you drive, you can take me to the hospital on the days you want to shop, use my car to do your errands and pick me up at the end of my shift. How does that sound?"

Realizing how much the doctor was doing for her made her suddenly uncomfortable with feelings of guilt.

"I think I'm going to be a lot of trouble," she said, trying to smile.

"Nonsense," he replied, "You can see that this house is in need of activity and it'll give me some peace of mind knowing there's someone here while I'm away. Now let me show you the rooms upstairs."

His explanation gave Ruth little consolation at this moment. Her thoughts were already in the future. *Will the doctor regret his magnanimous decision to have me move in?* She took a minute to check the baby before following the doctor up the stairs. He was still asleep and hadn't moved at all. Gene showed her the three bedrooms and the hall bathroom.

"We'll have to share the bathroom up here," he said, "but I'm usually out of the house by 5:30... 6:00 at the latest. Since the baby will be sharing your room, I've moved my things to the bedroom at the end of the hall and given you the larger bedroom."

"But I don't want you to put yourself out on my..." Ruth started to protest.

"Don't worry about it," he interrupted, "I've given it a lot of thought and I've got everything arranged. I'm going to go back to the hospital for a few hours now, so you'll be here alone. I know there's some coffee in the pantry and some bread and cold cuts in the refrigerator. I'll call you later to see if there's anything else you need."

He started back down the stairs and Ruth followed. When they reached the living room, the doctor walked over to the couch and stood for a moment looking down at the baby.

"He is a beautiful boy, Ruth."

The doctor had tossed his coat on the chair when they came in. Putting it on, he said, "I have to leave now. While I'm gone, I want you to become familiar with the house. Anyway, you'll feel more at ease when I'm not around making you nervous. Please try to relax. I'll see you later."

There was a second when Ruth wanted to call out, "Please don't go," but she didn't. Ruth sat down next to the baby, still loosely wrapped in his blankets. Feeling a little uncomfortable, she stared at the front door thinking the doctor might come back but he didn't. The car backed out of the driveway and Gene drove away.

She took the baby's bag with the ready-made bottles of formula and walked to the kitchen to put them in the refrigerator. The nurse had told her that, without sufficient milk to breast feed, she would have to supplement with formula. That seemed all right. The nurses were kind enough to have several bottles prepared for Ruth before she left the hospital and gave her six cans of Similac powder to be mixed as was needed later.

In the refrigerator, she found the cold cuts, a loaf of whole wheat bread, a quart of milk, some butter and a dozen eggs. One by one, she proceeded to open each kitchen cabinet to see what was inside. She found the one that held the dishes; a service for six that looked as though it had never been used. Another held an unopened box of saltine crackers, a box of shortbread cookies and some peanut butter. *There's enough here to do me for a while but he shouldn't be eating in restaurants all the time,* she thought, walking back to the front room. *That's too expensive, even for a doctor.*

With the baby in one arm and his bag of clothes in the other, she started up the stairs. The bedroom the doctor had assigned her was quite large. There was a dresser with a mirror and a highboy, with ample room for a crib when she could afford one. The baby stirred when Ruth laid him on the bed and removed his sweater and cap, but went right back to sleep again.

Despite some trepidation and a feeling of embarrassment at doing something she knew was wrong, curiosity made her walk to the doctor's room. There was much more she needed to learn about him but nothing in the room seemed unusual. A closet held several suits; one of them was a very expensive silk suit. In the drawers were white shirts, underwear, socks. A comb and brush lay on the dresser. There was also a bottle of men's cologne. An irresistible urge compelled Ruth to unscrew the cap. She sniffed it once and then once again. It was delightful, a manly scent that would stay in her mind for a long time.

She went back to her room feeling a little disappointed that there wasn't anything mysterious about the man but at the same time relieved because she'd found nothing unusual. The baby began to stir so Ruth went down to the kitchen to heat his formula. Just as she finished, the phone rang. She hesitated before lifting the receiver off of the phone on the kitchen wall. "Hello?" It was Gene. She thought, *it's so good to hear his voice.*

"Is everything all right, Ruth?"

"Yes, everything's fine." She wanted to say, "I wish you were here."

"Do you need anything, for you or the baby?" he asked.

"No. I was just fixing his bottle before putting him down for the afternoon."

"All right, then. I'll see you later."

"Good-bye," she said, and hung up the phone.

Ruth went back upstairs. Overwhelmed with mixed emotions, she lay down next to her baby. He was her life now. She needed him as much as he needed her, perhaps, even more. Then her thoughts turned to the doctor. *What about Gene? Will he need us as much a year from now as we need him now?* Soon, Ruth and the baby were asleep.

It was the sound of dishes rattling that woke her. Ruth opened her eyes to a darkened room. She experienced a moment of panic and confusion, thinking she was back in Mrs. Travis' house, but quickly realized where she was. Rolling off the bed, trying not to wake the baby, she gently put a pillow on each side of him, even though she knew he couldn't turn over yet, and tiptoed out of the room. She went down stairs and walked toward the kitchen, where the doctor was doing something at the counter.

"There you are," he said, when he turned and saw her standing in the doorway. "If you're wondering why I was making so much noise, it's because I didn't want to be quiet. I was hoping you'd hear me and come down. It was still early when I left the hospital so I decided to stop for a bottle of wine. I thought we should drink a toast to our newfound friendship and the birth of your son. What do you say?"

"I say you're a very generous, compassionate person to bring a perfect stranger into your home; two perfect strangers, in fact."

With a frown on his face as he stared at her, he answered, "Well, maybe you do look a little strange." She knew he was joking. They both laughed. "Oh, my God!" He'd had a sudden thought and whispered, "we're celebrating you and the baby, while I'm making all this damned noise and forgetting he's upstairs. Did I wake him? I don't hear him crying."

"No, he's sound asleep." Ruth couldn't hold back a chuckle, seeing the concerned look on Gene's face. Her thoughts moved him closer in her mind. "I don't think he'll be a light sleeper after hearing all those crying babies in the hospital." She said.

"That's a relief."

Gene took two wine glasses from the top cabinet above the stove, filled their wine glasses then raised his. Ruth touched his glass with hers. For a moment their eyes held. He was the first to turn away.

"I haven't eaten," he said, "and since it appears nothing here has been touched, I guessed you hadn't eaten anything either, so I made some sandwiches."

They sat down opposite each other at the small table in the kitchen.

After taking a couple of bites of her sandwich, Ruth said, "This is very good. I am hungry. Thank you, Doctor."

"Ruth," he began, "since we're no longer doctor and patient, I really want you to call me Gene. No," he continued. "I insist that you call me Gene. Okay?" He smiled.

"Okay!" she smiled back.

"Now, I know you must think I'm crazy, but from the moment I saw you, especially after I heard your story, I felt this compulsion to do something about the distressing situation you got caught up in. As soon as you're up to it, I want you to help me find that house where you stayed so we can put those evil people where they belong and stop their cruel business of human trafficking."

What Gene said brought on fleeting feelings of the mental anguish she had endured in that frightful place. Ruth felt a shudder move through her body.

Will I ever get over what happened there? She thought. *They say time heals, but I wonder. How long will it take to heal me? Gene wants to see Mrs. Travis and the others put out of business, that's for sure. I admire him for that, but going to that house again would make me feel...* She shook her head and said, "I'm not sure where it is but I'll know it if I see it again. I can't help thinking of *my* last night there; those frightful hours spent trying to hide from them, all the while following an unfamiliar road that, thank God, led me to the church. Maybe you can contact the ambulance that brought me to the hospital. They can tell you where they picked me up."

"That's a good idea," Gene said. "We'll start there. Although, I have a feeling that these people will find another place to operate very quickly. Since you managed to escape, they'll figure you had to get help getting away; especially with the baby about to be born. Questions would be asked that would get the authorities involved. With the little information we have, it might take some time to find them."

"That's one thing I've got plenty of right now." Ruth didn't care how long it took. She and the baby were safe and that's all that mattered to her.

They finished their sandwiches in silence; the baby's cries broke the almost uncomfortable silence. Ruth got up from her chair.

"I'll take care of the baby then clean up," she said.

"There's not much to clean," Gene said, standing. "You take care of the baby and I'll take care of things here."

They brushed against each other as Ruth started for the refrigerator. He touched her arm. She smelled that scent again; the scent from the bottle on his dresser.

She heated the baby's bottle and went upstairs.

"You are so beautiful," she said to Robert, as she cradled him in the crook of her arm. Between wakefulness and sleep, she realized the house had become quiet. The noises from the kitchen had stopped. Hearing the sound of the shower in the next room gave her a comfortable sense of peace. She didn't feel friendless and alone. She felt... "At home," she sighed.

For a little while, friendly visions filled her head. Her thoughts went back to the peaceful, unhurried life of the orphanage and the sisters who had raised her. There had always been a feeling of safety while living with them. They had loved and cared for her. There had never been a time when no one had been there to comfort her after she'd had a bad dream. Nor had she ever had to concern herself with things beyond what her young mind had been able to comprehend. Now, lying in a happy, tranquil state beside her son, she felt safe again. It seemed that her bad dreams had, once again, disappeared.

The baby's stirring woke her. Untroubled sleep had been a stranger for so long that, for a moment, she felt a irritating hint of guilt when she opened her eyes.

She thought, *it must be 5:30 or 6:00*, as she listened to the racket the birds were making. She looked out the window and saw a huge maple tree. It had been planted so close to the house that one could reach out and touch its branches. *I'm going to have to get used to the noise these little beauties make every morning*, she thought. The baby had awoke only once during the night and was satisfied with mother's milk before falling asleep again.

Because the baby might disturb Gene, she took him downstairs while fixing his bottle. It was 6:30 by the clock above the kitchen sink. Remembering that Gene said he was usually out of the house by 5:30 or 6:00 a.m., she realized that he wasn't home to be disturbed. She thought of the long day awaiting her. Robert started crying and soon the baby in her arms took all her attention. Ruth couldn't take her eyes off him as she watched him drink. She touched his little head and caressed his tiny hands.

"My son," she said to him. "I'm all you have. It's a shame you'll never know your father. You'll never have grandparents to spoil you. It's my fault, and I'm sorry. I made some very bad choices and I regret them but I don't regret having you. Please don't hold my sins against me when you know the truth, and you will know it when you're older. We're lucky to be here now, so let's try to be happy and not lose sight of our good fortune."

Ruth spent a portion of the day becoming familiar with the house. She had seen the upstairs and the main floor, with its sunny, enclosed back porch, so, now it was the basement that needed exploration. Ruth found the light switch on the wall when she opened the door leading to the basement. Slowly, she descended. The basement was virtually empty. Ruth assumed that it was because Gene hadn't had the house long enough to gather a lot of possessions. Stationary tubs were under the window at one end of the basement. An old wringer washing machine stood next to the sinks. Other than that, the basement was empty. *Well, that didn't take long,* she thought.

Ruth returned to the first floor. She intended to clean but there didn't seem to be a need for that, since the tables were bare of knick-knacks and the floors didn't need attention. She wondered if Gene had someone come in to clean the house. If he did, she would insist he dismiss them so she could do the housework. That would help pay for the inconvenience of living here with the baby. She smiled, remembering his first offer. "He did say I'd be housekeeper... but I can't accept a salary. It wouldn't be right. Room and board for us is more then enough."

It was 6:30 when Gene arrived home that evening. Ruth felt butterflies in her stomach when she heard Gene's car pull into the driveway. Realizing that most of her day had been spent in anticipation of his arrival, she wondered if it was just loneliness or an actual desire to be with him, to feel the security that his being there gave her.

There was a moment of awkwardness when he came in through the kitchen door. They exchanged hellos and, to Ruth's surprise, his next words were, "How's Robert?" Without waiting for her answer, he walked past her and started for the stairs. She didn't have the heart to tell him that Robert had been irritable most of the day and had finally fallen asleep. When Gene came down, she heaved a sigh of relief. All was still quiet upstairs.

"Oh!" he exclaimed, "I stopped to pick up dinner but left it in the car, I'll be right back."

Ruth couldn't believe the little-boy look on Gene's face when he realized what he'd done. It was another side of this outwardly stoic, in-control man she was beginning to know. She had to smile at that pleasing revelation.

"I have a day open tomorrow," Gene said during dinner. "I'll drive you around town so you can become familiar with the area. You and the baby need some clothes and I want to pick up a crib for Robert. He needs a bed of his own, and so do you."

Ruth was ready to protest, but she didn't. To what would she protest, his kindness or his generosity, or that she was penniless and had no way of repaying him. Instead, she said, "I was wondering if you had a housekeeper. It's my understanding that this was to be a reciprocal situation and I want to do my part. I know you're giving me much more than I can ever give in return, but I want to do whatever I can to compensate for the kindness you've shown."

"Ruth, the house is yours. I'm leaving everything in your care. You have to promise me one thing, though."

"Yes, anything."

"When I come home, whenever that may be, I want to see a smile on your face

CHAPTER 13

It was now winter. December had come too soon. The trees were bare and snow dusted the ground. The summer had gone by too quickly but it had been a wonderful summer. Ruth had watched as the garden slowly came to life and brought forth sweet smelling blossoms. Then, with the chilly winds of autumn, she saw the leaves turn to beautiful shades of red and gold. Now the trees were bare and stark against the winter blue sky.

Gene had bought a stroller so that Ruth could take the baby for walks whenever the weather permitted. She used it almost every day it was warm enough. When it got cooler, she continued to take Robert for short walks, bundling him in his warm snowsuit and hat.

Through the changing seasons, Ruth continued to find contentment. She enjoyed a new stability in her life. Thoughts of the past subsided as each day brought new pleasures. Being in charge of things, as if it were her house, had been the first of those pleasures. Cooking and cleaning and being able to shop were enjoyable responsibilities. Listening to the mellifluous sounds that Robert made when he was bouncing around in his crib, trying to decide which stuffed animal to cuddle before falling asleep, made this house really feel like home.

Robert was seven months old on December seventh and was already crawling. *He's growing up too fast,* she thought.

It took Ruth a good twenty minutes after Robert went to bed to gather up all the toys that were strewn around the house. She didn't want Gene tripping over anything when he came in, even though he told her that it didn't matter. It was he who kept bringing more toys home.

The most rewarding thing for Ruth was the attention Gene paid to the baby. It was obvious that Gene loved him and Robert showed he loved

Gene in return. Gene's face showed pride when they were out shopping and someone would remark that he had a beautiful baby. They were like a family, except for one thing; Ruth and Gene's relationship remained platonic. Unaware of each other's feelings, both were reluctant to make the first move toward intimacy for fear of ruining a comfortable, happy situation.

On Saturday, Gene came home early. He was excited as he came through the door. His enthusiasm was obvious in his laughing eyes and cold-reddened cheeks.

"Come on," he said, "Get your coats on. Santa Claus is in town and I think Robert should pay him a visit."

"My goodness! You could give a person some advance notice." Ruth chuckled.

"I didn't know myself until one of the nurses talked about taking her two children. Anyway, let's go before Santa leaves the store."

Ruth put Robert in his snowsuit. Gene held him while she put on her coat and hat. A light snow was falling, just enough to stick to the trees but not enough to make the roads slippery.

Fortunately, a car was pulling out of a parking place in front of Goldblatt's Department Store.

"Now, aren't we lucky," Gene said as he backed the car into the space with one try. "I hope we're not too late." Once out of the car, Ruth handed him the baby and they hurried through the revolving doors. They took the elevator to the second floor. Holiday music could be heard throughout the store. Decorations and colored lights twinkled everywhere. Surprised by all the activity going on, Robert kept turning his head from left to right in order to see everything around him. Ruth and Gene laughed at his wide-eyed fascination.

Winding their way through the aisles, they found Santa. "We're in luck," Gene said, with a sigh of relief, "He's still here." He removed Robert's hat and opened the top of his snowsuit. There were three children ahead of them. When their turn came, Gene put Robert on Santa's lap.

"Well, who have we here?" Santa said in a loud voice that made Robert's lip quiver. He didn't cry, but he didn't want to get too close either, so he leaned way back. His eyes were as big as saucers and never left Santa's face.

"His name is Robert, Santa," Gene said.

Santa tried talking to Robert but the smile they were anticipating never appeared. Even after hearing Santa say his name, Robert didn't respond. He just kept staring and frowning. Finally, he began to whimper so Gene took him back. Santa called, "Merry Christmas," as they walked away.

"At least he made it long enough to get his picture taken," Gene laughed.

"I know. I was waiting for him to start screaming."

"Not my boy," Gene whispered in Robert's ear, but Ruth heard him, too.

What a wonderful evening, Ruth thought, as they pulled into the driveway. Her heart was overflowing with love for this man. *I believe he loves Robert. I wish he felt the same about me.* Once inside, Ruth took Robert upstairs and got him ready for bed. He had been dozing on the drive home, so after he was tucked in, he went right to sleep. Ruth went back downstairs. Gene was relaxing on the couch. There were two glasses of wine sitting on the coffee table.

"Sit down, Ruth," he said. "It's still early. I thought you'd like to join me in a glass of wine before we retire."

"I'd like that very much," she said. There was a moment of hesitation when she wasn't sure where to sit, next to him on the couch or in the chair. She chose the chair.

"I have to tell you, it was fun tonight," Gene smiled. "Robert's a great little guy."

"I had a good time too, and you were so patient with him, Thank you *so* much!"

They both sipped their wine in silence for a little while.. Ruth searched his face for signs of something; of what, she didn't know. She only knew she couldn't read anything in his expression.

"Ruth," Gene said, after a pause he devoted to swirling the stem of the wine glass, "I'm sure you must be aware that I am very fond of Robert. No, more than that. Maybe I'm taking too much for granted but I've come to love him."

"I thought so, the way you look for him the moment you walk through the door. And you're always bringing some new toy home. Do you think that's a good idea? I mean I don't want him spoiled, thinking he can have everything he wants."

"He won't be spoiled. I know when it's necessary to say no." For a second, he thought about what he had just said. He lowered his head. "That sounded terrible, didn't it? I mean, it sounded like I'll be in charge of his upbringing. I'm sorry. You can tell me to mind my own business any time, Ruth."

He set his glass down then picked it up again and took a sip. He used the motion to ease the uncomfortable feeling he had just given himself. Ruth reached for her glass and sipped slowly.

She shifted in her chair. *How am I supposed to answer him?* "I don't know what to say," she began. "I know you love him and he loves you, but Robert isn't your responsibility," she said, shifting again in her chair, trying to find the right words. She wondered how she could say that she wanted everything to stay the same. In her heart, she knew Gene would make a perfect father. She decided to come right out and tell him how she was feeling.

"I don't know what your plans are for the future," she began, "I only know that we're happy here and Robert loves you. So, as long as we're welcome, we'll stay. I know that a child needs a father, and it would make us both happy if you were that person." Ruth stared into her glass of wine and wondered if she had said too much. Had she put him on the spot? "I mean, only if you want to be," she quickly added. "I mean while we're here.

Gene moved forward, set his glass down and looked into Ruth's face.

"I don't know if you realize it but you've just made me the happiest guy in the world. I don't want you to leave. My house feels alive now, and I want it to stay this way. I've been alone too long." He raised his glass and said, "Now that we've got that settled, here's to the three of us - one happy family."

Ruth raised her glass. *What does he mean by that? If we're a family, where do I fit in? And what does he mean; he's been alone too long?* Gene settled back with a big grin on his face. "I'll try to get home early again next Saturday," he said. "We need to get a Christmas tree." He was thoughtful for a moment, and then added, "We don't have any lights or decorations. Oh, well! We'll pick those up, too. Do you want more wine?"

"No thanks. But you go ahead and have another."

"No more for me either. I'm off to bed, how about you?"

"In a little while. I'll finish my wine, and then I have to fold the diapers I washed this afternoon." Gene started to take his glass away. "I'll take care of the glasses," she said

"Okay, then, Good night."

"Good night."

Christmas Eve was a particularly busy day for Ruth. Tomorrow would be Robert's first Christmas. She spent the day preparing foods for their holiday dinner. She didn't know exactly what time Gene would be home this evening or tomorrow, but she wanted to make this holiday a special one for all of them.

The tree was beautifully decorated with colored lights and ornaments, thanks to Gene. Too many presents waited beneath the tree, again thanks to Gene. Ignoring her protests, he kept buying more.

After her chores were done and Robert was sleeping soundly, Ruth looked around and smiled. With only the tree lights on, the house felt cozy with peaceful warmth. Not wanting to retreat from her contentment just yet, she decided to have a glass of wine and relax in the glow before going to bed. One glass led to a second, as she drank in the silence as enthusiastically as she drank the wine in her glass.

Mesmerized by the shimmering lights before her, she became aware of an emotion she refused to identify, but couldn't repress. Turning the stem of the glass between her fingers, she closed her eyes. A tingle of awareness whispered across her skin. She thought of Jon and tried to remember their romantic nights, thinking his memory had encouraged the eruption of these emotions. Now those intimate meetings seemed distant and vague. She tried to see his face, but it was a blur. Instead, it was Gene's face that captivated her thoughts. It was Gene's body that aroused her. But most of all it was his scent hibernating in her memory. Her thoughts became convoluted.

What's the matter with you? Aren't you the one who said you would never trust another man? Never get close enough to love again! You know you're lying when you tell yourself that your feelings for Gene are purely out of respect and gratitude? Are you really ready to make a fool of yourself again? There was little hesitation before Ruth answered her thoughts out loud. "Yes, I am" she said emphatically. "I really am." Blushing, she looked around as if someone might be listening.

She emptied her glass and stood up. Feeling a little light-headed, she grabbed the back of the chair to steady herself. A giddy but nice sensation washed over her. Laughing at herself, she said, "We must do this more often."

Taking her glass to the kitchen, she rinsed it, set it on the dish drainer and started up the stairs thinking that a nice warm shower would feel good.

She turned on the shower, checked the water temperature, but changed her mind. She would treat herself to a long soak in the tub, something she hadn't done in a while. There had never seemed to be enough time until now. While the tub was filling, she began to undress, letting each piece of clothing fall to the floor around her. Stepping out of the circle of crumpled clothing, she stepped into the tub and lowered her body into the soothing warm water.

Gene opened the back door expecting to hear some activity but the house was quiet. All the lights were out except for the Christmas tree. He thought, *Ruth either forgot to turn them off or left them on for me to enjoy and, perhaps, light my way through the house.* Standing there and looking at the lighted tree, he smiled. *I am really home?*

When the warmth of the house finally got to him, he removed his overcoat and draped it over the back of a chair. He removed his sweater and tie, and draped them over his arm. Still standing there admiring the tree, he slowly unbuttoned his shirt as if he were getting ready for bed. Finally, he picked up his overcoat and walked through the house to hang it in the front closet. It was then that he noticed a light in the hall at the top of the stairs. It was coming from the open bathroom door. *Another light she forgot to turn off,* he thought, and grinned.

While in the process of putting his coat on a hanger, he heard the soft humming of "We Wish You a Merry Christmas." *Oh, boy, what do I do now? She didn't expect me home this early. I don't want to frighten her. I suppose I could wait down here. I'll just creep up the stairs, hurry past the bathroom and go right to my room.*

Starting out on tiptoes, hoping the stairs wouldn't creak and give him away, he slowly took one step at a time. When he reached the top of the stairs, Ruth was just coming out of the bathroom. Catching her by surprise, she drew back when she saw him, but didn't automatically clutch the towel to make sure she was sufficiently covered.

They did nothing at first but exchange stares, Ruth, wrapped in the towel that just covered her torso, and Gene, with his shirt unbuttoned almost to the waist. Seeing her standing in the doorway with the light on her wet hair and water droplets glistening like diamonds on her skin, he was immediately overcome with desire and wondered how he'd been able to resist the urge to take her in his arms for so long. Their gazes still locked, he was the first to speak. His voice was husky with a slight stammer.

"I… I'm home," he said. "

With her free hand, she brushed away some wet hair that stuck to her face, thinking, *this is very awkward. What a sight I must be.* She couldn't see the tantalizing woman standing there in near nakedness. All she could say was, "I wasn't expecting you so soon." *Now that sounded stupid,* she thought.

"I know . . . I'm sorry." More silence. Gene took two steps towards her. The uneasiness of anticipation lay beneath the steady look they exchanged.

Ruth fought for control when, suddenly, she felt her body becoming aroused by his unexpected presence. *Surely, he must feel the same,* she thought. *Why is he just standing there? Doesn't desire show on my face? What is he waiting for? Maybe he doesn't find me attractive. Maybe he's afraid to make the first move. What if I do and he rejects me? Will I spoil everything? Will he think I'm a terrible person? Damn it, Gene! Do something!*

This was too much for her. The tension was all consuming. She looked away and then back again. *Oh, well, I guess there's only one way to find out.* She let the towel fall to the floor. She could hear the rush of air as he sucked in his breath. His eyes found her every curve as they slowly worked their way up the platinum flesh, from the tip of her toes, past the trim waist and the firm breasts, to the bright blushing pink in her cheeks. Gene lowered his arm and the tie and sweater dropped to his feet. Slowly, he walked to her until they were as close as two people can be without touching. For a moment they stood facing each other.

Ruth saw it then; the hunger in his eyes. His hand was trembling as he reached up and touched her hair. He put both hands on her shoulders then slid them down her arms till he had her hands in his. Ruth lifted her chin in anticipation. She left no doubt that there would be no resistance.

He bent to kiss her lips. His touch was soft and quick at first. Then, his hands went around her waist as he crushed her into him. Ruth rose up on her toes and wrapped her arms around his neck. Her mouth found his. The passion she had known so long ago came rushing back. There was no hesitation; her body was so ready.

Their lips were stuck to each other when Gene lifted her up. Her feet never touched the floor as he carried her to his room. Standing beside the bed, Ruth didn't want to let him go. She could hardly believe how much she wanted him to come into her. Her body was actually trembling. He had to take her arms from around his neck so he could remove his clothes. She stood, waiting to feel his skin against hers, and the moment they were naked and in each others' arms, she could feel the trembling of his body. Desire was so intense that it became an ache. It was a hunger that required immediate gratification. He eased her gently down. As he covered her with his body, she thought she must have been scalding him with the heat of her yielding flesh. She arched against the weight of him.

"Ruth, Ruth." He repeated her name while trying to slow the pace by kissing her neck, her shoulders, and her breasts. Moving his tongue around each nipple, he took them into his mouth. He worked his way down her body. He slid his lips over her stomach, penetrating her navel with his tongue. He eased her legs apart and caressed his way up her inner thighs to the warm wetness of desire. She stopped him there by taking his head in her hands. He knew the signal and brought his body back to rest on hers. She was too aroused for foreplay. That would come another time.

She loved the weight of him as his hardness pressed between her legs. He kissed her hard, forcing her lips apart as his tongue found the inside of her mouth. She sucked his bottom lip and for a second held it between her teeth. The instant bite was a surprise that sent his desire to the limit. With a moan, he slipped inside her. Ruth inhaled sharply with the initial entry. Tight with the first stroke, her muscles quickly relaxed, welcoming the combustible force pulsing inside her. They moved together, slowly at first, until Ruth ran her hands down his back, pressing his tight buttocks trying to pull him closer. Desiring deeper penetration, she raised her hips and wrapped her legs around him. Responding with the abandonment of a woman who wouldn't be denied, Ruth met each thrust with one of her own.

A master of self-control, Gene brought Ruth to climax again and again until they ended in blazing, panting completeness. Breathless sounds of pleasure melted into quiet moans, until nothing was left but a whimper. Ruth was overcome with the wonder of it all. Gene slid his arms under her and took her with him as he rolled off her.

They clung together till their breathing relaxed. She buried her face in the hollow of his neck. They had become as one. He was now a part of her. Time stood still as they lay cloistered in each other's arms.

"I love you, Ruth," he whispered.

"I love you, too." Now, Ruth looked down at him and smiled. "Why did you wait so long?" she asked.

"I was afraid I'd scare you away. You don't know how stressful it's been to want you so badly and not be able to take you in my arms, or how hard it was to resist kissing you. I tried not to get too close; afraid I might lose control and cause you to run out of my life."

"Isn't this ironic?" she said, "you wanting me and me wanting you, yet both afraid to destroy a beautiful relationship?"

Ruth let her full weight rest upon him. She could feel Gene beginning to rise.

"This could go on until morning," she laughed.

"You're right! Any objections?"

"No, sir, not I," she laughed, and kissed him hard

It had been so long for both of them. She wriggled against him until he was between her legs; she began teasing herself by tightening her thighs and thrusting her pelvis back and forth. Gene was hard again. He grabbed her around the waist and lifted her high enough to be able to find his way into her. She helped with the insertion. Once more, he became a part of her. Once again their bodies became entangled, exploding into a pulsating union that was so incredible, more than either one had ever known. He fell away from her after they climaxed again. For a while they rested, exhausted and out of breath. Gene turned to her and roughly pulled her into his arms, holding her so tight she could barely breathe.

"Don't leave," he demanded. "Stay here, with me. This is the way I want it to be from now on. I want you here in my arms all night… every night." He loosened his grip and turned Ruth's face up to his. "Robert is sleeping soundly now. Let's not take the chance of waking him. Don't go."

Ruth felt the firmness of his muscular body, the sweet smell of his flesh, her tender kiss that tasted the sweat that lingered on his brow, and knew she would never leave. She loved the safety of his arms and desperately wanted and needed the love she knew he had for her.

"I love you, Gene. I never thought I could let myself get close to another man. I vowed no one would ever hurt me again. Now here I am, loving you, taking a chance again. Only this time, I feel that it's right. I'll never leave. You'll have to tell me to go."

He gave her a quick squeeze and said, "You're stuck with me for life, Honey."

It was late and they were both tired, or there might have been another round of lovemaking. Ruth lay in the shelter of his arm with her head on his chest, while Gene's hand cupped her breast. That's how they fell asleep.

Gene woke up to numbness in the arm that Ruth was lying on. Ever so gently, he slid his arm from under her. Ruth didn't awaken. The clock on his dresser said 5:30. *Time to get up anyway,* he thought. Slipping out of bed, he went about his morning routine. He left the house, quietly closing and locking the door behind him.

After a while, Ruth reluctantly awoke. She squinted at the morning light trying to squeeze through the half-open blinds. Taking a deep breath, she turned onto her back and stretched. Her thoughts immediately returned to Gene and the night before, she raised her head to see if he was still beside her. He was gone.

Lying back, she stared at the ceiling as a smile spread across her lips. Last night and the wonder of it all came rushing back. She couldn't get it out of her mind. Not that she wanted to, as she lay there luxuriating in the after glow of their lovemaking. After running her hands over the impression remaining beside her, she rolled into the mould. She hugged the pillow that held the scent of the man she was sure she would never get enough of, the man whose arms had held her all night long. In retrospect, she became giddy and that feeling returned again and again in the months that followed.

CHAPTER 14

Ruth stood at the kitchen sink washing last night's dinner dishes. Once again, they'd been left in the sink. Robert was sound asleep when Gene got home, and after a quick reheated meal, Gene and Ruth couldn't wait to be in each other's arms. She had a silly grin on her face thinking about the nights when Robert's contented squeals would interrupt her reverie, as if he were giving permission.

He was a happy child upon waking and amused himself with soft toys and looking at things around him. She decided to finish the dishes and take a quick shower before Robert, who normally took up most of her day, required her attention.

After her shower, Ruth went about her normal routine of cleaning and dusting while Robert played with his toys in the middle of the living room floor. He was walking now, which meant the tables were bare of breakables. As she worked, Robert, still a little cautious, crawled to the couch and hauled himself up to stand. When Ruth wasn't looking, he walked along the couch till he came to the end table. He noticed the knob on the table drawer and yanked on the pull. The drawer slid out easily spilling the contents onto the floor. Ruth turned with a frown on her face when she heard the crash, but the look of surprise and fear on Robert's face made her laugh. "Robert, you're a real nuisance at times!" she exclaimed, and put him back among his toys in the playpen.

Ruth knelt down to pick up the things and put them back in the drawer. There were letters and a few pictures. She sat down on the floor and began looking at the pictures.

There was a picture of an older man and woman sitting on a sofa next to a huge fireplace. Ruth thought they must be Gene's mother and father. The woman had a small round face with blond hair and was wearing a sweet smile, while the man looked rather somber in his suit, white shirt and tie. His hair was still mostly dark with touches of grey at the temples. He looked very distinguished but not at all pleasant. The corners of his mouth drooped in what must have been a perpetual frown.

There was the usual assortment of family photos; pictures taken at the zoo, at birthday parties, at Gene's college graduation, at parties on the lawn and at Christmas. There were several pictures of Mom and Dad with two boys. Ruth thought that the other boy must be Gene's brother. She didn't open the letters, even though she was tempted. She picked up the mess and put everything back in the drawer, trying to be neat but not knowing how it had been arranged before Robert spilled it.

Gene Parker came from a wealthy family, the second son of George and Alice Parker. His older brother, George Jr., was the apple of his father's eye, while Gene was his mother's favorite. The boys were friends, but their parent's inconsistent attitude toward them, drove the boys in opposite directions. Knowing he had his dad's approval no matter what, George ignored the urging and encouragement to become a lawyer and join his father's firm. He couldn't see himself tied to a desk trying to solve everyone's problems. Instead, he took the easy way and preferred having fun on his father's money.

Gene, however, sought his father's approval. So much so that he took pre-law classes upon entering college. Mid-semester, he realized law wasn't for him either. He felt himself drawn to the medical field. Albeit not law, he thought his choice would be good enough to make his father proud. He wrote to his parents about his career change, hoping for a positive response. His mother wrote back to say that she was proud of his decision and joked about having a doctor in the family. There wasn't a mention about his father's feelings. That disappointed but didn't surprise him.

Ruth was curious about Gene's past, and his family, but didn't know how to bring up the subject without feeling guilty about looking through his things. A couple of days passed before she was given the opportunity to do so. She was unaware that the change in her demeanor showed. But Gene's question proved that it did, and it gave her the opening she needed. Ruth was seated on the couch in the living room and Gene had just poured them a glass of Riesling.

"What's bothering you, Ruth?" Gene asked as he set their glasses of wine on the coffee table and sat down beside her. "You seemed preoccupied the last few days. Talk to me."

"Well," Ruth began. "Robert and I had a bit of an accident the other day."

"What kind of an accident?" Gene said anxiously. "Is Robert okay?"

"He's fine. He just pulled the drawer out of the end table and the contents spilled out. I tried to put things back like you had them but I couldn't help looking at the pictures that were there. I hope you're not upset. It did make me curious though. Are those your parents in the pictures, and do you have a brother? I'd really like to know about your life before we met, if you'd care to tell me."

Gene was quiet for a few moments. He picked up his glass, took a sip of wine and put it back on the table. Ruth thought she might have brought up things he wasn't ready to discuss.

"I had intended telling you because you have a right to know," he said. "But that would have been a bit later. I actually haven't thought about my past in a long time. The only thing that's been on my mind lately is how happy I am since you came into my life. I realize that finding the pictures would naturally make you curious."

"If you don't want to tell me now, you don't have to."

"No, it's just as well we get it over with."

"Gene, please. You seem a little anxious about this."

"I'm not anxious at all," Gene said, after picking up his glass and taking another sip of wine. He rose from the couch and walked slowly to the window. He looked out as if trying to think of a way to begin. "I just needed a place to start," he said, "and, thanks to Robert, the pictures you've seen proved to be the perfect opening."

Gene hesitated another moment before continuing. "For one thing, my dad and mom didn't agree on how to raise kids. When a situation regarding us boys was discussed, it always ended in an argument. Of course, my dad, being the high and mighty, pompous ass that he was, always won. The situation was very distressing for my mother, since she had to make decisions when he wasn't there and then prepare herself for his wrath when he came home. He wasn't an affectionate person. Everything revolved around business so he never made time for her. I know my mom needed love, because I could see the quiet desperation in her eyes many times. I didn't understand it very well the, but I do now." He walked back to the couch and sat down.

"That's sad. I can almost feel your mother's pain. How did she cope with that situation?"

"She took a lover."

"Good for her. Did that work out?"

"Not really. The guy turned out to be a heel. He used my mom because he thought she had money. When he realized that a divorce would leave her a pittance, and even if my dad died, all of it would go to the kids, he disappeared."

"I know exactly how she felt," Ruth said. "I've been there!"

"That's not the end of it. My mom pleaded with my dad to take her back, but he wouldn't. He was so pissed that he called her a slut and didn't care who was around to hear. My brother and I had to hear the whole thing. I felt sorry for my mom. My brother, George, just stood there. We looked at each other and I waited for him to say something, but he just walked away. My mother began to cry hysterically. My father turned his back and told her to get out, that he never wanted to see her again. Later that day, I overheard my dad talking to his attorney on the phone. He was making arrangements for my mother to receive minimal support each month. My mom moved to a three-room apartment in town. My father forbade us to have any contact with her or he would disown us. He never found out that I used to visit her. Each time I went, I could see her sinking deeper and deeper into depression. At first, I thought my visits would be of some comfort to her but they weren't. She would ask about my brother and if my father had changed his mind about her. I had to tell her no. She began drinking heavily. Over the next few months, I often found her in a drunken stupor. There were times when she didn't even know who I was."

"Oh, Gene," Ruth exclaimed. "How awful, I'm so sorry."

Gene got up and walked to the window again. Ruth waited while he stood looking out for a moment or two. He took a deep breath and, without turning, continued. "I remember it was a Saturday. We were having breakfast when my dad, very casually, announced, 'By the way, I have something to tell you. Your mother is dead.' My father showed no emotion whatsoever. It was almost as if he'd told us it was going to rain. At that moment, I knew I hated the man."

Gene turned, walked back to the couch and settled beside her again. He seemed in deep thought as he sipped his drink. "That was a long time ago, Ruth. It doesn't bother me anymore. My hatred turned to apathy. Two years later, the man died of a heart attack while playing golf."

"Where was your brother during all this?" Ruth asked.

"I'll tell you exactly where he was. He was busy gambling wherever there was action. He was popular with the trash he hung out with, because he was a big loser and they knew he could always get the money to pay his gambling debts. My father helped him out of several scrapes, each time warning him that it would be the last. He was being threatened by his so called friends at the time my father died, but he got out of that one when he promised to pay with his inheritance. Of course, it didn't stop there. He gambled away what was left of his money. Now there was no one to bail him out. I don't think I was aware of the seriousness of the situation at that time, because when he called me asking for money, I refused. I never forgave him for the way he didn't stick up for my mother."

"I can see your point, Gene," Ruth said. "I would probably feel the same."

"That's not the end of it". Gene continued. "Some months later, I was called to identify my brother's body in the morgue."

Ruth shifted in her seat and was about to take a drink but stopped with her mouth open when she heard this. "Oh, that's terrible," she said.

"I'm sure he'd been threatened and when he didn't pay, he was literally beaten to death. His skull was crushed. That's the way those people operated."

"And you've had to live with this for so long," Ruth said sympathetically.

"You know, Ruth, I did feel guilty at first, but after talking to one of my colleagues, I was shown how selfish my brother had been all his life. He knew he could get away with anything and he always had. He was tenacious about wanting it all, no matter who he hurt to get it."

After listening to Gene's story, Ruth lowered her head looking very unhappy. Gene took her face in his hands and raised her head. Looking into her eyes with a smile on his face, he said, "But all that's in the past and, as I said, I couldn't be happier now that you and Robert are in my life."

Ruth managed a weak smile. "Maybe it was fate that we found each other."

"Who knows . . . and, who cares! Now, let's get on with our lives." He kissed her softly on the lips. "Let's finish our wine and then make love."

CHAPTER 15

Ruth lived in a state of euphoria; she felt nothing could go wrong. Life had made a complete turnaround. She actually felt guilty for being so happy, as if she didn't deserve it but, nonetheless, she took pleasure in enjoying every minute.

It was Sunday morning and Gene wasn't home. It was his weekend to be on duty at the hospital. Ruth sat at the table drinking a cup of coffee while watching Robert concentrate on trying to eat the breakfast cereal she had prepared for him. She glanced at the calendar.

"Guess what, Robert? You're going to have a birthday next month. Can you believe you're going to be one year old? What a big boy you are!"

Frowning, Ruth looked at the calendar again and gasped as she quickly covered her mouth with her hand. She had a moment of déjà vu and it startled her. "My God!" she exclaimed, "I missed my period!" She turned and looked at Robert, on the verge of panic. "I think we might have a problem," she said.

Robert looked at her in bewilderment; as children do when they don't understand, but he smiled and went right back to stuffing food into his little mouth.

Ruth spent the rest of the day trying to decide how to break the news to Gene. Her mind drifted back to the experience with Jon. *Will Gene be pleased about having a baby?* After asking herself that question, she knew he would. Still, thoughts about her last pregnancy filtered in. *Would she and Jon have stayed together if she hadn't gotten pregnant? Was it because a baby was on the way that made his mother dislike her? Did it make that horrible woman think that Ruth was not only low class but an easy woman as well?* In spite of her concerns, Ruth was excited to know that she was carrying the child of the man she loved. Then, another thought crept in. *Didn't I feel that way about Jon, too?* She shook the thought from her head. *Forget all that. That was then and this is now. Gene is genuinely in love with me… and Robert.*

Ruth had dinner ready when Gene arrived. After a few welcome home kisses and hugs, the three of them shared a meal of meat and potatoes. They shared smiles and laughter as well, as they watched Robert, who was making a mess of his chopped chicken, potatoes, carrots and applesauce. She was teaching him to feed himself and in the process, he spilled most of his food all over his high chair tray and himself.

"How was your day, honey?" Ruth asked.

"Same old stuff. I'm really tired tonight, and I have early rounds in the morning. A group of young interns will be following me around trying to impress me by asking a million questions. How was your day? Did you and Robert go for a walk?"

"No. Actually, we stayed in all day. I went through Robert's clothes. He's outgrown so many of his things, I thought about taking some to the hospital."

"That's great. I don't have to tell you how much these things are needed."

"I said I *thought* about it. I mean, we should return some kindness to others, but perhaps we should wait a while before giving all Robert's things away"

Gene put his head back and yawned. "I'm sorry," He said. "Go on. I'm listening."

"No," Ruth replied, "I'm sorry. You look tired, honey. Why don't you treat yourself to a long, hot bath? I'll clean up and put Robert to bed."

Gene laughed. "I haven't taken a long hot bath in years. I can't get over the feeling that it's a waste of time. I know it may sound silly but it's a guilt thing, like I should be doing something more productive than soaking in a tub for an hour."

"Maybe you get that from your father who never knew anything but work."

"Probably, but you know what, I'm going to give it a try? Will you wake me if I fall asleep? I don't want to soak too long. I don't want to drown either"

"If you can last about twenty-five minutes, I'll be there to scrub your back," Ruth said as she stood up and started to clear the table.

After Ruth finished all she had to do, she walked into the bathroom and removed her clothes, letting them drop to the floor. Gene was lying back with his eyes closed.

"Wake up, sweetie." Gene opened his eyes. "Sit up now," she said.

He moaned as Ruth began washing his back. "Mmm, I could get used to this."

"You can call on me anytime," Ruth laughed. "I can please in other ways, too, you know."

"You sure can, and don't you ever quit!"

She washed him all over, and then concentrated on the area between his legs. She could see the calm look on his face change to a grin as she played with him until he was ready.

"You devil," Gene laughed as he pulled her into the tub. She squealed as she fell on top of him. Even in the confines of the hard, inflexible tub, once again, it was a beautiful, crazy reunion of love.

Later, in the solitude under the covers of their bed, their naked bodies warming each other, Ruth kissed him on the cheek and said, "Do you realize that Robert will be a year old next month?"

"Yes, I do," Gene said, sleepily.

"Do you think it's wise to raise an only child?"

"I don't know," Gene replied, "I never thought about it."

"If we had another child, I mean, yours and mine, would you want it to be another boy or a girl?"

"Ruth, I don't know what you're talking about," Gene mumbled. "I love you, sweetheart, but can we talk about this tomorrow? I'm really tired."

"Of course, honey. Goodnight."

"Goodnight. I love you."

"I love you, too."

Soon, Ruth could hear his breathing become slow and even and knew he was asleep.

The following night, Gene was already in bed when Ruth finished showering and stood looking at herself in the full length mirror in the bathroom. Was the life she thought might be growing inside her really there? Her right hand made circular strokes over her abdomen. *Is it another boy or a girl? Gene might be happy to learn we're having a baby. I'm just not sure if he'll feel it's the right time.*

Ruth slipped into bed, snuggled up next to Gene and gave him a quick kiss. "Remember last night when I asked you how you felt about raising an only child?" she asked.

"Vaguely," he answered, "but I was too tired to listen to everything you said. What were you trying to tell me?"

Ruth hesitated. "That Robert isn't going to be an only child."

Gene was quiet for several seconds, and then quietly said, "I don't understand why you're bringing this up." He chuckled, "Are you trying to tell me you're pregnant

"Yes, I think I am, and I was wondering how you'd feel about it. I mean, does it upset you?"

"I'm not upset, Ruth, just surprised. I *had* hoped that one day you and I would have another child. I just didn't expect it to happen so soon."

"Well, you're the doctor and you know we don't use protection. What did you expect?" Ruth laughed and gave him a gentle shove. "I didn't expect it either but it's our baby and I couldn't be happier."

"It's not every day that you find out you're going to be a father. That's an important event. No, I didn't expect it to happen so soon but I'm happy about it, too." Gene grinned and pulled her tightly to him. "That doesn't mean that we have to stop having fun, does it?"

"Well, I don't have a headache," she said, giggling.

"Then, let's celebrate, as if we needed a reason."

Later, when their passion had subsided, she snuggled against him, happy that he was open to the fact she might be pregnant. "Gene, this is going to have an effect on you socially, isn't it? I mean, our having a baby."

"Why do you say that?" he asked.

"Well, we aren't married. How will that look to your friends at the hospital?"

"Almost everyone that matters knows that you're living with me and I think by now they presume we've been sleeping together. I've never tried to hide my feelings for you."

"Then it's okay if we just go on the way we are?"

"No, it isn't, because I know what you're thinking. I'm sure the fact that we're not married is bothering you, right?" He didn't wait for an answer. "So, I think we ought to do something about it."

"That's what I've been thinking. Oh, Gene, I'm so glad you feel that way. I want our baby to be legitimate." She smiled and touched his face.

"And while we're on the subject," he continued, "I would like to adopt Robert. What do you think about that?"

Ruth put her hand to her mouth to muffle a choke as tears came to her eyes.

"Now you've got me talking about it, so you know exactly what I've been thinking." He waited for an answer. "So, what do you say?"

"I don't have anything to say." Ruth wiped her eyes, fighting back the tears.

"Shall we make an honest woman out of you?" Gene said, trying to put some humor into the conversation.

"I should resent that but I don't," she said. "Okay, when?

"When what? Gene replied, teasing.

"When can we get married, silly?" she asked.

"That all depends on what kind of ceremony you want, my dear," Gene said.

"Now I don't understand," Ruth replied, sitting up and looking right into his face.

"Well, are you looking for a white dress and tuxedo formal affair, with all the trimmings, or will a few minutes with a judge in his chambers be enough?" he asked with a chuckle.

"Anything that's legal, Gene. I'm so damned happy! I love you so much."

"I'll call an old colleague of my father, Judge Walker. I'm sure he can work us into his schedule tomorrow, unless that's too soon for you." And he gave her a wink.

"Oh, my goodness! That *is* too soon. I'd like to look nice on my wedding day. I don't have anything special to wear. Do you think I can get something new? A new dress would be nice."

"You can get anything you want, honey, and I don't care what they think at the hospital. I told you they know all about us so I'm sure they won't be surprised. They'll be happy for us."

"Are you sure?"

"Yes, I'm sure.

Ruth spent the next three days looking for the perfect dress. Her dream wedding dress was supposed to be white, low cut, flowing, beaded skirt and fitted at the waist. That's what she expected to wear when she thought she would be marring Jon. What she found now was a beautiful, low cut, powder blue, chiffon sheath with puff sleeves, fitted at the waist that fell just about a foot above her ankles. Her dream of a formal wedding was something she thought she would have, but that was long ago; another place, another time and another man. Gene's love and devotion were everything for which she could have hoped. He was real and not a dream.

Ruth heard Gene's car in the driveway. She was ready to show off her wedding dress and hoped he would be pleased. He came in the back door, as usual, and when he didn't see Ruth, he called, "Honey, I'm home."

"I'm in the living room," Ruth answered.

Gene stopped in the living room doorway. There, Ruth was posing in her new dress. As she twirled, Gene thought she was the most beautiful woman he'd ever seen.

"Do you like it?" she asked.

"My God, you're absolutely gorgeous!" he exclaimed.

"But do you like the dress?"

"Of course I like the dress, but it's you that makes the dress. You're beautiful. I think you better take it off though, before I mess it up taking it off."

"Are you sure you like it?"

"Honey, I love it."

"I'm so glad. I want to look perfect for our wedding day."

"Can I make the arrangements now?" he asked, with a chuckle.

"Yes, please," she sighed.

Gene got the license and set the appointment with a Justice of the Peace, because Judge Walker was out of town. The following Saturday, Ruth and Gene exchanged vows. Vern Mitchell, a colleague of Gene's, and his wife, Susan, acted as witnesses. After the ceremony, the two couples went to dinner at the Palmer House to celebrate.

On their way home from dinner, Gene said; "Now it's time to start the adoption proceedings."

"Gene," Ruth said, her voice showing her surprise. "I can't believe you're thinking about this now. I mean, I think it's wonderful that you want Robert to be your son and I love you all the more for wanting that but this is *our* wedding night. Can we talk about Robert later? Tonight, you're mine, all mine!"

On Monday morning Gene called Patrick Walker.

"Good morning, Judge. This is Gene Parker."

"Well, Gene, it's been a long time since we've spoken. How are you?"

"A lot has happened since my dad died. I just married a wonderful lady."

"Congratulations, Gene! It's about time you settled down with someone."

"Judge, she has a little boy and I want to adopt him. How do we go about this?"

"What about the father, Gene? Where is he?"

"The guy left her when she told him she was pregnant and she's not seen him since. He's not on the birth certificate."

"Are you telling me that this girl wasn't married to the father?"

"That's true, Judge, but she thought they were going to marry, then the guy took off. She accepted her responsibility to her child and decided to go it alone."

There was a lengthy pause before the judge continued. "Well, she must be pretty special. If you're sure you want to do this, come to my office on Thursday and we'll start the proceedings. Gerry will help you fill out the necessary papers. I'm looking forward to meeting this young lady."

"Thank you, Judge. What time should we be there?"

"About nine will be good; I'll be in court from one o'clock on."

"Thanks again. See you on Thursday."

Later that week after Ruth had finished lunch with Robert and put him down for his nap, she was ready to take a shower and then lie down and rest for a while. Humming a tune, she stepped in the shower. The warm water felt soothing and relaxing, as usual, as it washed over her body. "Mrs. Gene Parker," she kept repeating as she caressed her body with lather. Suddenly, she felt a stabbing pain in her lower abdomen. It was so severe that she grabbed the soap dish fastened to the wall and sank to her knees. Blood droplets began to cloud the water running down the drain on the floor.

"Oh, my God," she gasped.

She began to bleed, a trickle at first, then a steady release. She watched the blood flow from her body, mix with the water and disappear down the drain. The pain and loss of blood persisted until she released a huge blood clot. The bleeding slowed. The pain eased somewhat. The jabbing sensations subsided.

She turned off the water, then grabbed a towel and held it between her legs.

Slowly, she crawled from of the shower stall. She was able to catch the hem of her robe that hung on the nearby hook, but try as she might, she couldn't unhook it. She finally just ripped it down. She sat there for a while with the robe wrapped around her, clutching the towel between her legs. When she felt she could stand, she hobbled to her room and fell onto the bed. Curled up in a fetal position beneath the covers, she began to cry. After a while, she reached for the phone and dialed Gene's office. She didn't want to worry him right off, so, trying to keep her voice calm, she said, "When will you be coming home, dear?'"

"I'm not sure, honey, why do you ask? Is something wrong?"

"I'm not feeling too well. If you can possibly get away early, I'd appreciate it."

"I'll be home as soon as I can arrange it. Is Robert okay?"

"He was taking his nap, but I can hear him now. He's awake but I can't go to him."

"What do you mean, you can't go to him?"

She had to tell him now. "I can't get out of bed. I've started bleeding."

"I'll be right there."

When Gene arrived home, he found Ruth in bed, crying.

"Ruth, I'm here," he soothed.

Looking up at him, her emotions making it difficult for her to speak, she sobbed, "I lost the baby."

Gene ran upstairs to check on Robert. Robert wasn't crying but was amusing himself with the toys in his bed. Gene picked him up and took him downstairs and put him in the playpen, just for a change of scenery to keep him occupied. Then he went back to tend to Ruth. Gene felt bad about Ruth losing *his* baby too.

Several weeks later, Ruth, Gene and Robert walked into the

courthouse at 10:30 in the morning and took the elevator to the third floor. Ruth made sure Robert was neatly dressed and had spent more time than usual on *her* appearance. She wanted her family to make a good impression. Gene was wearing his suit, looking handsome, as usual.

Gerry Dombrowski, the judge's research clerk, and an excellent attorney in her own right, rose from her desk as they entered the room.

"Gene," she said, "It's been a while. How are you?"

Gene took her extended hand and said, "I'm wonderful now. I'd like you to meet my wife, Ruth, and this little guy is Robert."

"Ruth, how nice to meet you," she said, taking Ruth's hand. She turned to Robert and put out her hand. "Hi, there, Robert"

Robert gave her a big smile and put his hand out for her to shake. "Hi," Robert said in his little voice. They all laughed.

"He's never said that before," Gene said, looking at Ruth and obviously showing pride in his little boy.

"Please sit down." Gerry motioned to the two chairs by the desk.

When they were all seated, Gerry said, "The judge tells me you want to adopt this little guy."

"That's absolutely right," Gene said and smiled. Robert was trying to pull the pen from Gene's jacket pocket. Ruth held out her arms, intending to take control of Robert, but Robert turned away and hugged Gene. Again, Gene beamed with pride. "I think this is just a formality to Robert. I'm already his daddy."

Ruth felt a twinge of jealousy. *That's my boy and I love him, too,* she thought, but quickly realized that this was exactly what she had hoped would happen between the two men in her life. She smiled and said, "I hope this won't take long. Robert has a pretty short attention span."

"Not long at all," Gerry replied. "I'll need some information about you," she said, looking at Ruth, "then I'll have the papers typed up."

Ruth answered all the questions as truthfully as she could but felt somewhat stressed by the time Gerry had finished. Uninvited thoughts of her bitter relationship with Jon came flooding back.

"I have enough information now. Let me get it to the typist." Gerry left the office through a door other than the one they entered by. As she opened the door, the sound of typewriters broke the silence. When the door closed, Ruth said, "How long do you think this will take?"

"It might be half an hour, maybe more. Just be patient, love. This will be over soon."

Robert continued to fidget on Gene's lap, trying to reach for things on the desk and protesting loudly when his hands were pulled away. Gene stood up and began walking around the room, trying to interest Robert in the pictures on the wall and looking out of the third floor window.

Twenty minutes later Gerry returned with the completed forms. "If you and Gene will sign by your names…"She turned the legal documents around and pointed to the appropriate place for them to sign.

Ruth signed and pushed the paper toward Gene, who had to stop Robert from grabbing the pen.

"You better take him," Gene said, holding the boy out at arms length to prevent him from clinging again. Ruth took Robert and immediately began consoling him. It was obvious that Robert wanted to be in his daddy's arms.

Gene quickly signed the paper and pushed it across the desk. He reached for Robert and the boy held out his arms and grinned contentedly.

"Let me take these papers into the judge and this will be finished," Gerry said, grinning at the happy little boy. "There's no doubt that you're already a family. I'll be back in a minute or two."

Gerry did come back in a minute or two. "Before the adoption can become final," she said, "there are certain procedures we have to complete. You say the father doesn't know the child exists so the one thing we'll do immediately is get a notice of the adoption in the newspaper. If no one contacts us protesting the adoption, mainly the child's father, we can proceed with the rest of the legal business."

"How long will we have to wait?" Gene asked.

"Thirty days from when the ad is published. It will read something like. This is to notify the father of the child born to Ruth Lawson on May 7th 1946, in Chicago, Cook County, Illinois, of the adoption of said child. You have thirty days from the date of this notice to contact the office listed below if you wish to contest this adoption. The number I put as contact will be mine."

"Thank you, Gerry," Gene said. "You've been more very helpful." They shook hands. Robert was funny because after watching everyone shake hands, he stuck out his hand for Gerry to shake again. She did shake his hand. Robert let out a delighted squeal and grinned with satisfaction. They all laughed. Gene was still carrying Robert as they left the office.

As they walked towards the elevator, Gene shifted Robert to one arm and took Ruth's hand. They looked at each other and smiled. Words weren't necessary. Ruth blinked to suppress the tears.

Once inside the elevator, Gene chuckled, struggling to contain his emotion, and said, "Well, now it's official! Robert is mine too, now."

"It's going to take thirty days, honey."

"I'm confident that no one will answer that notice. This baby is mine! Let's celebrate and have lunch downtown."

Ruth squeezed his arm and said, "That's a great idea! Where shall we go to have a bite to eat?"

Gene walked from the courthouse with a grin on his face. "Where would you like to have lunch?" he asked.

"Anywhere you wish," Ruth replied, "but I see a sign. There's a restaurant on the corner at the end of the block. We could eat there."

"I've eaten there before," Gene said. "It isn't fine dining but the food is good."

"That's just the place then. We don't want fine dining with Robert along. Anyway, he'll probably make a mess," Ruth laughed.

"That's my boy," Gene said as he gave Ruth's hand a squeeze and bounced Robert.

Gene pulled open the restaurant door and waited for Ruth to enter. He followed her as she walked toward the back of the restaurant. As she passed one of the tables, she sucked in a quick breath and paused for just an instant, as if something startled her. She seemed to compose herself quickly and headed for the last booth. When Gene slid into the seat across from her, he could see that she was upset about something.

"What's the matter, honey?" he asked, reaching for her hand.

"Do you remember when I told you about Mrs. Travis, the lady who was stealing babies?" Ruth whispered.

"Of course," Gene said.

"Well, I'm sure that's her, sitting with that pregnant girl. Gene, she's still at it! I'm scared. What if she recognized me?"

"I see them," Gene said. "Are you sure that she's the same woman?"

"I'm absolutely sure!"

"I don't think she'll recognize you, honey. You certainly don't look like the person who came to the emergency room that night."

Ruth gave a deep sigh. She looked as if she were about to cry. "Gene, we have to do something."

"We can't do anything now." Gene said, suddenly understanding why Ruth was so shaken. "Short of calling the cops…" He shrugged helplessly. "But they won't do anything. What could we tell them? The woman and the girl look like two ordinary people having lunch. Look, I've lost my appetite. I can't eat anything now, and I know you're too upset to eat." Gene thought for a moment and said, "I have an idea. You take Robert home and I'll stay until they leave. The first thing we have to do is to find out where their place of operation is located. I'll follow them and then we'll have something to take to the police. Now, let's get a cab for you."

"I'd rather be with you," Ruth said.

"If she does recognize you, she might hightail it," Gene replied. "It's best if you just go home and let me do this alone."

"Just be careful. I don't want anything to happen to you," Ruth said.

The waitress was suddenly standing there. "What can I get for you folks?" she asked.

"Just coffee for me," Gene said. "The lady has to leave as soon as I can get her a taxi."

"Well, whadaya know. We can fix that right now." The waitress turned and looked at a poorly dressed man, sitting at the counter, still wearing his cap. "Hey, Herbie, you ready to go back on duty?" she called.

Gene could see the man nod his head as he stuffed the last of his sandwich into his mouth.

"Yeah," the man said, still chewing. "The cab's out back." Getting up from the stool at the counter, he headed toward the kitchen door.

"There's your cab, mister," the waitress said. "I'll bring your coffee. You need cream?"

"No, thanks, but tell me. Why is the guy going out through the kitchen?" Gene was suddenly concerned with Ruth and Robert's safety.

"It's hard to find a place to park with the court house and all, and since Herbie eats here every day, the boss lets him park behind the restaurant in the alley."

Gene felt better. He turned to Ruth. "You and Robert go home now, honey. I'll see you later."

Ruth nodded. "I love you," she whispered as she slid from the booth. She picked up Robert, who, for the last ten minutes had been squirming on Gene's lap trying to reach for things, but was now starting to doze in his arms. Ruth was relieved to have her back to the two in the booth as she left. The swinging doors of the kitchen closed behind her, leaving Gene feeling just a little uncomfortable.

He sipped his coffee, hoping that the woman and girl would leave soon. The waitress came by to ask if he wanted something else or just more coffee. "Just more coffee," he replied.

Gene couldn't hear what the woman and girl were saying but their discussion seemed to be coming to a close. The woman patted the girl's arm as they both stood up to leave. The young girl looked as if she were about to deliver at any moment. Gene left four dollars on the table as he slipped from the booth to follow them. He could feel his stomach trying to send him into a panic. He quickly took a deep breath and swallowed, trying to quell the sensation.

As the two women left the restaurant, he walked slowly to the door to keep an eye on them. A station wagon pulled up to the curb. The driver got out and opened the door to the back seat to let the women in. Gene knew that he had to get to his car before they got too much of a head start.

He hurried out of the restaurant, and ran the half block to his car, jumped in and started the engine. When the station wagon pulled away from the curb, Gene pulled into the traffic lane behind it, allowing it to stay a safe distance ahead but keeping it in view. The driver turned north on Randolph and then west on Lake Street. Gene followed about a block behind them as they drove through the worst part of town.

About twenty minutes later, the station wagon pulled onto a dirt road. Gene pulled to the side of the road and stopped the car. He could see what looked like an old farmhouse at the end of the road. This was obviously where Mrs. Travis brought her girls. Gene waited there for about fifteen minutes trying to figure out what should be done. When he realized her new location was still in Cook County, he knew they were still under Uncle Pat's jurisdiction and he would know what would have to be done. Gene made a u-turn and headed for home.

Ruth had been waiting anxiously for Gene's return. Robert was in a cranky mood because he was overtired, and Ruth had lost patience with him. Finally, she fixed a bottle for him and carried him upstairs to his room and put him in his crib. Nothing seemed to satisfy him. Ruth said firmly, "Robert, I know you're not happy right now, but Mommy's upset, too, so I'm going to let you cry it out. Be a good boy and go to sleep. I love you." She leaned over, kissed him on the head then left the room and closed the door behind her. Robert's normal naptime had come and gone which was why he was so cranky, but soon all was quiet upstairs. That left Ruth feeling less guilty about leaving him alone and crying.

Pacing in front of the picture window, Ruth saw Gene pull into the driveway and ran to the door to meet him. He gave her a quick peck on the cheek when he walked through the door and went straight to the telephone. Opening the personal directory, he flipped to the W's, ran his finger down the page till he found the judge's number and quickly dialed. The receptionist answered.

"Judge Walker's office. How may I direct your call?"

"This is Doctor Parker. I'd like to speak to Judge Walker."

"Judge Walker isn't in at the moment. May I ask what this is about?"

"No. It's imperative that I speak only to the judge and as soon as possible! When do you expect him to return?"

"He won't be back until tomorrow morning. He usually arrives about ten. May I take a message? Does he have your number?"

"Let me speak to Mrs. Dombrowski."

"She's gone for the day, too, sir."

"Well then, can you give her a message for me?"

"Yes, Dr. Parker, I can do that."

"Tell her to have Judge Walker phone me as soon as possible. Say that it's an emergency. She has my number"

"Yes, sir, I'll leave it on her desk before I leave tonight."

"Thank you. Good-bye." Gene hung up the phone and turned to Ruth. "I'm sure Uncle Pat will be able to help us."

"Gene, you don't know how worried I've been. Those people didn't see you, did they? If they found out you were following them, there's no telling what they might have done. Are you sure they didn't see you?"

"Yes, honey, I'm sure," he said, hoping it was true. "I found out where they took the girl. It's not that far, still within the city limits. You heard the message I left for Uncle Pat. I know he'll want to know about this.

He'll help us. Do you think we can have a bite to eat now? We did miss our lunch. Did you eat anything?"

"No, how could I? I was too worried about you to eat. I'll fix something now." Ruth kissed him and headed for the kitchen. On the way she began telling him about the ride home with the cab driver. "That Herbie guy never stopped talking."

"Who's Herbie?" Gene asked as he followed her.

"That cab driver, dear. He was a wealth of information. It was like a tour. He had something to say about every neighborhood that we passed through. It was good, though, because the more he talked, the less I was able to think about what might be happening to you."

Gene was pleased to see Ruth relaxing again, and thankful that she wasn't aware of his growing uneasiness.

The next morning, Gene called Gerry Dombrowski. He was worried that the receptionist might not have left his message. When Gerry answered, he said, "Gerry, can you have the judge call me as soon as possible? This is really important."

"I got the note to call you, Gene. I was just about to do that. Does this have anything to do with the adoption?" she asked.

"No, it's a personal matter and it's imperative that I speak to the judge about it."

"He's in court most of the day," Gerry said, "but I'll give him the message when he takes a break. I have some papers he's waiting for."

Gene didn't want to miss the judge's call so he was able to get one of the other doctors to cover for him while he waited at home. Gene was surprised, though, when the judge's call came before noon.

"What's this all about, Gene? Gerry said it was urgent," Walker said.

"It's about a gang of baby thieves, Uncle Pat. I have a lot to tell you"

"Baby thieves! How the hell did you get involved in something like that? "

"Like I said, it's too much to talk about over the phone and you have to hear the whole story. Can you meet me after court today?"

"Yes, I can meet you. I have to hear about this. Where do you want to meet?"

"I know you're busy," Gene said. "I'll come to you. How about if I meet you in the cafeteria on the lower level?"

"Sounds good. I'll see you about three."

Ruth walked in as Gene hung up the phone. "What did the judge say?" she asked.

"I'm meeting him at the courthouse later this afternoon. I told him it was about baby thieves and he asked how the hell I got involved."

"You told him that?"

"Well, it got his attention."

Gene arrived at the cafeteria about two forty-five. He chose a table in the back corner. He drank two cups of coffee before the judge walked in. He spotted Gene, nodded to him, stopped to buy a cup of coffee and walked to the table. Sitting opposite Gene, he took a sip of coffee. "They have really good coffee here," he said. "Now tell me what the hell this is all about."

Three more cups of coffee and forty-five minutes passed by the time Gene finished telling the story,

"I don't know what to say, Gene. As you know, this is a serious situation, and you say Ruth was involved in all of this?"

"Yes, she managed to escape from the house they were using and almost didn't make it to the hospital. That's how we met, you know. We hoped that one day we would find these people and put them in jail, so this may be the opportunity we've been waiting for."

Somebody dropped a tray interrupting the conversation. The servers were noisy as they removed platters from their cases.

"Go on, Gene," the judge said, as they turned their attention back to each other. "Let me hear the rest of this."

"Well, Ruth spotted the woman sitting with a young, pregnant girl in a restaurant yesterday. Ruth was afraid the woman recognized her, but I assured her that she couldn't have. I told her she looks nothing like the disheveled girl I met in the hospital. We're sure they're still operating in the area."

"What makes you so sure they are?"

"When they left, I followed them to their new location, so I know where they are." Gene took a sip of his coffee and a deep breath, and then continued. "So far, it's only Ruth's word about all this. We need proof that they're stealing babies. Many of the girls that go there are planning to give up their babies. They think they're going through a proper adoption agency where the prospective parents have to go through an extensive investigation. The ones that don't plan on giving up their babies are the girls that are being victimized. They don't know that their babies are being stolen, and then sold. The girls are told that their babies were stillborn. That's why Ruth ran away. They planned to steal her baby." Gene finished his coffee and said, "I'm going to get another cup of coffee, how about you?"

"No thanks. If I have any more, I'll float out of here. Is there anything more you have to say?" The judge was drumming his fingers on the table. Gene could see he was getting anxious about the whole situation.

"Uncle Pat, we need someone with authority to start the ball rolling. I know the police have to be involved, but without evidence, they can't do anything. You can get the thing started...if you believe me, that is."

"Oh, I believe you, Gene. It's just that I never thought I'd be called on to start an investigation. You know, of course, that kidnapping is a federal offense? In essence, that's what you're telling me. Ruth seems to be pretty level headed. I doubt she'd make up so fantastic a story."

"Uncle Pat, I saw her when she was brought into the emergency room. She was a mess! So, will you help us?"

"I'll talk to Captain Flynn. He'll jump on this one, if only for political reasons."

"What do you mean?" Gene asked.

"He wants to be police commissioner and knows the public will eat this story up. My personal opinion is that he'll make a good commissioner, but that's beside the point."

"Thanks, Uncle Pat. Ruth and I really appreciate your help."

"I'll keep you informed, Gene, and tell Ruth not to worry. You two are doing the right thing." The judge stood up and put out his hand. Gene stood to shake Pat's hand and they both left.

Robert heard the car pull into the driveway and ran to the back door. "Daddy, daddy," he called.

Ruth smiled and said, "Yes, Daddy's home."

Robert's arms were outstretched waiting for Gene to pick him up. Gene swung Robert into his arms and said, "How's my big boy?"

Robert giggled with excitement and wouldn't take his arms from around Gene's neck. "Okay, okay," Gene said, giving Robert a kiss on the cheek, "Can I take my coat off now?" Putting Robert down, he hung his coat on the back of the chair and said, "Mommy's turn." He walked up behind Ruth as she stood by the sink and kissed her on the neck.

"Stop that," she laughed, "you know it tickles."

"And I know you like it," Gene teased.

Ruth turned and gave him a quick kiss on the mouth. "Now let's stop this," she grinned. "Dinner's almost ready. Besides, I'm anxious to know what Pat had to say. Did he believe anything you said about Mrs. Travis?" She began setting the table.

"Yes, he did, and he's turning it over to Captain Mike Flynn. He's sure the future commissioner will jump on it. There'll be an investigation, of course, and they'll be looking for proof before they can do anything." He put his hands on Ruth's shoulders and made her turn to him.

"You'll have to tell your story again. Are you up to it?"

"Yes, I can do it. Now that we have someone on our side, I'm not afraid anymore."

"I feel better too," Gene said, as he dropped his hands and walked to Robert, who had been standing there watching them.

"We can relax now and let the law handle things." He picked up Robert and put him in his high chair then sat down in his usual place. He looked over at Ruth and suddenly grinned.

"You know," he said "I think this calls for a celebration. I'm going to open that bottle of wine we've been saving."

"Gene, you're always ready for a celebration. Okay, but you know what a little wine does to me," Ruth warned.

"By all means, we're having wine tonight," Gene said firmly. Robert giggled and pounded on his tray with his spoon.

A week passed before Captain Flynn came to the house to get Ruth's story about her experience while staying in Mrs. Travis' home for girls. As thoroughly as he questioned her, Ruth's story never changed. At times, he seemed almost brutal in his questioning. At times, he had Ruth near tears.

At one point, Gene asked angrily, "Do you need to be so goddam hard on her?"

When it was over, Ruth looked at Flynn's face. There was no sign of emotion. She frowned and said, "Don't you believe me?"

"It's not a matter of me believing you," Flynn said. "I have to make sure the facts are consistent. I do apologize if I seemed too harsh, but I had to make sure there were no holes in your story. Now, we'll start surveillance at the organization's location and keep you informed. Just remember this may take a while."

Gene stood up and said, "Would you like a cup of coffee or maybe something stronger before you leave?"

"No, thanks. I'm on duty and I need to call the judge. He insisted I let him know the outcome of our meeting so we can start the ball rolling."

After Flynn had gone, Gene took Ruth in his arms. "That turned out well, don't you think so honey?" He kissed her cheek. "I need to get back to the hospital for a while. Are you going to be all right?"

"I'll be fine. I think I'd better lie down for a while. That detective really had me going."

As much as Ruth wanted these people to be caught, there wasn't anything to do but to wait. She kept thinking how shrewd Mrs. Travis and Dr. Roman had been at keeping things as honest as was necessary to keep the law off their backs. But, the wheels of justice were turning now.

CHAPTER 16

June of 1949 blossomed into a beautiful month. The balmy weather and the little rain that fell satisfied the thirst of the new growth in the yard. Ruth always found a great deal of satisfaction working in the garden. However, she had to slow down some now that she was expecting again. It surprised her to feel so lethargic with this pregnancy. She hadn't felt this weary while carrying Robert.

Ruth would play games with Robert in the yard, just to get him to do some of the weeding. She would say things like, "Now don't pull off those drooping stems or the plant will cry." And of course, Robert wanted to see the plant cry. Or, "If you put all those dead branches in a pile, the squirrels will hide there." He had fun doing that for a while, but very soon he just wanted to play on the swing set and the slide.

Robert had turned three in May. Ruth had a birthday party for him and invited his playmates from the park with whom they'd become friendly on their many visits. Gene came home just as the guests were leaving, but they all got to meet him.

Gene had his own practice now and was very comfortable on his own which made his hours considerably more regular than they were at the hospital. Kelly, the E.R. nurse, had been looking for another position. When Gene heard about her desire to leave, he asked her to join his staff and she jumped at the chance to come to work for him. Gene felt very fortunate that she agreed to work for him.

There was little word from Flynn about how the investigation was going. Gene called the judge a few times, but the judge's remarks were always the same, "The investigation is ongoing. If anything comes up, Flynn will get back to you. How's the rest of the family?"

"We're fine, Judge. Oh, by the way, Ruth's going to have another baby. She's two months pregnant"

"Well, well, so the family's growing. That's nice, Gene. How's the little guy, Robert? That's his name, right?"

"That's right, Uncle Pat. He's just fine. How about your family?"

"Everyone's okay here. We'll talk again soon. Take care."

The months that followed passed quickly and without incident. The days became shorter now and the autumn winds were sometimes bitterly cold. October 19, 1949 was another cold, blustery day. The weatherman had predicted snow for the day and by ten that morning flakes had begun to fall. It was very early for snow. It was a wet snow so the flakes were big and fluffy. Most of them melted when they hit the pavement. Robert was happy to see the snow.

"Mommy, Mommy," Robert called from the window, "Santa Claus is on the ground."

He was smart enough to associate snow with Christmas and, of course, presents.

"It'll be a while before Santa comes," Ruth called from the kitchen. She was clearing the breakfast dishes from the table when she had to sit down again. Her back was bothering her. This pregnancy didn't seem to be going so well.

Later that evening, there was a call from Mike Flynn. Gene answered the phone.

"Gene, I think we have something on that baby racket."

"Really! That's great! What did you find out?"

"The guys on surveillance picked up a girl who was trying to leave that house. She was picked up running down the road. There was a guy who came out and started running after her but he ran back into the house when he saw the Mars lights go on. We picked her up and took her to the hospital. She didn't have a coat on and was talking hysterically. If this girl cooperates, we'll be able to start investigating."

Gene could hardly contain his excitement as Mike continued. "Judge Walker asked me to call and let you know what's happening, but you're gonna have to talk to him to find out the details. That's all I can tell you right now."

"Thanks for calling, Mike. My wife is going to welcome this information. Good-bye" Gene hung up the phone. "Ruth!" he exclaimed as he walked to the kitchen.

"Don't tell me you've come to help me with the dishes," she chuckled.

"No, sweetie."

He went on to tell her about his conversation with Mike Flynn. Ruth's knees became weak and Gene put his arms around her to keep her from falling. She sat down. He pulled up a chair and sat down in front of her. He took her hands.

"This is what we've been waiting for, honey."

"I know, and it's great. It's just that it's taken so long; I almost forgot it ever happened. The happiness I've had with you has given me a real sense of security but I want to see this through. I will see this through!"

The next morning, Gene left another message with Gerry Dombrowski. "Have the judge call me as soon as possible."

It was two long days before Gene heard from the Judge. When he finally did, they made arrangements to meet at Gene's house the following night.

"Will you be able to make it for dinner Uncle Pat?" Gene asked.

"Sorry, but I can't. I should be there around seven thirty or so. Will that work for you?"

"We'll be waiting."

The next evening, Ruth made an early dinner and by 7:30 Robert was sound asleep. She made a pot of tea and sat down with Gene at the kitchen table to wait. Sitting in silence, they both jumped a little when the doorbell rang at 7:50. Gene went to the door.

"Good to see you, Gene," Pat said as he walked in.

"You, too, Uncle Pat," Gene said, as he took Pat's coat and hung it in the hall closet. "We were just having some tea. Would you like some?"

"Yes, thanks. That should warm me up a bit."

"We were in the kitchen. I'll have Ruth bring our cups in here."

"No, don't do that. I'd rather sit at the table."

Ruth was standing there in front of the stove, looking a bit apprehensive, but put on a smile when she saw the judge. "Hi, Uncle Pat," she said.

"Ruth, you're looking well. How're you feeling?"

"I'm good." She wasn't. She was shaking on the inside and trying to look calm.

Ruth put another cup of tea on the table and they all sat down. The judge slowly sipped his tea. Ruth and Gene waited.

"I know you're waiting for me to let you in on what's been happening." The Judge smiled. "I can read your faces. So I'll get right to the facts."

Ruth and Gene turned to look at each other, waiting anxiously.

The Judge continued. "According to Mike, the girl the cops picked up went through a situation similar to Ruth's experience. The officers took her right to the hospital. She needed to be examined. In addition to that, we didn't want to lose her or have anything happen to her. We have an officer stationed outside her hospital door. It could be the same girl you saw in the restaurant with that Travis lady."

"I'd like to talk to her," Ruth said.

"You will and, hopefully, you can identify her as the girl in the restaurant; otherwise, they can claim Travis never set eyes on her." He turned to Gene. "Gene, you saw the girl as well, right?"

"Yes, and I'm pretty sure I could identify her."

"Good. That makes you a witness, too." Pat paused and shook his head. "Yes, they did see the girl run out of the house but those people can claim she wanted to be taken in and, since there was no room, she ran out hysterically, " Pat speculated. There's a hundred stories they can contrive.

Gene could see Ruth biting her lips and tensing up. He put his hand over hers and she turned to face him. His simple gesture made Ruth heave a sigh and smile. It was the same as saying, 'I'm here for you.'

"We need your story and the girl's story, before we can take this to court, Ruth," Pat went on. "We may find other girls if we put out notices, but that might be wishful thinking." Pat took another sip of his tea before continuing. "Mike's trying to get a search warrant. I'd issue one but that's not my jurisdiction. We'll know more after the place is searched. The lady and the doctor were questioned and let go. The house is padlocked and closed to everyone. We need the warrant to get access to the files. We also need a good reason for the warrant and that's not going to be easy without help from the girl and you, Ruth."

"How long will the girl be kept in the hospital?" Ruth asked.

"I don't know. That's another thing we have to work out. She needs a safe place to stay. It'll be a while before we can cover everything."

"Why can't she stay with us?" Ruth asked.

"Yes," Gene chimed in. "She can stay here. We've got plenty of room."

"We'll have to think about that. We don't want to put your family in danger. We're dealing with unscrupulous people and we don't know what they're capable of. They won't go down without a fight, that's for sure. Let's face it. They're not about to lose a very profitable business if they can prevent it. They don't know anything about you or where you are and we want to keep it that way."

"I think I'm getting scared again," Ruth said. "I know how ruthless these people can be. I saw them in action."

"That's why we have to keep your location secret." Pat said.

Ruth forced a smile. "I know you won't let anything happen to us. We'll do whatever you say. You know what's best,"

"I've got to run now," the Judge said as he stood up.

"Thanks for coming Uncle Pat. We really appreciate your help." Gene stood also. They both started for the front door. "Let me get your coat." Gene helped Pat put on his coat and opened the door.

Turning back, Pat called, "Bye, Ruth, You take care now."

"Hello," Gene said.

"Hello, Gene. This is Mike Flynn"

"Hi, what's up?"

"Judge Michael told me to call you. We've got Justine — that's the girl's name — over at Gerry's house. She agreed to help us out. I'm supposed to set a time for Ruth and Justine to get together and compare stories. Justine is just as anxious as you are to get these people out of the way. So what would be a good time for you?"

"Can you hold on a minute? I'll ask Ruth."

"Yes."

Gene put the phone down and ran up the stairs to Robert's room where Ruth was getting him ready for bed.

"Ruth, Detective Flynn's on the phone. He wants to know when you and the girl can get together."

"Oh, my gosh! Tell him I can be ready any time... But I'd like you to be there if possible"

"I'll try but, if I can't make it, you have to go any way. You know that?"

"I know."

"Flynn, you still there?" Gene said as he picked up the phone.

"I'm here. What did Ruth say?"

"She said any time."

"Good! I'll pick her up around seven tomorrow evening. Bye now."

Ruth had the chills all the next day. Was it the weather or was it the anticipation of meeting someone who had gone through the same dreadful experience that she had? Gene called Ruth earlier to say that he was able to re-arrange his schedule and would leave work in time to accompany her to Gerry's. That eased her anxiety.

Mike Flynn arrived promptly at 7:00.He rang the bell but went back to wait in the car for Ruth and Gene. They didn't talk much on the way to Gerry's. When they arrived at the apartment, they were buzzed in. Gerry was waiting in the open doorway when they got to the second floor.

"Good to see you two again." Gerry said. "Sorry it has to be under such unpleasant circumstances."

"We are, too," Gene answered. "But it's what we've been waiting for and we can't thank you enough for helping us."

"I'm glad I could do it. Why don't you take seats in the living room? I'll get Justine. She's been resting while waiting for you."

Ruth couldn't quite remember the girl she saw in the restaurant. At the time, she had only been interested in seeing Mrs. Travis, but when Justine walked into the room, Ruth could have cried because she looked so familiar. Justine could have been Carol. Ruth realized how much she'd missed Carol and wondered where she was.

Justine was short, slight of build and had blond hair. She had a pug nose and thin, perfectly shaped brows over big blue eyes. Her skin was fair and she had a friendly smile when she saw them. Yes, she was Carol.

Gerry introduced everyone. Mike stuck to business as he reminded Ruth and Justine why they were here.

"Justine, were you the girl in the restaurant with Mrs. Travis?" Mike asked.

"Yes. I answered Mrs. Travis' ad and was told to meet her there. Mrs. Travis was very nice at first. She treated me like a daughter. She showed concern and I was grateful. I had no where to go."

"That's just what happened to me." Ruth exclaimed.

Ruth and Justine exchanged looks. It was sort of closure for Ruth to know that someone shared her fears and understood what she had gone through.

"We need to know what happened to make you realize that your baby would be taken," Mike said.

"Well, I was there for a little over a month." Justine began. "There were two other girls there when I arrived, but shortly after I got there, they had their babies less than a week apart of each other and left. Both of them were planning to give up their babies. The rest of the time I was alone. Everything seemed okay to me."

Justine changed positions in her chair and took a shallow breath. "Mrs. Travis began to frighten me then. Almost every day she would talk to me about giving up my baby. She said I was selfish and that it wouldn't be fair to the child if I kept it. She said, 'You have no money and no place to go. A child shouldn't be raised without a father.' I refused to give up my baby and that's when I realized that Mrs. Travis wasn't going to let me do that. I ran at the first opportunity."

As Justine spoke, she twisted the handkerchief she held in her lap; what lap there was with her huge protruding belly.

Listening to her story, Ruth began to perspire. The thought of her ordeal was creeping back. There was an end table between her and Gene. She wanted him close. She wanted him to hold her hand. When Justine's voice began to fade, Ruth forced herself to remember where she was, that she was safe and needed to concentrate on the present.

Justine's voice began to tremble as she tried to continue. Gerry walked behind the chair and put her hands on Justine's shoulders.

"Take your time, dear. Do you want a moment to compose yourself? Can I get you a drink of water?'

"No, thank you. I'll be all right." Taking another deep breath, Justine went on with her story.

"I don't remember what night it was, but I woke up about three in the morning. I heard a car pull into the driveway, so I got out of bed and looked out the window. It was Dr. Roman. It was too late for him to be there and, as I said, there were no girls in the house who needed attention. I was curious, of course, so I quietly opened my door and tiptoed to the top of the stairs. They were in the dining room and they were whispering.

I crept halfway down the stairway so I could hear what they were whispering about.

Dr. Roman was saying that he had a couple who wanted to adopt a baby and that they were very well off. They had tried another agency but were refused. He didn't say why. If he did, I couldn't hear. I'm sure he didn't care anyway.

He said the man's job was taking him out of state in about two or three weeks and they wanted a baby before they had to leave. Then he asked Mrs. Travis about the one that was still here, meaning me, and Mrs. Travis said, 'She may not be ready to deliver.' Then Dr. Roman said, 'We could always give a sufficient dose of Pitosin to induce labor and make sure she has a large dose of anesthesia. Then, of course, we'll tell the girl what we always say, that the kid was stillborn.'" Justine's voice got louder and tremulous, "That's when I realized what was going on."

Justine's hands were shaking now and she became silent for a moment. Her eyes began to dart around the room as she tried to clear her throat. It looked like she was fighting back tears, but then she continued.

"I almost gasped when I heard that, I tripped on my nightgown trying to hurry up the stairs and back to my room. Thank goodness, they didn't hear me. I didn't turn on my light but sat by the window till I heard the doctor's car pull away. Of course, I couldn't sleep, knowing they were going to steal my baby. I cried all night."

"I was still awake when Mrs. Travis knocked on my door. She announced that breakfast was ready and I said I'd be right down. She sat down next to me at the table and asked me what was wrong; why was I picking at my food? She looked kind of worried. I told her nothing was wrong, just that I didn't have much of an appetite and that I slept well all night. I told her if we'd had a tornado, I wouldn't have heard a thing. She seemed to relax after that. I could see it in her face that she was wondering if I heard anything of her and the doctor's conversation. I knew I'd said the right thing. I stayed in my room the rest of the day. At lunchtime, I said I wasn't hungry.

Everyone could see that Justine was getting tired. The others had been sitting quietly listening intently to Justine's story.

"Let's give the girl a break now," Mike said

"That's a good idea," Ruth said. She rose from her chair and walked over to Justine, put her hand on her arm and whispered, "I know what you went through. My friend and I went through the same terrifying experience. My friend never knew that they stole her baby. I found out after she was gone. They would have taken mine if I hadn't managed to escape. You did a brave thing by running away too. It's over now and you're safe. And you have your baby." Justine touched Ruth's hand and, with misty eyes and a grateful smile, looked up at her, but said nothing.

Gerry came in with a tray of soda. Everyone took a glass and thanked her. There was an awkward silence as they sipped their drinks. Each one knew what the other must be thinking. How could this sort of thing go on? And how many other girls had been victims?

Finally, Mike asked, "Shall we continue? Justine, are you ready to go on?"

"Yes," she said, after taking a few sips of soda.

"I didn't know how or when I would get out of that house, but I knew that I had to. I came down for dinner that evening, but still didn't have an appetite. I had to make a showing of being all right though. Then, everything happened so fast. I did what I did without thinking. The dining room is off the front entrance. Stanley was coming in with some things he had picked up for Mrs. Travis and he had his arms full. Mrs. Travis was just coming from the kitchen. Without thinking, I ran out the door. Stanley didn't know what happened. Mrs. Travis saw me run out and yelled to Stanley, 'Go after her.' Stanley dropped the packages and started after me. I think I was screaming as I ran. It was then that the police car turned on its lights. I didn't know why they were there but I was grateful that they were there and didn't wonder why. Stanley ran back into the house. That's about it. You know the rest of the story."

Justine took another sip of her soda. The room was quiet for a moment.

"Well, that takes care of one story," Mike said. "What I would like now - not tonight but soon - is for Ruth and Justine to get together and work out a comprehensive story," he turned to address Ruth and Justine, "from your own experiences, about how these people treated you and proof that they intended to steal your babies. If Gerry is willing," he turned to face her and smiled, "I'd like her to take all the info down and help us prepare our case. What do you say, Gerry?"

"I'm pretty busy with the judge's work, Mike."

"If I can clear it with the Judge and make it work, will you?" Mike asked.

"I'll do it as long as we talk to the judge first."

"Okay, that's it then," Mike said. "Thank you all for coming. Let's call it a night."

They were all quiet on the way home. Ruth broke the silence. "Justine looks like a girl I met when I stayed with Mrs. Travis. I thought about Carol tonight and wondered where she is. She was the sweetest person. Is there any way we could find her, Mike?"

"It's a possibility," was all he said.

"I'm so glad you were there tonight," Ruth whispered to Gene. "When you're with me, I feel I can handle things. I feel safe."

Gene whispered back, "It went well tonight. You were wonderful."

CHAPTER 17

Ruth stood in the vestibule and waited for Gerry to buzz her in. She was anxious to talk to Justine about her experience but, at the same time, she was apprehensive. Now she would have to think about everything that happened to her while living with Mrs. Travis in that horrible place. Her life was so organized. She was happy. Now she would have to remember those painful months and relive them. She knew it had to be done and would be worth it if these people could be stopped.

When the buzzer sounded, even though she was expecting it, it startled her. Quickly grabbing the handle before the buzzer stopped, she pushed open the door and stepped inside. For a moment she hesitated, then walked up the stairs to Gerry's apartment. Once again, Gerry was waiting in the open doorway. Justine was standing behind her. They greeted each other as Gerry took Ruth's coat and hung it in the closet. Gerry led Ruth and Justine to the living room where they made themselves comfortable. Ruth felt she needed to be more secure with the closed arms so she chose the overstuffed chair. Justine took the couch.

"Would you ladies like something to drink?" Gerry asked. "The coffee's made and there's hot water for tea or a soft drink if you prefer."

"Nothing right now, thanks," Ruth answered.

"I'll wait, too," Justine said.

Gerry sat down at the other end of the couch and picked up her legal pad from the end table. "Are we ready to start?"

"Is Martha Turner still the cook?" Ruth asked Justine.

"I think so," Justine answered. "Is she a big woman with short bushy hair, kind of tough looking, with a deep rough voice?"

"That sounds like Turner, all right. That's what we called her. She wasn't a bad sort, if you didn't cross her. I know Stanley is still there. He's the one who chased you when you ran out of the house, right?

"Yes. That was Stanley. He never says much, just does whatever Mrs. Travis tells him to do. He was kind of scary," Justine admitted.

"He looked scary to me, too. When I first saw him on that snowy day when he picked me up," Ruth said, "I almost didn't get into that station wagon. But I don't have to tell you, when you're alone and need someone, you take chances and do what you have to do."

Gerry let them talk a little longer until they were completely at ease with each other, then she reminded them that they needed to compare experiences while she prepared notes that the judge had to look over before they went to court.

It wasn't long before Gerry could hardly keep up with them. For Ruth, who was at first hesitant to relive her frightening experience, it was a catharsis. There was someone with whom to share her nightmare and who understood.

Ruth told Justine about her friend, Carol, and how they stole her baby.

"Oh, my God, Ruth." Justine's eyes filled with tears and Gerry got up to get them some tissue. "That's what was going to happen to me."

"You and I are lucky," Ruth assured her, "But, we'll never know how many girls weren't so lucky and ended up like Carol. I'd love to see Carol again but, if I do, I would feel compelled to tell her that her baby is alive somewhere even though that would be crueler than not knowing. When I think of her, I pray that she has made peace with what can't be changed and that she's made a new beginning."

This went on for two hours. When there was a lull in the conversation, Gerry took the opportunity to jump in. "I don't know about you guys but I need a break. Can I get you something to drink?" Both said they were ready for a break, too.

When they finally ended the meeting, Gerry was satisfied that they had covered so much. Ruth and Justine hugged and agreed that when all this was over they would remain friends.

"I wish you could have been there," Ruth said to Gene when she arrived home. She was almost giddy with excitement. Gene had picked up Robert from the sitter and was doing the lunch dishes that Ruth had left in the sink.

"Honey, you don't have to do those," she chided.

"I know that," Gene said, "but I had to do something until you got home. Tell me how your meeting went." Ruth sat down at the kitchen table and began to relate what took place at her meeting with Justine. "Honey," Gene interrupted, "I think I can wait until you take off your coat." They both laughed.

Gerry handed the judge the notes she took at Ruth's and Justine's meeting. "I haven't had time to type these yet, but just look them over quickly."

The judge took the tablet and looked at Gerry.

"I'd like to read them, Gerry, but I can't read shorthand."

She had a smile on her face. "Oh, sorry, Judge. Anyway, things are going according to plan. The Judge just stood there without saying anything. Gerry frowned. *What's the matter?* She thought. *Why doesn't he say something?*

"I hate to tell you this," he said. "The notes, the meeting, and all that we've gone through haven't been wasted effort. It's just been put on the back burner."

"What do you mean?" Gerry asked in surprise.

"I mean, we finally got the search warrant but when we got to the house everything was gone. There wasn't a thing to confiscate. The place was empty. *I mean empty!* They took the file cabinet, all the furniture and equipment, and disappeared. Empty rooms were all we found. I think they knew the jig was up and took off to wait until the heat was off a little. They cut the padlock off the door and took everything. We don't know where they are now."

"And after all our work, is there anything we can do?"

"Not until we find them and, if they left the state that may never happen."

"Excuse me, Judge… but, God damn it!" Gerry turned around and shook her head vigorously. She hadn't expected to hear this.

The judge put his hands on her shoulders in an effort to show that he felt the same. "I agree, Gerry. I am as disappointed with this turn of affairs as you are. I'm sorry I had to tell you this."

Gerry turned. "Now I l have to tell the girls that these people have once again given everyone the slip. How do you think they're going to take this, knowing that these people are still at large and will continue their rotten business?"

"I know how you feel, Gerry, but what can I say? We tried. That's all there is. I know you hate being the bearer of bad news, but there you have it."

"But stealing babies is a federal offense," Gerry insisted.

"Yes, of course, and something is still being done. The case remains open. This will all be turned over to the FBI and now they'll take over. I feel sure the people left town but more likely they'll leave the state. That's where the problem comes in. It's going to take quite a while to find them again."

"You know, this has been extremely exasperating for me. There is so much about me that you don't know, Judge," Gerry said.

"Gerry, I know more than you think, but let's not go there now. We have to tell the girls the bad news, and they're going to be very disappointed."

"Okay. I'll take Justine to the Parker's house and tell them the bad news. This has been pretty hard on me, Judge. I feel as bad about all of this as the girls will be. I wanted those people caught."

"I know, and I can't thank you enough for all the personal time you spent on this, Gerry."

Gene and Ruth were expecting Gerry and Justine. Ruth had coffee and biscuits ready for them. When Gerry called earlier to ask if they could come over, Ruth and Gene were expecting to hear exciting news about an arrest, so when the doorbell rang, Ruth jumped up from her chair and yelled, "I'll get it."

When they were all settled at the table and Ruth had poured the coffee, she and Gene waited for Gerry to begin. Ruth had felt a strange uneasiness from the moment they walked in the door but she shrugged it off. Gerry wasn't as excited as she was supposed to be, and Ruth thought Justine's eyes looked a little red, as if she had been crying.

"Well, we're waiting," Gene said. "Tell us the good news."

"I'm afraid we have no good news," Gerry said. Justine began to cry openly.

"What do you mean?" Ruth asked. "I thought everything was ready for an arrest. What happened?"

"Yes, what happened," Gene repeated, frowning.

Gerry tried to calm Justine before going on with the details. She couldn't hold back the bad news when she got home because Justine kept insisting Gerry tell her what happened. Finally, Gerry had to tell her the bad news, and Justine hadn't stopped crying since.

"The judge is very upset about the whole thing," Gerry said. "But he wants me to tell you that it's not over. He said they used up too much time and money for all of this to be wasted by dropping the case. The FBI is going to take over. These people are in deep, deep trouble." Gerry was trying hard to keep them from thinking the situation was completely hopeless. "Sooner or later, there *will* be a conviction," she finished.

There was a long silence, except for an occasional sniffle from Justine. Each was lost in their thoughts of disappointment.

"What's going to happen to Justine?" Ruth asked.

"She's going to stay with me until the baby comes, Gerry said, "and then she'll have some choices to make about where she wants to go."

"Well, that's that!" Gene said, angrily. "Now we're supposed to go back to living our lives like nothing happened?" He stood and walked to the window, something he did when he was upset and needed to calm himself. "Let's hope they did leave the state, maybe even the country, so we won't have to worry that we'll bump into them again around some corner."

"I'm so sorry," Gerry said again.

Ruth got up and stood behind Gene. She put her hands on his shoulders. It was more for her security than to calm Gene. Her stomach was suddenly churning and she had to fight the nausea that was welling up inside of her. Swallowing hard, she managed to regain composure.

"I know you're upset, dear. We all are, but we'll be all right. Justine will have her baby. We can be thankful for that at least. Maybe because of being so close to getting caught, they'll decide not to open another shelter."

"You're right, honey. I guess I overreacted," Gene said. "But I'm really angry about this,"

"You know, Ruth," Gerry suddenly announced. "I think you've just given me a brilliant idea. Why don't we get the state to investigate the possibility of opening legitimate shelters? Maybe we can get a grant to get the ball rolling. That would certainly put any other unscrupulous organizations out of business. What do you think?"

It took a while before the idea sank in. Finally, Ruth said, "I think you've given me a cause." She looked at Gene and smiled and they all looked at each other. "That's a great idea, she said.

Soon, they were all talking about how to go about starting this new enterprise.

CHAPTER 18

It was eleven P.M. when Ruth woke with a start. The pain she felt was unmistakably her first contraction. She reached over and shook Gene.

He rolled over on his back and mumbled, "What?"

"I've just had a contraction," she said.

"It's only the first one, honey. Wake me when you have another."

Ruth lay there waiting for the next contraction and when it came, it startled her. She had dozed off again. Glancing at the clock she was surprised to see it was almost an hour later. She shook Gene again and said, "Honey, I just had another one."

Gene, still half asleep, said, "How long has it been?"

"Almost an hour."

"Honey, it's probably going to take hours."

"Gene, I'm worried. Let's not wait. It's really bad out there. It's been snowing all night."

"Okay. Why don't you get started? You know, get your bag ready and call Margaret."

"My bag has been ready for over a week, but I'll call her."

Margaret wasn't too happy about being awakened in the middle of the night, at least that's what she called it, but she said she would be over as soon as she dressed. It was about forty-five minutes later when the doorbell rang.

"I'm so sorry, Margaret," Ruth said. "I know it's late and the weather is bad. Thank you for coming. You know the routine. Help yourself to whatever you need. Robert is sound asleep, and I've put blankets on the couch so you can go back to sleep."

"I know I sounded crabby and I'm sorry," Margaret said.

"Don't worry," Ruth laughed. "Gene's having a hard time waking up."

"Are you ready?" Gene called as he came down the stairs.

"Just waiting for you, Sweetie," Ruth called back. She and Margaret smiled at each other.

Gene put Ruth's case in the back seat and helped her into the car. When he opened the garage door, a blizzard greeted him.

"Jesus, look at this weather! You sure picked a bad time to have my baby."

"That's why I wanted to leave before the contractions were too close." She no sooner spoke those words when another contraction hit her.

The world was white around them. The road was completely covered with several inches of snow. Gene drove on what he thought was the right side of the road, always looking for the edge of the road, where it ended and where the ditch along side began.

Ruth had another contraction. *Not as severe this time,* she thought. If she kept a little conversation going, it would ease the tension.

"Will you call Gerry and tell her I can't make the meeting with her and Justine?"

"Of course I will."

"I'm so glad Gerry is letting Justine and Tommy stay with her. They seem to be getting along just fine. Justine's baby is so sweet. I know those two are going to spoil the heck out of him."

Ruth was getting really nervous now. She couldn't see the road and wondered if Gene was having an easier time because he had driven this road to the hospital so many times. In an effort to keep Gene from getting too anxious, she tried unsuccessfully to hide the contractions but Gene knew what was happening.

"How close are the contractions, Honey?"

"I don't know. They could be every fifteen minutes."

I'm working on instinct, now." Gene said. "I haven't seen any other cars and we're on the longest uninhabited stretch of the road."

"We're not going to make it, are we?" There was a tremor in her voice.

"Ruth, I'm going to stop for a minute so you can get into the back seat."

"Why, Gene?"

"Because, if anything should happen, you'll be safer back there."

Gene slowed and tried to stop. As he did, the back wheel slid off the left side of the road and into the ditch. He had been driving on the wrong side of the road.

"Gene, what happened?" Ruth yelled.

"We're all right." Gene patted her hand.

"Gene, I don't want to have my baby in this car," she shouted. "I would rather have had it at home! Why didn't we stay home?"

"Honey, we didn't know how bad it was until after we started out."

"Yes, we did! What are we going to do?" She began to cry.

"Ruth, I'm here with you. We'll make it. Remember, I'm a doctor."

"I don't want to be here," she yelled as another contraction grabbed her. "I want to go home."

"Ruth, you have to get in the back seat. Cover your head. It's windy and cold out there. I'll come around and help you." Gene stepped out of the car. The snow was over his ankles and got deeper as he slid halfway down the slope. He held onto the door handle to keep from falling. Digging each foot into the snow for support, he managed to make it up to the road. Walking around, he opened Ruth's door. The snow blew in from both sides now.

"Be careful, dear," he said as he helped her out of the car. The snow lashed hard in their faces. When Ruth was settled in the back seat, Gene leaned over the front seats to close the door on his side. The wind had blown the snow into the car when both doors were open so it had a snowy cover over everything. He sat down next to Ruth and took her in his arms. She moaned when each contraction hit her.

Now that the doors were closed, the car was warming up. Gene left the motor running even though he was low on gas. He was hopeful that help would come before the tank was empty.

"Gene, am I going to be okay?"

"Yes, you are," Gene said, trying to make a joke. "Just think how much the children will like hearing the exciting story of how our baby was born in a car in the middle of a snow storm on a lonely road."

Ruth forced a smile. It was something to think about.

Gene couldn't think of anything else to say to allay Ruth's fears. He thought of the county snowplows as another means of salvation because it was obvious they hadn't come this way yet.

Fortunately, the pains subsided for a while and Ruth dozed off still nestled against Gene's chest.

Soon, the gas gauge registered empty and after a few sputters, the engine died. Gene had to tell himself not to panic. He couldn't let Ruth see how worried he was, but as it grew colder, he began to fear the worst.

There was the sound of a motor. Gene thought at first it was the howling wind, but it became louder as the vehicle came closer. It was the sound of a truck. He turned to look out the back window. There were two headlights, beacons out of the swirling darkness, slowly approaching.

"Ruth, honey," Gene said excitedly, "There's a truck on the road! It's coming our way!" With a dying battery, the lights on Gene's car had dimmed until they were practically out. Gene leaned over the front seat to blow the horn. It made a short, quick, pitiful beep. The dying battery took care of that. Anyway the wind had to drown out what little sound there was. He jumped out of the car and began waving his arms. *If they don't see me in this storm, I'm a dead man.* The truck gave a couple honks and flashed its lights. *Oh, thank God, they've seen us.*

The truck slowed to a stop beside the car. The driver lowered the window and a husky voice asked, "Is anyone hurt here?"

"No one's hurt but my wife is having a baby and we were on our way to the hospital. Do you think you can help?"

"Hell, let's get her into the truck and I'll drive you right to it."

"God bless you." Gene helped Ruth out of the car. She could barely keep her footing with the weight of the baby and the slippery road. The driver got out of the truck. He was a big burly man. Without even asking, he picked Ruth right up and carried her to the passenger side of the truck. This took Gene by surprise but he didn't say a word.

"Open the door," he yelled to Gene as he walked around the truck.

Gene kept slipping but managed to keep from falling as he hurried to the passenger side and opened the door.

"Can you make the top step, lady?" the driver asked.

"I'll try," Ruth answered, breathing hard. She struggled into the truck, glad to be inside.

"You get up there beside her, now," the driver said, motioning to Gene.

Gene wasted no time getting in the truck. He felt the cold. His hat was in the car. He put his arm around Ruth and she leaned into him. When the driver got in, his large frame took up more than his share of the seat.

"My name is Gene Parker," he began. "I'm a doctor at the hospital. Ruth was afraid she would have our baby in the car. Actually, I was too. If there were any complications, that wouldn't be a good place to deliver. You're a lifesaver."

"I'm Lester Williams," he said. "I got a late start, tonight, the weather being so bad and all. Lucky for you, I did."

"You can say that again."

Lester had a plump, pleasant face and wore a woolen cap that covered his ears. Gene looked at the cap with envy.

"I come this way a lot so I know where the hospital is. I'll take you right there."

"Mr. Williams, we can't thank you enough. If I can be of help to you, anytime in the future, please don't hesitate to call on me. The hospital always knows how to locate me. I'm not just saying this. I mean what I say."

The deep snow helped the truck maintain reasonable traction. It slid a few times but stayed on the road. When this happened, Gene would become frightened and clutch Ruth a little tighter to him. He could be heard sucking in an anxious breath as they were jostled about.

"We're okay," The driver assured him. "Been through these storms lots of times."

Gene could tell that Lester was in control. He was a very good driver, but still, that didn't assuage the uneasiness that wouldn't leave him.

When the lights of the hospital appeared through the snow-streaked windshield, he sighed with relief. Ruth had kept her face nestled in his chest and used his body to muffle her moans. Cradled in Gene's arms and so in tune with her own body, she was oblivious to the precarious situation they'd been in.

Soon, Lester pulled the truck right up to the emergency entrance.

Gene jumped out and ran through the revolving doors. In seconds, there were a couple of orderlies with a wheel chair helping Ruth out of the truck. It took two of them now because Ruth was doubled over and unable to walk.

"Be careful with that little lady," Lester called.

"Jesus, how'd she get up here?" one of them asked.

"Just watch where you're going, these steps are slippery," the other one answered.

Gene followed them in. Just inside the doors, he ran out again to wave goodbye to Lester, who was slowly pulling away. Lester saw him and waved back.

Ruth was moved to one of the curtained-off spaces in the emergency room and helped onto the bed.

Gene hadn't worked in the emergency room in quite a while. There were new faces there. He knew the nurse, Cindy, but couldn't remember her last name.

"Dr. Parker, What's happening?" Cindy asked.

"It's my wife. She's about to deliver. Call upstairs and let OB know she's here, will you? I believe Doctor Meyer is on duty tonight."

"He is," Cindy answered.

"Wonderful! I was hoping he would be." Gene sounded relieved.

Gene took his coat off and threw it on the chair, then helped Ruth with hers. He held her hand while they waited. The baby wasn't going to cooperate.

"Gene," Ruth yelled, "the baby's coming, the baby's coming!" She squeezed his hand so hard he winced.

"Don't push, Ruth, we've got to get you upstairs."

"Oh, for God's sake, I can't hold it! Take my pants off."

Gene made sure the curtains were closed then removed the blanket from Ruth and started to remove her maternity pants. Although they had elastic around the waist and were plenty big, Gene fumbled as he struggled to get them from under her. She was squirming too much and her moans unnerved him. He no sooner yanked them off, along with her panties, when Ruth let out another yell. The nurse heard her and rushed in.

"Doctor, what's happening?"

"We've got a baby that won't wait!" Gene exclaimed.

Ruth let out a groan, the urge to push overwhelming her. That's when her water broke.

"Gene, my water just broke. What are they waiting for?" She pulled at his shirt.

"We're waiting for the orderlies."

"Oh, my goodness," Cindy said, "I better call upstairs again."

Gene tried to sound calm. "You're doing fine, honey," he said through clenched teeth. *Where the hell are they?* Just then, he was relieved to see the orderlies come in. They quickly covered Ruth and moved her out.

Gene ran alongside trying to hold onto Ruth's hand as they hurried to the elevator.

When the elevator doors opened at the obstetrics floor, Dr. Meyer was waiting there in the hall.

"Gene, nice to see you. It's been a while. How's the little lady doing?"

"Dr. Meyer, I was glad to hear that you were on duty tonight. Ruth's contractions are coming rapidly now. She had quite a scare on the way here. Actually, I did too. We were stuck on the road until a truck driver gave us a lift. If it wasn't for him we would probably still be stranded."

"Thank goodness for good Samaritans." Dr. Meyer said. "Too bad there aren't more of them. Let's get Ruth to delivery and get her prepped."

About two hours later, the doctor announced to Gene, "You have a beautiful baby girl, Dad. Ruth and the baby are doing fine."

CHAPTER 19

With two children and a husband to care for, Ruth had no time to feel sorry that everything she'd wanted to accomplish had to wait for its time to come. She rarely thought about the doctor and Mr. Travis.

With Pauline already a year old and Robert in Kindergarten, Ruth fell into a comfortable routine that was both satisfying and exhausting. And the years passed almost too quickly.

Robert started high school and Pauline felt left out because she was just ten and in the fifth grade. It was Robert that pulled her out of her sour mood by having her sit with him while they studied. She quickly saw how difficult high school would be.

"Good thinking, Son," Gene had said at the time. "Now she understands how good she has it."

The next four years were the shortest that Ruth could remember. Robert had been accepted at Perdue University and Pauline could hardly wait for the next school year to begin, because she would be in high school and no longer a little kid.

"Now, maybe somebody will give me a little respect," Pauline said, haughtily.

Robert just laughed because his kid sister didn't realize that she'd, once again, be at the bottom of the social ladder.

Ruth had long ago gotten used to her children's sibling rivalry but still had to get between them at times. And, as always, the years continued to roll by.

When Robert left for college, Pauline cried. It was the first time that she and her brother would truly be parted. "This is the worst!" she complained. "Who will I argue with now?"

Robert put the last piece of luggage in the car while Ruth, Gene and Pauline stood on the porch and watched. Ruth was almost in tears as she watched her grown-up son getting ready to leave the nest, almost for the last time. This was his last year at Perdue. The school was a long way away and the visits would be few and far between. Even Gene was having a hard time keeping a dry eye. Pauline ran to Robert's arms as he started walking back to say goodbye.

"Good bye Robby," she said, throwing herself at him. "You have a good time in school. Don't do anything stupid."

"Thanks, sis, I'll try not to." He let her go and turned to Gene. "I'll be seeing you, Dad." Robert waited for a response, but words didn't come easy. Gene put his hand out but when Robert extended his hand, Gene pulled him into his arms.

"Goodbye son. You take care now. Don't forget to write. You know your mother is going to worry if she doesn't hear from you."

"I won't forget."

Ruth was crying now.

"Come on, Mom," Robert laughed, trying to ease the tension. He put his arms around her. "I'll write often and come home every chance I get. Purdue's not that far away."

"I know I'm being silly but I can't help it. I love you."

"I love you too, Mom," he said, and turned to go.

He stuck his arm out the window and waved as he pulled away. They all waved back. Gene put his arm around Ruth and guided her inside. She was dabbing her eyes with a tissue.

"This is almost as bad as when I had to leave him when he started kindergarten," Ruth sniffled. "Where did all the time go? He was a baby just last year, wasn't he?"

"No, dear. It had to be at least three or four," Gene replied, and wiped his eye.

Robert was true to his word. All the years he was at Perdue, he wrote once a week and called every two or three weeks. Now in his last year at the school, the letters suddenly became less frequent, and Ruth began to worry.

"He's met a girl and is spending all his time with her," she complained. "I just know he has."

CHAPTER 20

Long dark hair, laughing brown eyes, a mischievous smile and a gorgeous figure; this is what caught Robert's attention as he closed his book and stood up. He was ready to leave the study center when she came in. She was headed in his direction and about to walk right past him. Without thinking, he turned and stepped out in front of her.

"Whoops, I didn't mean to get in your way, beautiful."

"Excuse me, buddy! Why don't you watch where you're going?" she asked snidely.

"Hey! Okay, I'm sorry. What more can I say?"

"You could get out of my way, if you don't mind."

"My name is Robert. What's yours?"

"None of your business," she snapped.

Robert turned to let her pass as she moved to walk around him. They were face to face again. "Whoops, again," he said. "Care to dance?"

"Are you trying to be funny?" she said. "If you are, it's not working. Would you please get out of my way, I have studying to do."

"No, I wasn't trying to be funny. I was trying to get out of your way, miss... what did you say your name was, Madame Butterfly?"

"Oh, pull-eeze!" She took a deep breath and let it sigh out as she turned her face trying to hide a smile. She wasn't about to let him see that he had gotten to her. She pushed past him and walked away.

Robert followed her with his eyes as she sat down. He watched as she opened her books and began to concentrate on her work until he felt the eyes of the other students waiting to see what he was going to do. He left the room knowing he would never get this girl out of his mind. He could still smell her perfume and feel her touch.

Christy sat there musing over what she considered a comical incident.

He was kind of cute, she thought. *I think I'd like to see him again although I don't know why. He might end up being a jerk.*

Robert haunted the student study center but didn't see her again for another week. It was Monday about three o'clock and he was leaving the center. As he walked down the stairs, she was coming up the stairs. Their eyes met and they smiled.

"Hi, there, Madame Butterfly," he said.

Christy had to laugh. "Still trying to be funny, I see."

"No, I just don't know your name."

"My name is Christine, but everyone calls me Christy."

"Well, Christy, my name is Robert. Not Bob or Rob or Robby but Robert... Parker, that is."

"Well, hello not Bob or Rob or Robby but Robert Parker, that is."

"Now who's trying to be funny?" he asked with a big grin.

"Well, you started it."

"Can we be serious now? Let me buy you a cup of coffee or tea or pop or whatever." When Christy hesitated, he went on, "You might as well say yes because I'm gonna keep asking until you do."

"You win." Christy began to relax. "I could use some coffee right now."

Robert took her elbow as they started down the stairs. Christy quickly turned to look him in the face but she didn't pull her arm away. Robert dropped his hand when they reached the foyer and left the building.

"You know, let's not go to the school cafeteria. There's a little café about two miles away. I think it's called the Pilgrim's café or something like that. Anyway, I've been there before. It's a nice place. My car is right here in the lot."

Christy turned and gave him a deep frown, and said "I can read your mind. You're about to say, 'I swear I just want to get to know you better. I'll be the perfect gentleman.' Well, I'm not sure I want to get to know you better," they both almost laughed.

The cafe was different. Robert and Christy made comment about the place. They agreed it looked like it might have been a retail store at one time because there were shelves along both walls. The windows went from the ceiling to the floor. They had gold colored rods that held short, laced cafe curtains at just the right height. Where there had been rows of tables stacked with merchandise, there were round tables with checkered tablecloths. Behind numerous pictures of old country scenes of people and places, the wallpaper had a busy little floral pattern. The shelves around the room, that at one time might have held canned goods and cereal boxes, held knick-knacks and relics of yesteryear. There was a man at the register shuffling receipts and counting money. Two ladies, the café's waitresses, dressed in long country skirts with white blouses and bib aprons, were clearing tables and setting out fresh napkins and flatware.

The salt-and-pepper-haired lady stopped what she was doing and came to the door as Christy and Robert entered. "Good afternoon. Will it be just the two of you?"

Robert said, "Yes."

"We're still serving lunch, or would you prefer the dinner menu?"

"We're just going to have something to drink, if that's all right," Robert said.

"Of course, follow me." She seated them at a table for two in the rear of the place. "Coffee?" she asked.

Christy answered. "I'll have Boston coffee, please."

"I'll have a large coke," Robert said.

The waitress was back with the drinks in less than a minute. She set them down and said, "Let me know if you need anything else."

They took a few minutes to sip their drinks then Robert said, "So tell me about you, Christy."

"You first," she said.

"Well, I'm in my last year and have been taking mostly pre-med classes," Robert began. "My dad is a doctor and I've been swayed in that direction. But I've been having some misgivings lately." He hesitated, as if he were giving what he'd just said a little thought. "I don't know if that's really for me. I'm sure my dad and mom will back me up no matter what I decide to do. I know my dad will understand. He's a great guy."

Christy sipped her coffee and waited for him to continue.

"We have a house in Winnetka; that's a suburb of Chicago. It's close to the hospital where my dad is registered on staff. I have a sister. Her name is Pauline and she's sixteen." He had to smile thinking about Pauline. "Most kid sisters are a bit of a pain, but I have to say Pauline and I have always been very close. She's always been a little unpredictable but she's great. Okay, I've told you a lot about me, now it's your turn."

"Okay," Christy began, "I'm in my first year and I'm not sure what my major will be. My dad wants me to pursue a career in business. My mom doesn't really care what I do. She's a socialite and, I'm embarrassed to say, they are both very materialistic. My dad tells me that my grandmother was like that."

"Nothing wrong with that" Robert said. "Someone has to watch the pennies."

Christy just shrugged, thinking, *he doesn't know my father.* "Well, that's my family. Anyway, I haven't decided what I want to do. I plan on talking to one of the counselors later. We did a lot of plays in high school and I find that I love the theater. My father says you can't make a decent living in that field. He says actors starve to death because they're always out of work. So I told him I would let him support me until I became famous. You should have seen the look on his face."

"I can imagine," Robert said. "That's kinda funny, though."

"My dad's not easy to know. I think there's a lot of family history that he doesn't care to talk about."

"Theater, that's interesting," Robert volunteered. "I did some acting in high school but I wasn't very good. I ended up working behind the scenes. I liked that, though. I learned a lot about sound and lighting."

They ended up talking through another coffee and large coke. They laughed a lot while sharing childhood experiences. They were so engrossed in conversation they hardly noticed the café filling up for the dinner hour. Christy was the first to mention it was getting late.

"Look how long we've been here. It's getting dark. I wonder why they haven't asked us to leave. All this time and we've only had drinks."

"Why don't we stay and have dinner?" Robert asked.

"I can't," Christy replied. "I have to study and I promised my friend we'd get together for dinner later."

"Okay, maybe next time."

Robert drove Christy to her dorm. She opened the door and started to get out of the car when Robert put his hand on her arm.

"I'm glad we had this time together," he said. "Thanks for putting up with me. Now you know I'm not such a bad guy." Robert became very serious. "I really like you, Christy. Can I see you again?"

Christy knew she liked him but was wondering if she should play hard to get. That's what all the love stories said a girl should do on a first date. After a moment of hesitation she answered, "Yes!"

Robert and Christy began seeing each other at every opportunity. They were both very studious and didn't neglect their studies, but on weekends or on days without classes, they always managed to do something together. They might go to a movie, a play, a concert or take a drive to a nearby town. They were both aware of the chemistry between them but, being uncertain of the other's feelings; both thought it best to keep it platonic.

One Saturday, they attended a play on campus. The theater group always put on good plays and the two of them never missed a performance. When the show ended there was a rush to get out, but that ended when the foyer was crammed with people looking out at a downpour. One or two at a time would venture out until there were only a few people left. Should they take a chance and get drenched or wait a little longer hoping the rain would stop. Robert and Christy were among those who had to make a decision. Robert suggested they chance it.

"My room is the closest sanctuary," Robert said. "Do you want to make a run for it? This rain might not stop for a while."

"We might as well. I don't think we'll melt and it's better than waiting here till God knows when."

They left the building. Robert took Christy's hand and, as the rain poured down on them, they ran to Robert's apartment, laughing all the way. Once inside, they couldn't stop laughing while trying to catch their breath. They were soaked.

"Christy. Get out of those wet clothes. There's a robe hanging in the bathroom, I'll go to my room and get out of mine."

Robert had one of the choice accommodations. It was small but he had two rooms instead of one, a bedroom and a larger room with a small, kitchen area; and he had it to himself. There was just enough space to squeeze in a tiny table and two chairs.

Robert came out first, wearing sweatpants and a tee shirt. His upper body was extremely handsome and the tee shirt was just tight enough to show off his well proportioned torso with his muscular upper arms and broad chest. He made some hot tea.

Christy emerged in the much-too-large robe with the sleeves rolled up and the robe having a big overlap in front. That look had a distracting effect and was enough to excite Robert as he tried to picture the body concealed beneath the robe.

"Well, if it isn't my Madame Butterfly, all dressed up in her finery."

"The latest from Paris, you know. I'm not "Poor" Butterfly," Christy quipped.

They laughed. It was their private little joke now. Robert put two cups and saucers on the table, put a teabag in each cup and poured in the hot water. Christy sat down across from his place. As she did, her robe parted slightly. Robert had to force himself to look away. He got the sugar, the spoons and a pitcher of milk. When he turned to put them on the table, he saw that she'd made no effort to close the robe again. Her breasts were straining to reveal their nipples.

"Be careful, it's hot," Robert warned. "Would you care for a cookie? I'm sorry, but that's all I have to offer you. "

"No, thank you. The candy bar I had during the show was enough sweets for one day. Don't laugh when I put sugar in my tea, though" she said as she reached for the sugar bowl. "I can't drink tea without sugar," The big sleeve caught her cup handle and turned the cup on its side spilling her tea. Robert jumped up, grabbed a towel from the counter and began to soak up the spill before it ran off of the table on Christy. He stood over Christy. The scent of her and her still-damp hair invaded his nostrils. She raised her head. He looked into her eyes and for a moment they stared at each other. Slowly, Robert lowered his head until he tenderly kissed her lips. He waited. She didn't move. He kissed her again. This time it was soft and lingering. Robert helped her to stand. Her robe fell open. He put his hands inside the robe and around her naked waist and drew her to him. She didn't resist but put her arms around his neck and pushed her body against him. He kissed her long and hard. He kissed her neck, her cheeks, her lips.

"What are we doing?" she finally whispered.

"Do you want me to stop?" he replied, almost in a pleading tone.

"No," she said with a sigh.

He turned her slightly and led her to the bedroom.

"Robert," she whispered, as they stood beside the bed, "I've never done this before."

"Christy" He paused to consider the consequences. "Neither have I," he said truthfully.

Sunday morning found them curled up in each other's arms. And that's how it would be on the weekend mornings that followed, and every other chance they had to be together. Robert wanted her to move in with him but she refused.

"Robert, there's barely enough room for you in this place. My clothes would fill up the whole apartment. Besides, what would I tell my folks if they happened to drop in unexpectedly on some weekend and find that I had moved in with some guy? My dad would probably have you shot."

"You're right," Robert said as he dropped his hands from her shoulders while she sat at the little table waiting for her coffee "I know I'm being selfish, but I can't stand being away from you. Do you feel that way about me?" He hesitated. "Christy, I love you."

Christy looked up at him and smiled. She stood, took his hands and put them around her waist. "Do you really feel that way?"

"Yes, I thought that was obvious."

"Maybe to you, but a girl has to hear it."

"I'll tell you how important you are to me, I want to marry you."

Christy was stunned. She took his face in her hands and kissed his mouth. "I love you so much, Robert. I want to be with you forever. It's too early to talk about marriage though. I'm too young and you are too. We can talk about this after graduation when we've both finished school. That is, if you'll still want me then."

"Of course I'll want you. Don't talk crazy."

"My parents will have a hard time putting up objections when I come of age," Christy continued.

As usual, Robert acquiesced. "You are the practical one and I love you. I love you. I love you," he said between kisses.

Time passed quickly for the lovers. They seemed to be perfectly suited for each other. They enjoyed the same things, and their ideas about life and the world in general were much the same. Even their temperaments were incredibly similar. They often studied together, which was especially beneficial for Christy because Robert was able to help her with problem assignments and would quiz her when she had to prepare for an exam.

December came too quickly. All they could think about during those last weeks was being separated during Christmas break and dreading the thought of being apart.

The last day of school ended early. Robert spent the afternoon in Christy's room watching her pack a few things. They made love all night long. The next morning, they spent their last hour together in the school's cafeteria waiting for Christy's parents to come for her. She had asked them to meet her there. She wanted them to meet Robert but he couldn't be in her room.

"I'll have to put on a happy face for my parents when I get home," Robert said, "But all the time I'll be thinking of you and wishing we were together."

"I know." Christy said. "I'll have to do the same or my father will be suspicious."

"What would he be suspicious about?"

"While I was growing up, he had to know my every move, and if a boy asked me out, he had him investigated. I think he thought every guy was going to have sex with me. Or maybe he just doesn't trust me."

"I can see how he'd be worried. You're a beautiful girl."

"You're a guy so you don't know about the pressures a girl has to bear because her parents are afraid she'll come home with a belly full. That sounds crude but that's what Dad said my grandmother would say."

"What a stupid expression," Robert shook his head. "Well, I'm a guy and I know how much I want you. It's because I love you that I want to make love to you. I'm so glad we waited for each other. I would never hurt you and I really wish I could kiss you right this minute!"

"I wish you could too but my parents are coming in the door right now."

Christy ran to greet them giving each one a hug. They walked back to the table where Robert waited.

"Mom…Dad, this is my friend, Robert Parker."

Robert turned to Christy's mom. "It's nice to meet you, Mrs. Malcolm." She didn't answer, just nodded her head. He then offered his hand to her dad. "How do you do, sir?" Mr. Malcolm didn't return the gesture. Instead, he glared at Robert and said," How long have you known my daughter?"

"Well, since school started, sir."

"Dad, I said he's my friend. I have lots of friends now."

"What are you doing down here anyway?" he said in an angry tone.

"We were going to meet you in your room and help you carry your things."

"I was so anxious to see you that I didn't look at the time. When I realized I was too early, I decided to wait here instead of alone in my room. Robert was here so I asked him to keep me company. Besides, all I have is this one bag. It's not heavy."

Ellen Malcolm put her gloved hand on Christy's arm. "You look lovely, my dear. College must agree with you. Are you eating well?"

"Yes, Mother, everything's just fine. Can we get going?" Christy wanted to get her father out of there before he started asking too many questions and if he were to look too closely at their faces, he might guess their secret. She turned to Robert. "Thanks for keeping me company. Hope you have a nice holiday."

"Thanks, you too, Christy. See you later." Robert had wanted to help her on with her coat but he was afraid to touch her in front of her father.

Mr. Malcolm picked up Christy's bag and the three of them started for the door. Christy turned for one last look at Robert. He waved.

CHAPTER 21

Ruth spared no time or expense making everything perfect for Robert's visit. The house was festive, outside and inside. The big pine in front of the house was decorated with lights.

Before Robert reached the top step, Pauline was there and opened the front door. "Welcome home, Robby." They hugged. "We missed you. Do you still like college? Did you miss us? Did you make a lot of friends? How long are you going to be home? Mom's been crazy waiting for you to come home. Dad says she's going overboard but he's more excited than he wants to show. He really misses you. We all miss you."

"Take it easy, little sister. I'll be home for a couple of weeks. We'll have plenty of time to catch up. I want to know about you, too. Can we go in now?"

Ruth and Gene were in the foyer and, of course, Ruth was trying to hold back her tears.

"Hey, Mom, Dad." He was surprised at how good it felt to be home again. Ruth had activities planned and Robert didn't fail to tell her and Gene how much he appreciated their efforts.

"The house is beautiful, Mom. And Dad, come on! That tree is huge. I see all the old ornaments are hung again. I can't believe you saved all the stuff we made as kids."

Ruth smiled. "It helps me remember when you and Pauline were small, and it makes me happy."

The days were busy, filled with visits to friend's homes and having friends over. Robert hung out with the guys a couple of nights. He was glad to relax with his friends. He didn't think he should tell anyone about Christy yet, but with his buddies, he felt sure they would like to know and he just had to tell someone. The guys congratulated him and, of course, teased him about losing his cherry.

Ruth kept everyone busy but they all had fun. Robert enjoyed the time with his folks but when he went to his room and crawled into bed at night, his thoughts turned to Christy. As much as he liked being home, he missed her even more. He held the pillow until he fell asleep.

It was his last evening at home and Ruth had prepared Robert's favorite meal of baked pork chops, mashed potatoes and broccoli. There was also a green salad and apple pie with ice cream for dessert.

When they finished the meal, Ruth poured coffee for her and Gene.

"You haven't talked much about school, Robert. Are you still taking pre-med classes?" Gene asked.

"Dad, I've taken all the pre-med classes" and hesitantly continued, "I hope you won't be disappointed but I'm not sure that's what I want."

"You know it's your decision son. I won't deny that I'm a little disappointed but I'll be happy no matter what you decide to do."

"Is that why you seem so preoccupied since you've been home?" Ruth chimed in. "You know your dad and I will always be here for you, no matter what you decide."

"There is something else I haven't told you." He suddenly smiled. "I've met a girl and I think I love her." He laughed. "No, I'm sure I love her."

Pauline put her two cents in then. "Robby's got a girlfriend. What do ya know? Robby has a girl!"

"Stop being a dork." Robert glared at her, "You sound like a five-year-old. This is serious."

"Just how serious are you about this girl?" Ruth asked.

"Serious enough to want you to meet her."

"Okay," Ruth grinned. "What's her name? What's her background? Where does she live? I only have a few hundred questions for you, Robert."

"Is she pretty? Do you have a picture, Robby?" Pauline asked.

"She's not only pretty, she's beautiful, and no, I don't have a picture."

"Gene, will you look at our little boy. I wasn't expecting this so soon."

"Ruth, he's a man. This was inevitable. Can I have another cup of coffee?"

"Seriously, Robert," Ruth said, ignoring Gene's request, "Why did you wait till your last night here to tell us this?"

"Because you're doing just what I thought you'd do, ask me a million questions."

"Well, can you tell us *something* about her?" Ruth asked again.

"Her name is Christy. She's in her first year at the college and she's eighteen."

"Isn't that a little young, Robert?" Gene asked.

"How much older are you than mom? Isn't it about ten years?"

"Yes," he said, raising his cup, "but she was older than eighteen when we met."

"Dad, we're not getting married next week. I just want you to meet her. I'm sure her parents would object to anything serious right now, anyway."

"Honey, he's right," Ruth said, taking Gene's cup and setting it down in front of him. "Let's not make more of it than what he's telling us. When can we meet her Robert?"

"I was hoping she could get away for spring break if that's okay with you."

"That will work for us." Ruth said.

"Great, we get to meet Robby's girlfriend," Pauline was sincerely happy for him.

"You'll like her, sis. You'll all like her."

"Well, that's that." Ruth said. "Your visit was too short. Did you get to see all your friends? What did they say when you told them you had a girl?"

"I didn't tell them," he lied. "No one else knows but you. Do me a favor and don't spread it around? It's too early to tell everyone."

"Of course dear, if that's what you want"

"How about you, Pauline?"

"My lips are sealed, big brother."

"It's going to seem like ages until we see you again. You won't forget to write, will you?" Ruth asked.

"I won't forget, I promise. I'll send some pictures too."

"I guess I don't get my coffee." Gene grumbled. "Pauline, will you help your mother clear the table?"

"Oh... okay," Pauline said reluctantly, getting up from the table.

"Robert, let's relax in the living room for a while. You've been pretty busy so I think you're ready for a little rest before you start packing."

"That sounds good, dad."

"I'll bring your coffee, dear," Ruth chirped.

Robert found himself speeding. *What the hell are you doing, jerk? You want to get back to school in one piece don't you? Watch those ice patches in the road.* "Yeah, I don't think Christy will be expecting a pile of broken bones. Now, you're talking to yourself, you ass. So what!" *Turn the radio on. Relax.* He saw the sign 'SLOW DOWN FOR MARTY'S TRUCK STOP 2 MILES'

I think I should stop for some coffee and take a twenty-minute break. I'm so anxious to see Christy, I'm not thinking straight. There was an old gas station exactly 2 miles from the sign. He decided to fill up even though he still had a half tank of gas. The twenty-minute rest and the coffee settled him. When he got back in the car, he was calm and turned his thinking to the happy times with family and then to the time when he would hold Christy in his arms again.

It was sundown when Robert pulled into the college parking lot in front of Christy's building. He jumped out of the car, slipping on the snow packed pavement, and headed straight for her room. He knocked several times but there was no answer. The girl next door stuck her head out the door.

"Christy won't be back until tomorrow or the next day. She's still with her folks."

Robert started to say thanks but she ducked back in before he took a breath. He turned, headed down the stairs and left the building. Back in his room, he went straight to the table and, without taking off his jacket, just sat there for forty-five minutes feeling sorry for him. The anticipation he felt while driving back evaporated into oblivion. He finally got up and walked to the bedroom. Christy's blouse was hanging on the doorknob. He picked it up and put it to his face. He could smell her fragrance. Flopping onto the bed, he stared at the ceiling and flipped her blouse over his face.

Robert waited all the next day but there was no sign of Christy. He sat in the cafeteria so he wouldn't miss her when her parents brought her back. Another night without her was going to be unbearably long. Sleep didn't come until three o'clock in the morning. It was almost noon when someone pounded on his door.

"Who the hell's that? Do you know what time it is?" Robert yelled.

"Yes I do. Its afternoon" Christy called back. "Open the door."

"Christy?" he said as he threw back the covers and jumped out of bed.

"Yes. Can I come in?"

He raced to the door and yanked it open. Christy threw herself into his arms. It had been snowing all morning and Christy was covered with the white stuff.

"Jesus, you're fucking cold. Take off that coat." He said as he began to help her unbutton it. The coat fell to the floor when he picked her up. He held her tight as he turned and kicked the door closed with his foot. He kissed her hard. Now the scent of her was real and he wanted more. So did she.

The sun was setting when Christy, leaning on one elbow, looked down at him and said, "I'm starving. Let's go get something to eat."

"Okay with me, I need something to keep up my strength."

"Yes, you do honey. Can we go to the Pilgrim's Café?"

"Any place. Just feed me," he said.

Once again in the Pilgrim's place, they gave the waitress their order and she came right back with their drinks. While they waited for their food, Robert asked how her visit with her parents went.

"My dad bombarded me with questions practically the whole time. He insists I'm getting too independent. He doesn't believe that you're just a friend who waited with me. He suspects I'm dating you and doesn't want me dating below my station."

"So I'm below your station, huh? He'll change his mind when he finds out my folks are millionaires."

"Your folks are millionaires?"

"Not really, but they're pretty well off. I told you my dad's a doctor."

"You know, I don't really care about any of that." Christy said in a disgusted tone of voice, as she almost slammed her drink on the table. "I'm so tired of listening to my folks talk about money. They're so materialistic. I wouldn't care if you came from the slums. I'd marry you just to spite them." Her tone suddenly softened as she put her hand over

Robert's just as he was about to raise his glass and take a drink. "Tell me about your visit now. How did it go?"

"Well, that was some tirade." he smiled. "Anyway, my visit was great. My folks are great. I told them about us. Of course, my mom asked a million questions. My dad was cool though. My sister can't wait to meet you. I know you'll like them. Hey, where's our food? I can smell those hamburgers."

The couple took up the old routine. There was nothing to complain about. Life was good. And so were their grades. They were in Robert's room when Christy said, "Dad's going to be pleased with my report, but I can't tell him that your help is what's gotten me there."

"You didn't need much help, honey, just encouragement. By the way, spring break will be here before we know it. Do you have plans that week?"

"My mom and dad have to take a business trip so they asked me to stay with my Aunt Martha. She's a wonderful person and I always have a good time with her. Why do you ask?"

"My folks are expecting me to visit during the break and I told them I would try to get you to come along. I want them to meet you. Do you think you can make an excuse to your aunt and come with me?"

"I don't know."

"Since I told them I'm in love, of course they want to see who their little boy is dating. My folks are great. You'll like them."

"Are you sure?" she asked.

"Yes. I told you, my mom already knows about you. I had to explain why I wasn't writing when I saw them at Christmas. She asked why my letters weren't coming as often so I told her I met a girl. Mom laughed and said, 'I guess that's a good enough reason.' So, what do you say . . . about your aunt, that is?"

"I'll say, 'Aunt Martha, the girls in the sorority are getting together for a field trip and its part of curriculum expectations. I'm sorry I can't be with you but I know you understand.' How does that sound?"

"That should do it, I hope. I could kiss you."

"Well, why don't you?" she giggled.

Robert called his mom as soon as Christy told him that it was settled with her aunt and that she would be accompanying him for spring break.

"That's wonderful, Robert, we were just talking about your visit and hoping Christy would be coming too. You say you'll be here on Saturday around dinnertime?"

"Yes, mom."

"Is there anything special you want me to fix?"

"You know I like everything you cook, mom, and Christy's not fussy."

"Okay, dear. We'll see you then." Ruth felt excitement welling up in her. She was happy about Robert's visit but felt some trepidation about meeting a girl who might take her son away; one day become her daughter-in-law. She sat down at the kitchen table and started planning her menu. Her thoughts began to wander. *Robert will sleep in his room and Christy will use the guest room.*

Robert had some bread and cold cuts in his refrigerator so, Friday evening, they had sandwiches in his room.

"I'm sleeping in my own room tonight, Robert." Christy said. "I'll need some time to pack a few things and I really want a full night's sleep."

"But honey, I don't want to be alone. I promise I'll let you sleep."

"Do you really think we can sleep naked next to each other without touching?" she laughed. "You have to pack too, and besides, I want to be fresh when I meet your family tomorrow. Whoever gets up first gets to call the other, okay?"

"What can I say? You've made up our minds."

"Thanks, sweetie."

"Oh, by the way, my folks, like yours, are kind of prudish so they'll have us sleeping in separate rooms. I want you to know that when you feel someone slipping into bed beside you in the night, it'll be me, so don't scream or hit me." They both laughed.

"Are you sure we've got everything?" Christy asked.

"Now is a good time to ask when we've already been driving for a half hour. I'm not going back even if we don't."

"Yes dear. I don't think we forgot anything though. Oh, look! Now that we're on the open road, I'll amuse you by reading the Burma Shave signs. I missed the one we passed, but here comes another one. She read...

DON'T STICK YOUR ELBOW...

OUT SO FAR...

IT MAY GO HOME...

IN ANOTHER CAR."

They both laughed at that. Christy moved closer to him and put her hand on his thigh. She was feeling frisky. She kissed his cheek and then his neck and moved her hand higher.

"Behave yourself now. You're making things very hard for me."

"You've never complained before."

"I know, and I don't want to stop you, but I think we should look for a diner and have a cool drink and some lunch."

"Yes, dear." Christy was being petulant.

CHAPTER 22

Pauline must have been watching for them. When Robert pulled into the driveway, she was out the front door and waving at them. Robert got out of the car then walked around to open the door for Christy. Pauline ran into him.

"Hold on, little sister, you almost knocked me over," he said as he hugged her. Letting her go again, he said, "This is my friend Christy. Christy, this is my crazy little sister, Pauline."

"Hi, Pauline," Christy said, as she offered her hand. "Robert says nice things about you."

"I'll bet." Pauline answered, as she took her hand and pulled Christy into a hug. "Robert's talked about you, too, and we were all anxious to meet you. Now you're here."

"Let's go inside, I want Christy to meet Mom and Dad." Robert said."

Ruth and Gene were waiting in the living room. Pauline burst through the door yelling "Here they are!"

"Mom, Dad, This is my friend, Christy," Robert said.

Gene spoke first. "Welcome to our home. We're glad you were able to come."

Ruth escorted Christy to the chairs in the living room. "It's nice to meet you. Robert said he would be bringing you. We're so glad you could make it. Please sit down and make yourself comfortable. Robert, why don't you get your bags and put yours in your room and Christy's in the guest room?" Robert and Christy exchanged glances before he left the room as a secret smile played on their faces.

Ruth asked Christy, "Can I get you a drink? I have soda, coffee, and tea. What would you like?"

"Nothing now, thanks. We stopped for a drink about an hour ago."

Robert came in with the bags and took them upstairs. When he came down, Gene said, "Why don't you take Christy upstairs to her room, she may want to freshen up. There's no hurry though."

"Robert," Pauline said, "I want to take Christy to her room."

Robert wanted to get Christy alone upstairs for a few intimate kisses but he couldn't very well refuse his sister. "Sure, go ahead sis."

"C'mon, Christy," Pauline said as she took her hand. They went upstairs.

"Hey, Mom, what's cooking? It smells good." Robert asked.

"Well, Dad and I discussed what we should have and the consensus was that we should make something everyone would like, and since you said Christy wasn't fussy, we decided to make... wait a minute... You'll have to wait to find out."

"Okay, Mom. I know it will be great whatever it is." He picked up his and Christy's suitcases and started up the stairs. Pauline was chattering away when Robert entered the guest room.

"Gee, sis, are you ever going to come up for air?"

"Oh, let her be, Robby. She's a sweetheart." Christy said.

"Robby? Did you say, Robby?" Robert frowned.

Christy started laughing and so did Pauline.

"I had to get used to putting up with one little pest in my life, now I can see I have two to deal with." The girls continued to laugh. Christy walked over to Robert and put her arms around his neck. "Do you mind if I kiss your brother?"

"No, and just to show how much I approve, I'll leave you two lovebirds alone."

As Pauline left the room, Robert pulled Christy close to him and whispered, "I love you so much."

Pauline turned in the hallway and watched them kiss. She smiled. *I like Christy,* she thought, *I hope they get married.*

Ruth was bringing food to the table. "Help me finish setting things, please, Pauline."

"Mom, I like Christy. She likes me too."

"Well, we've only just met the girl, but I'm sure Robert knows what he's doing. At least we hope so. She seems very nice." When everything was ready, Ruth asked, "Pauline, will you go upstairs and tell them dinner is ready? I'll get Dad. He's in his office."

When everyone was seated, the mood seemed pretty formal at first. Gene broke the ice by saying, "Well, how do you like the dinner your mother and I prepared?"

"Excuse me, *we* prepared? Oh, that's right. Your father did peel the potatoes."

"You did well, Dad, and Mom the pot roast is delicious." Robert answered.

"The meal is wonderful, Mrs. Parker." Christy said. "Robert told me what a good cook you are."

Gene turned to Christy. "Robert hasn't told us much about you, young lady. How serious is your relationship, may I ask?"

"Dad, we're just friends," Robert broke in. "We like each other a lot but finishing school is our top priority. Christy's in her first year, so she has a long way to go."

"You sound a little defensive, son."

"I'm not, Dad. I'm just trying to tell you the way things are."

Ruth put her hand on Gene's arm. It was meant to keep things in perspective and to keep things calm. Turning to Christy, she said, "Christy, lets you and I talk a little. What are you studying?"

"My dad wants me to go into business administration, but I know I won't like that. I'm hoping I'll make up my mind by the time I complete my two years of required curriculum."

"How does your mother feel about your future?"

"My mother has nothing to say about my life. My dad's in charge of everything. My mom's kind of a socialite. She likes to keep the Malcolm name on the front pages, so to speak."

"What did you say your name is?" Ruth was taken aback.

"Well, my friends call me Christy, but my full name is Christine Malcolm."

Ruth's fingers tightened around her fork. That was a name she'd fought hard to forget. *How ironic,* she thought.

"You don't mind my asking about you, do you?" Ruth asked.

"No, I'd like to get to know all of you as well."

"What does you're father do for a living?" Gene asked.

"He's president of Malcolm Enterprises, but don't ask me anything else because I don't know what the company does."

"Whatever he does, he's successful." Robert chimed in. "He doesn't know Christy and I are friends yet. He gets upset if he sees her just talking to a boy. When you talk about a dad protecting his daughter, Mr. Malcolm is a very unreasonable man. He was upset when Christy left for college. Now he has his watchdogs checking on her every movement."

Christy nodded in agreement to everything Robert was saying.

Ruth was stunned into silence. She could feel the bile rising in her throat. Her hand began to shake as her fork clattered onto her plate. Panic drained the color from her face.

"Mom, is anything wrong?" Pauline asked.

"I'm not sure, honey. I suddenly feel a bit queasy."

"Why don't you go upstairs, Babe? I don't think the kids will mind clearing the dishes," Gene said.

"Yes, Mom, go lie down," Robert said. "Christy and I will do the dishes. Pauline can help us. She knows where everything goes."

Ruth was embarrassed. "I'm sorry if I'm spoiling the evening. I think I will lie down for a while. Pauline, you can help, dear."

"Ruth's been so excited about your coming that she exhausted herself with preparation," Gene said. "Let's go, honey." Gene took Ruth's arm and started for the stairs. When they reached their room, Ruth lay down on the bed. She began to shake.

"What's wrong with you, honey?" Gene asked as he helped her settle, covering her with the quilt. "You look like you've seen a ghost."

"I'm not sure. My insides are shaking so much, it's making me nauseous."

It wasn't the food or anything else causing Ruth to feel this way; it was the girl Robert had brought into her home.

Gene went to the bathroom to wet a washcloth and came back and put it across Ruth's forehead. Ruth said it felt cool but nothing could chase away what was weighing on her mind. *Could it be a horrible coincidence? I can't tell Gene what I'm thinking. Not until I know for sure. I don't know what he might do. He loves Robert. And Robert loves him. Gene is the only father he knows. Both of them will be hurt if what I'm thinking turns out to be true.*

"I'm going to take your temperature." Gene was getting anxious about Ruth's condition.

Ruth put her hand on his arm. "Don't bother, dear, I'm beginning to feel a little better." Ruth forced herself to close her mind so her shaking would subside. Gene was taking this too seriously, and the more he pressured her the nearer she came to telling him what was nagging her and making her ill.

"I'm going to be the doctor now," Gene said, "by insisting you don't worry about the kids and get into your night clothes and stay in bed till morning. I'll go down and keep them company for a while. It sounds like they're having a good time without us."

The three of them actually had fun cleaning up. They laughed at Pauline's dumb jokes that every high school kid tells. Christy was funny too, telling some jokes that surprised Robert. Her relaxation in his home brought him such intense pleasure that he had a hard time resisting the urge to take her in his arms. He also felt closer to Pauline because of the warm acceptance she showed Christy.

By the next morning, Ruth had composed herself enough to hear Robert say, "You look much better this morning, Mom. Did Dad figure out what was wrong with you?" It was presented as a joke but also as a serious question.

"Thanks for asking son. It went as quickly as it came. No need for a doctor."

"I can see where my services are no longer wanted around here?" Gene laughed.

"Daddy, you know we couldn't get along without you." Pauline said. "Just think how much we save on doctor bills." They all laughed.

Ruth had several activities planned for their stay. There were dinners with some of Robert's friends and tickets to see *'Hello Dolly,'* which was playing at the Schubert Theater. The whole time Robert and Christy were there she felt that, at any moment, she would have a nervous breakdown. She couldn't eat without going to the bathroom to throw up. She didn't sleep well either. She would often stay awake reading while Gene fell asleep as soon as his head hit the pillow so her wakefulness wasn't noticed. She was great at hiding her misgivings.

An afternoon came when Ruth didn't have anything planned. This gave Robert and Christy a day to relax before starting back to school. They sat on the back patio, sipping iced tea, while Ruth fussed in the kitchen.

Robert noticed a plant on the patio still in the nursery packaging.

"What kind of bush are you going to plant, now, Mom?" he called. "It doesn't look like there's a plant you don't already have."

"It's a rose bush, son. I don't have any yellow roses," Ruth called from inside.

Robert nudged Christy. "What do you say we plant the rose bush for her? There's nothing else to do. I think it would make Mom happy."

"I've never planted anything before. We had a gardener do that kind of stuff," Christy replied.

"Well, there's a first time for everything. Come on. I'll be doing most of the work anyway." Robert took their glasses and put them on the table. "Let's go!" he said, as he took her hand and pulled her out of the chair.

They got the tools from the shed and Robert called, "Where were you planning on putting this thing, Mom?"

Ruth stuck her head out the door and pointed to the corner of the house.

"I thought it would look nice over there."

"Okay, Mom," Robert called back and started digging.

Ruth could hear their laughter and the noise they made as they succeeded in putting the bush into the hole they'd dug. She had to smile at the fun they seemed to be having, but all the while she hoped that they were doing a good job. She didn't want to have to replant the bush.

The day the kids departed was a great relief for Ruth. She stood on the porch with Gene and Pauline, smiled and waved as they drove away.

Things went back to normal in the Parker household for everyone but Ruth. She went about her daily activities, trying to function normally, but the questions and doubts that filled her head occupied every waking moment. When Christy and Robert weren't looking, she had studied them trying to find any shred of resemblance. Maybe if Christy had been a boy there might have been something more to find but the fact that she was a girl left reason for doubt. While peeling potatoes, she thought their eyes had a similar shape. Making the bed, she was sure the corners of their mouths turned up at the same angle when they smiled. Was it Jon she was trying to see or herself?

She kept all her thoughts and feelings from Gene. She would wait until she had the answers that she knew would come in time.

Christy and Robert fell back into their routine. They had their assignments completed on schedule but they weren't looking forward to the end of the school year, as most of the other students were. Being separated for Christmas was one thing but being separated for the whole summer wasn't part of their plans.

One balmy evening, they lay together, each one quiet, lost in love. Christy broke the silence. "Robert, I have something to tell you."

Robert answered in a sleepy voice. "What is it?"

"Well, you know how we made all those plans for our future, like waiting to finish school and marriage and all that stuff?"

"Yes, so?" he said in a sleepy voice.

"Well, you know what they say about the best laid plans?"

"What are you trying to say, Christy? My brain's been on overload so let's have it."

"I'm almost afraid to tell you because it will spoil everything."

"Christy, for God's sake, what is it?"

"I'm pregnant."

Robert sat up on one elbow and looked at her. "You're pregnant? How can that be? We always used protection."

"Honey, all I can think of is that one night when we didn't have protection. I'm sure it happened when you didn't pull out fast enough." Christy looked like she was about to cry. "What are we going to do?"

Robert fell back. He didn't know what to say at first. It seemed like an eternity to Christy. "I guess we'll have to get married right away then."

"Do you mean it?" Christy seemed relieved. She got up on her knees and looked down at him. "What about school and everything?"

"This doesn't change things, it just rearranges them. You'll stay in school until the baby comes. We can stay at my place. I know my folks will help us. What about yours?" Robert sat up and gave her a kiss on the cheek.

"What about mine?" Christy said. "My parents are going to kill me."

Robert took her face in his hands. "I couldn't blame them if they wanted to kill *me*. After all, you are only eighteen. I'm starting to feel guilty about this whole thing. It really is my fault, Christy. I got you pregnant"

"It's *our* fault and it really isn't a fault at all. We love each other. Maybe I shouldn't feel good about this, and at first, I didn't, but now I'm getting excited thinking that I am carrying your... our baby. Our love has made another human being, Robert. Can you be believe it? Can we try to be happy about this?"

"It's going to take me a while to get used to this but the more I think about it, the easier it will be to accept. Imagine me, a father."

"Yes, and me, a mother."

That eased the tension. They laughed.

"Jesus, what have we gotten ourselves into?" Robert said, as he pulled her to him.

CHAPTER 23

Christy's arrival home from school put her father in an exceptionally good frame of mind. He had his baby girl home again. Christy had to put on a happy face but all the while she was waiting for an opportunity to talk to her mother alone. Mom could help her break the news to Dad.

The time never seemed right until one night her father was late coming home from a business meeting and Christy and her mother were eating dinner alone. They chatted during the meal until finally, Christy just blurted out, "Mom, I'm pregnant."

"That's nice dear. We're having a get-together at the country club tomorrow… What? What did you say?" If she'd had food in her mouth, she would have choked.

"I said I'm pregnant."

"Christy, that is not funny! How can you be pregnant? You don't even have a boyfriend. You're only eighteen, for God's sake. What do you mean, you're pregnant? You'd better be kidding or prepare yourself for your father's wrath."

Christy lowered her head. "I know what you're thinking. I'm a disgrace to the family. I'm sorry but that doesn't change things. I love Robert and he loves me and we're going to get married."

"Who's Robert?"

"He's the boy you met when you picked me up for Christmas vacation."

"That boy! He didn't look like much to your father and me. We don't know anything about him. We never should have let you go to that college."

"His father is a doctor, Mom. Is that high enough on the social register for you? I met his parents and they're wonderful people."

"Do they know about this? And do they approve?"

"No, they don't know. I'm sure they're not going to be too happy about it either."

"Oh, My Lord, have mercy." Mrs. Malcolm said with a sigh, as she rose from the table wringing her hands as she walked away. "I need a glass of wine to calm my nerves."

"Jesus Christ, son, what the hell were you thinking? That girl's only eighteen. You kids are… just kids." Gene pulled over to the side of the road. "I have to catch my breath, son."

"Dad, we didn't plan on this, but now that it's happened, we're going to make the best of it. You know, look at the positive side."

"Positive side! What the hell is so positive about having a baby at your age? You're not thinking of quitting school, are you?"

"No. We're both going to finish our education. We won't let the baby change our direction. We were planning on getting married after graduation anyway. I guess I never told you and Mom that. We love each other, Dad, so what's the difference if it's now or later?"

"Because, a baby means time and money, and that's something you don't have. What do Christy's parents say about all this?"

"I know they won't be pleased with us. I mean, you're right, she's probably telling them right now. I hope they're not too hard on her."

Gene pulled back onto the road. "Let's go on and get the stuff your Mother wants. When we get back home, you can tell her the good news."

They waited in silence in the living room for Jon, Christy biting her nails and Ellen sipping her wine. Soon, they heard Jon's car pulling into the garage.

"Please, Mom, you tell him first. I'm afraid of what he'll say or do."

"I'll tell him, but don't be surprised when you hear the uproar. You stay here. I'll take him into the study."

When Jon walked into the room, Ellen stood up and said, "Dear, I have something I want to tell you. Let's go into the study."

Jon looked at her, frowned and looked at Christy. "What's this all about?" he asked.

"Just come with me." Ellen said, taking his arm. He turned to look at Christy again as they left the room.

Christy could hear her mother talking but couldn't make out what she was saying. She started to shiver. Then, she heard her father speaking, softly at first but with increasing volume until Christy was sure his voice could be heard by the neighbors. She didn't like the sound of it. It wasn't what he was saying but the anger in his voice. She put her hands over her ears. Suddenly, there was an ominous silence. *Say something, do something,* she thought. Her father came out of the study first, red-faced and scowling. He slowly approached, then stood silent in front of her staring at her face. She started to stand but her legs wouldn't hold her. She fell back in the chair. Jon drew a hand back in anger but froze as he realized what he was about to do.

"How many boys have you had?" Jon asked, glaring at her with anger in his eyes.

Christy's voice shook when she answered. "Just one, Daddy, and we're going to get married. I love him and he loves me"

"You let some smooth talking jerk seduce you and you think you're in love? How stupid can you be? Don't you know he's not interested in you? A boy will say anything he thinks you want to hear just to get you into bed."

"You're wrong, Daddy. We love each other." His comment suddenly let doubt creep into her mind. She ruthlessly shoved it away.

"After all we've done to bring you up to be a respectable lady, you embarrass us by turning into a little whore."

"Jon, watch what you're saying." Ellen shouted. He ignored her completely.

Jon paced. "I'll arrange everything," he said. "You'll have an abortion and transfer to the Community College in Morris Town. No one will be the wiser." He turned to his wife. "You know we have to do this, don't you, Ellen?"

Before she could answer, Christy shouted, "Daddy, you can't make me do this. Mother, tell him not to make me do this. I don't want an abortion. Why would I abort my child? Why would you even think of such a thing?"

"Surely you can't be thinking of raising a bastard child. What will people say?" Jon asked.

"Daddy, I told you we're going to get married. I don't care what people say, and I don't care about your precious reputation."

"Well, we do! What about your education? How is this, what's his name, guy going to support you and a baby? You're just a baby yourself."

"I'm eighteen, father. That's legal age isn't it? Robert and I will manage."

"Robert is it? Who is this bozo?" Jon said, clenching his teeth.

"I told mother. He's the boy you met in the cafeteria."

"Well, then, I'm not surprised. He looked a little guilty to me. Both of you did if I remember! What do you know about this boy? He can't be much of a man if he hasn't got the guts to suggest meeting your parents."

"He did want to meet you and mother. I'm the one who kept putting it off until I could get you used to the idea that I was dating someone."

"Christy, I still think he's not good enough for you," Ellen started to sniffle.

"I told you he's not a nobody. His father's a doctor."

"What do they think about their little boy getting you knocked up?" Jon smirked.

"They'll probably feel the same way you do, but I'll bet they won't ask me to have an abortion."

"You better think twice about this. You stand to lose much more than you realize."

"I don't want your money, Father, if that's what you mean, and I'm sorry but you can't tell me what to do."

"Who the hell do you think you're talking to?"

"I said I'm sorry. There's nothing left to talk about." She rose from the chair and walked past them to the stairs.

"You ungrateful little whore!" Jon screamed at the top of his lungs.

Christy didn't look back even though that bitter epithet tore through her heart like a red hot knife through butter. Tears welled to the surface and spilled over as she took the stairs two at a time. She ran to her room and slammed the door as hard as she could. She could still hear her parents talking, and it sounded like her mother was crying. Then the conversation apparently ended. She couldn't hear anything. Christy was afraid her father would be knocking on her door any second to continue berating her. She sat in the middle of her bed, still very angry and terribly disappointed with her father but no longer crying. *He's being totally unreasonable,* she thought. *I can understand his being upset, but not like this. I'll never forgive him for calling me that!*

A knock on the door interrupted her line of thought, tightening the knot in her stomach. "What?" she spat.

"May I come in?" her father asked, seemingly more in control of his emotions.

"It's not locked," Christy replied, and swung her legs over the side of the bed to face him.

Jon was grinning as he entered. Christy knew it was insincere. He could play the part of a concerned rational person and had done so many times, but tonight she'd seen his ugly side.

"I just wanted to apologize for being so..."

"Cold hearted and out of control?" she interrupted.

"I wouldn't put it that way but... I was a bit too adamant. I will admit that. As I see it, you've made some very poor..." he hesitated. "Very unfortunate choices and I just know that we can work this out." Christy tucked her legs up under her and waited to hear what new garbage this man was going to spew.

"First of all, you mustn't return to that school. I want you closer to home."

"Dad you aren't in control of the situation. I am! No one coerced me. I went to bed with him willingly. We've been seeing each other since the second week of school. I told you, he loves me, and I love him."

"Like your mother said, he's not good enough for you." Jon said calmly.

"That's for me to decide, not you, Dad. That's the end of it."

Once again, his demeanor changed. "We'll see about that," he said coldly. "You do what you're told, or you'll be cut out of the will without a penny. Then let's see if you can live without all the luxuries you're used to."

"You just do that, *Dad!*" she emphasized the word Dad, turning it into sarcasm. "If that's what will make you happy."

She could see his face getting red as he stared at her. She saw his hands clench into a fist before he stormed out of her room, slamming the door behind him. Christy heard him muttering to himself all the way down the hallway. She was shocked at her own behavior. She had never spoken to her father or mother like that before. *What have I done?* She thought. Doubts about her relationship with Robert and her attitude tonight began to invade her thoughts. *What if he doesn't love me? What if he never wants to see me again and doesn't want this baby? What a fool I am! What a mess I've made of my life.* She jumped out of bed, stripped off her clothes and flung them in the corner. She stalked into the bathroom and turned on the shower, then stood in the corner crying while the water pelted down on her.

Jon went to the kitchen where Ellen was standing In front of the sink taking tissues from the box on the shelf and dabbing her eyes.

"Stop that blubbering, Ellen. I'll handle this."

"What are you going to do?" she whimpered.

"First things first. Tomorrow I'll set a detective to tracking this Robert kid. Before the week is over, we'll know everything there is to know about him. After that, I'm certain Christy will see things our way."

Ruth could tell something was wrong when Gene and Robert walked into the room. They were quiet and looked kind of sheepish. She spoke to both of them.

"What's wrong?"

Neither one answered.

"What's wrong?" she asked again, her voice at a higher pitch as she rose from her chair.

Gene spoke. "Robert has something to tell you."

Ruth looked at Robert and frowned. "What is it, dear?"

Robert hesitated. He knew he was going to hurt his mother with the news. Finally, he said... "Mom, I love Christy."

"Well, I don't think that comes as much of a surprise." Ruth said.

"We've been seeing each other since... since the second week of school."

"Continue." Ruth said.

"Christy is pregnant."

It's a good thing the chair was right behind Ruth because she simply plopped down on it. "Oh, my goodness, Robert, what have you done?"

Gene jumped in. "I already laid into him about this, Ruth, so the question now is, how we handle it?"

Ruth couldn't answer. Her elbows were on the table with her face resting on her hands. What could she say? She had such plans for her son.

"Mom, I'm sorry. We didn't plan this. I want to marry her so the baby will have my name. It's not the end of the world, just a little detour. Please say you don't hate me."

"Robert, how could I hate you? You're my son! I don't know what to do about this. I guess there really isn't anything we can do except to try to be there for you while you work it out."

Robert walked to his mother's side, bent down, and gave her a tight hug. "Thanks, Mom – Dad. I love you both."

Ruth was suddenly terrified, as the realization of Christy's true identity struck her again.

"Robert, has Christy told her parents?"

"She probably has by now. I haven't talked to her."

"Since Christy will soon be part of our family, will you please tell us all about her? I mean where she lives and all about her parents and their attitude towards this."

"Yes, I will. I don't know everything, but I'll find out. What I know so far is that her dad's name is Jon, and her mom's name is Ellen. They live in a town called Mayfield, in a section called Brandon Hills."

"What did you say her last name was?"

"Malcolm, its Christine Malcolm."

Beads of sweat appeared on Ruth's forehead. What she was afraid to face had come to pass. She thought, *so Jon married and had a daughter. And why, in God's name, of all the girls in the world, did Robert have to meet her? His half sister!*

"Do her parents know who you are? Have you met them?" Ruth asked.

"Just briefly, in the school cafeteria. They weren't too friendly. Her father seemed like he was real strict. Christy said he monitors her every move. I'm worried about her when they find out about us..."

"Do you have their telephone number? Maybe your father or I should talk to them."

"Yes, I do, but let's wait till I talk to Christy."

"All right, son." Ruth said.

Robert left and went to his room, relieved that everything was out in the open.

Ruth took a deep breath, "Gene, I have something to tell you now and I want you to be prepared to be shocked."

"Another surprise?" Gene said.

"I said a shock."

"All right then, tell me." He waited.

"Robert and Christy," she hesitated, "are half brother and sister."

"Ruth, what are you saying?" Gene was truly taken aback. "How do you know this?" Is there something you haven't told me?"

"I never told you who Robert's father was."

"I don't care! I *never cared.*"

"Christy's father, Jon Malcolm, is Robert's father."

"Jesus Christ!" He ran his fingers through his hair and began to pace.

"I know. I know... I thought I would never hear that name again. Gene, the kids will have to be told. This is really going to hurt them."

"What about the baby? Isn't that considered incest?"

"You tell me. You're the doctor."

Gene heaved a deep sigh and sat down; as if that would ease his mind and dissolve the problem and make everything go away.

CHAPTER 24

Christy left the shower and put on her robe. Just then, her phone rang. It was Robert.

"Robert, I'm so glad you called. I miss you so much."

"I miss you too, honey. How did your parents take the news about us?"

"My parents are furious. My father says I have to have an abortion."

"An abortion? You mean kill the baby?"

"Yes. He said you don't love me, that you just said those things because you wanted sex. That got me thinking that maybe he's right. Is that the way it is? Is he right, Robert?"

"He's wrong, Christy. I love you and I'll love our baby. Don't let him put those thoughts in your head. We knew our folks wouldn't be happy about this. They weren't going to welcome us with open arms, but that's only natural. Now we have to face the facts and take charge. I'm not sorry, are you?"

"No, I'm not either. I want to be with you though. When will we be able to be together? I know I can't wait all summer"

"I can't either. I'll find a way, honey. I told my folks. Like I said, they're not pleased but I'm sure they'll help us out if we ask them. Do you want mom or dad to call your parents?"

"That might work but let me talk to my folks again. My dad has to settle down first. Right now he's mad as hell. He really hates you. Maybe he'll cool down tomorrow and listen to reason. But... Robert, what if he doesn't?" Her voice was getting shaky. "What will we do? I can't stay here. Where will I go?"

"I have the place off campus, remember. We can stay there until we decide what to do. Don't worry, honey, I'll take care of you. Right now, my body is aching to hold you. Will you call me tomorrow or should I call you?"

"I'll wait for you to call. If I say, you have the wrong number and hang up, that means someone is listening, so try again later. I need you to hold me too. I love you, Robert. Please don't leave me."

"Don't even think like that. I'll call. I love you. Goodnight."

"Goodnight."

"The boy's name is Robert Parker. Father's name, Gene Parker; Mother's maiden name is Ruth Lawson. Father's a doctor and they live in Winnetka, Illinois. Robert is Ruth's natural child and Gene's adopted son. You might be surprised to learn that his mother, Ruth, was born right here in Mayfield. When she was about six years old the state took her away from her father. She was raised in an orphanage because the father was an alcoholic. She came back years later to take care of her father until he died, then she left Mayfield. You wouldn't have known her though. Her family lived on the other side of town."

As the detective talked on, Jon was shocked into silence. *This can't be,* he thought. There were times when his thoughts had taken him back to the past, and he wondered what had become of Ruth and his child, but he never took the trouble to try to find them. Jon leaned back in his desk chair and covered his face with his hands.

"Are you all right, sir?"

"How accurate is all this information?" Jon spoke through his fingers.

"Very, sir. There's more in the written report, such as addresses and phone numbers."

"That's all then. You can go," Jon said abruptly. "Send me a bill with the report."

Later that evening, while Christy was waiting for a call from Robert, Jon burst into her room without knocking and ripped her telephone wire out of the wall.

"What are you doing?" Christy asked her eyes wide with surprise.

"I'm making sure you don't communicate with that Robert boy. Where's your purse?"

It's over there on the dresser. Why?" Christy was too stunned to say more.

"I want your car keys," he said as he dug into her purse. "I don't want you to meet him again either."

"Daddy, why are you doing this? You're making me feel like a prisoner!" She started crying and threw her pillow at him.

"I have my reasons, more than ever now. You two cannot be together. I had a detective investigate your friend and he brought back some interesting facts. You're upset now but when you're ready to calm down, I'll tell you all about it."

"Tell me now!" she shouted. "What did you find out that's so terrible?"

"You have to understand that what I tell you will have to be our secret. I don't ever want your mother to know. You have to trust me and swear you won't say anything. Can I trust you to keep this between us?"

"You want my trust when you've been so unfair about my relationship with Robert? Now you want me to promise I'll never see him again."

"Actually, you have no choice. I don't want to put a guard on you but, if I have to, I will."

"That wouldn't surprise me." Christy got off of the bed and sat on the settee. "Okay. You win, Father. Tell me. I'm calm now," she lied.

Jon took a deep breath. Christy could see the change in his face as he struggled to find the right words with which to begin. He suddenly looked drawn and somewhat confused, if that was even possible for a man like him. She could see the small beads of perspiration forming on his brow. She became more anxious as she saw the change in her father.

"Well, Dad, what are you waiting for?"

"Okay, Christy." He coughed a couple of times. "A long time ago, when I was a young man… This was long before I met your mother, of course. I met a beautiful young girl. I became infatuated with her. Her name was Ruth and we dated for a while. She worked in a bookstore and she was very much in love with me. I had one thing in mind when we started dating. Because she loved me, I was able to take advantage of her.

"You mean like my friend Robert has done to me?" Christy said, sarcastically.

"Don't get smart with me, young lady! This isn't easy for me…" He took a deep breath. "She thought we would get married, but your grandmother forbade me to marry her. It wasn't very difficult for her to convince me because she threatened to leave me out of her will if I did. Your grandmother was a control freak and had enough money to put teeth into the threat. I know I get a little of that from her."

"As if we didn't know that," Christy said sarcastically. "Go on. What happened to this lady?"

"When she told me she was carrying my child, I realized I cared about her more than I'd ever cared about any girl. I thought my mother would relent for the child's sake and tell us we could get married, but she didn't. She told the girl to have an abortion and that she would pay for it. I let Ruth face my mother alone when my mother told her this. It was cruel, I know, but that was how I was back then. The girl refused to have the abortion but was smart enough to take some of the money my mother offered and left town."

"Imagine that! Just like Robert and me, right?"

Ignoring her, Jon continued. "She was an intelligent, proud individual and later I wondered if I'd made a mistake by listening to my mother. When your grandmother died, I never thought of looking for her and the child. I was too busy enjoying my freedom."

"Is that all? What has this got to do with anything? That was your mistake."

"As I said, Christy, I don't want your mother to know anything about this. You have to swear you won't tell her. Nothing would be gained by telling her. It would hurt her terribly."

"I said I wouldn't. So what else do you want to tell me? There has to be more."

"Through my investigation of Robert, I learned he has a mother named Ruth. Ruth married a man named Gene Parker who adopted Robert." He paused, waiting to see if Christy was catching on to what he was telling her.

"Dad, that's my Robert and his parents you're talking about?"

"Yes! And since Robert is adopted, who do you think his father is?"

"Wait, you met a girl named Ruth and she had your baby?"

"Yes."

"And Robert's mother's name is Ruth?"

"Yes."

"The *same Ruth* your mother wouldn't let you marry?"

"Yes."

"Oh, my god! Oh my god!" Christy screamed. "That makes Robert… that makes Robert…

"My son."

"And my half brother! Oh, my god." She screamed again.

"Quiet! We don't want your mother to hear." He walked to the settee and sat down next to her. Putting his arm around her, he pulled her head into his chest trying to quiet her. "You're getting hysterical," he said. "Please calm down."

Christy was sobbing now. "I hate you, I hate you!"

"I know and I can't help that. Now you know that this makes having an abortion a necessity. It's more than just reputation."

Christy became silent. She just sat there, her face streaked with tears, staring into space. Her whole life was tumbling down around her and it was too much to handle.

"It's going to be alright, honey. Daddy will make things better." She turned and looked into his face, her eyes glazed over. All she wanted at that moment was to die.

Ruth was still waiting to gather the courage to tell Robert about Christy until one morning, during breakfast; Ruth noticed his mood had change and mentioned it.

"You seem quiet, Robert. Is something bothering you?" She secretly hoped he had found out from someone else, maybe Christy, and that would save her the task of having to tell him.

"I've tried to call Christy several times and can't get through to her. I know something's wrong."

Now might be the right time, Ruth thought, *but he's feeling so bad, I know this will just devastate him. Come on Ruth, You know you're just putting off the inevitable. He's going to be hurt and that's that. Get it over.*

"Robert, I've been putting off telling you something because I can't stand to see you hurt, but it has to be told."

"What do you mean?" What do you have to tell me that's going to hurt?"

"Maybe the reason Christy doesn't answer your phone calls are that she's already talked to her parents about what I have to say."

"Mom, what's wrong?" Robert had been picking at his food and now he put down his fork. "Has something happened to Christy that you're not telling me?"

"Nothing's happened to her but what I have to tell you will break your heart."

"Mom," he was becoming agitated, "just tell me what it is! Stop procrastinating."

"When I was young, I met a man and fell in love with him. I thought we would marry. What I didn't know is that he didn't love me. So, when I became pregnant with you, he left me. Then, I met your father. He took us in after you were born. We soon fell in love and were married. He adopted you and loved you from the start."

"I know all that, Mother. He's my real dad."

"Yes, he is, but the man who got me pregnant is... Jon Malcolm."

The frown on Robert's face deepened with every passing second as he processed the information that was just presented to him. He whispered in disbelief. "Mr. Malcolm is my biological father?"

"Yes."

"Mr. Malcolm is Christy's father!"

"Yes." Ruth walked around the table and stood behind Robert's chair. She was about to put her arms around him when he jumped up. If she hadn't been there, he would have knocked the chair over. This was the first time Ruth saw her son, now a man, with murder in his eyes. He frightened her.

"Robert, I'm so sorry!"

"Sorry! Sorry! Do you realize I've fallen in love with my half sister and she's going to have our baby?"

"I know dear, I know how you feel."

"No! No, you don't know how I feel! There is only one person in the whole world who knows how I feel and that's Christy! She must know everything by now too. That's why she won't talk to me." Robert sank into his chair. Leaning on the table with his head down on his arms, he began to sob.

CHAPTER 25

"Do you mind if I have another patient coming in earlier this morning, Mr. Malcolm." The doctor asked Jon.

"Not at all, as long as this other person doesn't know my daughter."

Jon had picked a Sunday, when most of the shops were closed and the chance of meeting someone they knew was unlikely. Even though they were in another town, he was covering all possibilities. Everything was arranged including the doctor, who was being paid handsomely for his services and for the special arrangements."

Jon pulled to the curb in front of a two-story brick building. There was a black painted door between two empty stores, each with dirty plate glass windows.

"I won't go in with you, Christy. Just go through that door and up the stairs. The people there will take care of you. I was told it shouldn't be more than an hour... maybe fifteen minutes more. I'll be back for you then so wait for me outside on the stoop."

She didn't answer. She still had that glassy look in her eyes, like a whipped dog, and followed directions without question. She walked to the black painted door without looking back and went in. The hallway was dimly lighted with the wallpaper peeling off the walls. She stood for a moment, looking up at the long flight of stairs leading to the semi darkness at the top. Filled with fear, dreading the unknown, she started slowly climbing the stairs. Halfway up the stairs she found the hand railing was out of its metal holder. When she reached the top, she knocked on the door. A female voice called, "Come in."

The room was poorly lighted. There was a small window in the front of the building that looked onto the street. A bare light bulb hung from the ceiling. The walls were brick and mortar, and the place looked like a storeroom. There were three cots, two on one side of the room and one on the other. A young woman lying on one of the cots moaned softly as she tried to sit up. There wasn't enough light to see her face clearly. A woman in a white smock entered the room just then.

"Come with me!" she commanded. Christy followed her to another room. The woman closed the door behind them and asked Christy's name.

"Christine," Christy said sullenly. When the woman asked her last name, Christy said "I'm not going to tell you." Christy was very aware of what was happening and felt guilty and thoroughly ashamed.

"That's all right. We don't really need it, dear," the woman said. "Please step behind that curtain and remove your panties."

Christy did as she was told. She lifted her skirt and slipped off her panties. When she came out, the woman ushered her to a table behind a heavy curtain in a far corner of the room.

The doctor was waiting there. He was a short, grey-haired, fat man with several days' growth of beard. He had a high-pitched voice that wasn't pleasant to listen to. "Get on the table, please, and lie back," he said. When she did, the nurse put a sheet over her. As close as Christy could determine, the woman was in her late fifties. The doctor told her to put her feet in the stirrups. She did as he said and he had her scoot down until her buttocks were almost off the table. The doctor put his hands on her knees and gently pushed her legs apart. Christy felt herself blushing and thought *He's looking at my vagina and I don't even know his name.* The man inserted a speculum to open her vagina. It was cold till the warmth of her body made it tolerable.

Christy's stomach was in knots. *What am I doing here? Why am I doing this?* Her mind was in chaos as she stared at the ceiling and the stains on the tile from water seepage.

Then she felt the pain and tensed up.

"This won't take long," the nurse said. "Try to relax."

Relax! Christy thought. *What the hell is she talking about?* The doctor was deep inside of her now, scraping out the life she would never see. Just when she thought she would scream from the pain, he said "It's all over," and removed the instruments.

She took her feet from the stirrups and struggled to sit up. She felt shaky. The nurse helped her to a sitting position and the doctor and the nurse assisted her off the table.

"There'll be some bleeding but it may not happen right away. Put this sanitary napkin in your panties just in case. You'll go back to your regular periods," the doctor said.

When she tried to stand, her knees were weak and her legs wobbly. "I can't walk," she said. "My legs won't hold me."

"Just stand for a moment and hold onto the table. You'll be fine," the doctor said.

The nurse walked her to the changing area, where she was told she could put her panties back on. "You're going to feel a little discomfort for a short while, so lie down on the cot in the other room and when you feel able, you may leave."

Christy held the nurse's arm and made it to the door. "I can walk now," she said. The girl that had been on the cot was gone. Christy headed for the bed on the opposite wall. She felt heavy cramps, worse than she'd ever experienced before a period. Resting in a fetal position helped a little. She didn't want to get up but knew her father would be waiting. She knew these people weren't expecting to have patients stay for very long. She wanted to sleep but, after about twenty minutes, she forced herself to get up. *Oh Lord,* she thought, *I hope I can make it down those damn stairs.*

She saw her dad's car parked at the curb when she opened the door to the street. Jon leaned over and opened the passenger's door when he saw her. "Is everything okay, honey?" he asked after she was seated. She didn't answer. "Are you all right?" he asked again.

"I don't want to talk about it," she snapped.

"Okay, I understand."

"No, you don't understand, and I don't want you to say another goddamn word. Leave me alone. Just get me home so I can go to bed."

Jon didn't say another word. He patted her knee, wanting to convey what he thought was reassurance, but she jerked it away.

"Now remember, not a word to your mother," Jon told her as they pulled into the driveway. "We just went for a drive to get you out of the house."

Ellen was in the kitchen starting to prepare dinner. Christy went directly to her room. Jon went to the kitchen and gave Ellen a peck on the cheek.

"Well, where have you two been?" she asked.

"We went for a drive, honey. I wanted Christy to get some air.

She's been cooped up in the house and I figured she needed a change of scenery."

"Where is she?"

"She said she was feeling a little tired and thought she might be coming down with something, so she went to lie down."

"I hope she feels well enough to eat when dinner's ready."

"If not, I'll take something up to her. Let's let her rest for a while."

Christy didn't come down for dinner. Ellen called up the stairs but there was no answer.

"She's not answering," Ellen said, walking back to the kitchen. "I'd better check on her."

"No!" Jon said in an anxious tone, as he got up from the table and started for the hall, "Let me go."

He knocked on Christy's door. She didn't answer so he went in. Christy was curled up in bed. Jon could hear her moaning softly.

"Christy, are you all right? Mom's concerned that you're not coming down."

"I'm in pain, daddy. I can't get up."

"I'll tell mother you'd rather have something brought up to you. I'll be right back with a tray." She said nothing but struggled to turn over trying to find a painless position. Jon went back to the kitchen.

"Christy's not feeling up to eating but I'll take a small plate up to her in case she regains her appetite."

"I can take her something, Jon, you finish your dinner."

"No, Ellen!" He realized he sounded harsh, so he softened his tone. "You can fix a little something for her, though. Let's both finish our dinner. There's no hurry. She's resting." Ellen gave him a questioning look but said nothing.

Later, Jon went up with a tray but Christy still refused food. "Can I get you something for the pain, Christy?"

"You can get me a doctor!" Christy snapped angrily. "A real doctor this time."

"It's Sunday, honey. Let me get you some aspirin. I'm sure the way you feel is to be expected. If you feel this bad in the morning, we'll go to the doctor and see what he has to say."

The pain worsened through the night. *Please, somebody help me,* Christy moaned. She kept changing positions. On her back...that was the worst, in a tight fetal position, on her hands and knees, then all over again, twisting and turning all night long. *Maybe this is what it feels like to have a baby,* she thought. *If it is, at least you would have something when it's all over. Robert, our baby is gone!* She was crying now.

Morning came and still Christy found no relief. Ellen was up before Jon and knocked on Christy's door. "Its mother," she called.

Christy called back in a weak voice. "Mom, help me,"

When Ellen opened the door and saw the messed up bed and Christy wet with perspiration, she shouted, "Oh my god, girl, what is wrong with you?"

"I'm sick. Call dad!"

Ellen ran downstairs to get Jon.

"Jon, you better get up. There's something wrong with Christy."

Jon awoke immediately, threw back the covers and leapt out of bed. Without taking time for robe or slippers, he raced upstairs in his shorts. When he saw Christy, he was visibly shaken and said, "I'm taking you back to the doctor right away."

Ellen was right behind him. "What do you mean, *back* to the doctor?"

"I meant *to* the doctor, we don't know what's wrong, but it's obvious she needs to see a doctor right away."

"I'll get dressed," Ellen said.

"No! We can't wait. It'll take me a couple of minutes to throw something on. I'll call you as soon as we know what's happening."

"I have to be with her, Jon!"

"I said wait here!" he said in a commanding tone. "I'll call you."

Before she could fully react to his firm instructions, Jon was dressed. It did only take him a couple of minutes. He made a call to the doctor from the phone in his room before helping Christy down the stairs to the door. Traffic was heavy on that Monday morning. He helped Christy out of the car when they got to the black painted door. The hallway had a faint odor and when he saw the looks of the place, the peeling wallpaper, the smell, the worn creaky stairs, the broken banister, he felt horribly guilty. *How could I have subjected my daughter to such squalor, such indignity?*

The doctor waited at the top of the stairs. He'd heard them open the door. The doctor and Jon each took an arm and literally carried Christy to the table behind the heavy curtain. Christy was helped onto the table. The doctor said to Jon, "Will you please wait in the other room?"

"I can't stand the pain, doctor, what's wrong?" Christy cried loudly. "You've got to stop the pain,"

"Just try to relax; it will be easier for me to help you." His voice was softer now. He seemed honestly concerned.

There's that damned word again. Relax! It's not easy to do when you're in agonizing pain.

She was asked to assume the same position as the last time she was on the table. The doctor inserted the instrument and Christy experienced a quick, sharp, lower abdominal pain.

"That's it," the doctor said, sounding relieved. "This is what was causing so much pain." Christy got up on one elbow. The doctor showed her the pan he was holding. In it was a blood clot the size of a grapefruit. "You never could have passed this," He said.

She just stared at the blob. *So that's the worthless remains of my evil, immoral act. I've let the devil take my child and my life; all this because of my own weakness.*

"You should be okay now, miss."

You think so? She thought but said nothing.

He helped her off the table and asked her to wait while he called her father to assist him. Jon rushed to her side and put his arm around her. "I'm here, honey. The doctor said you'll be okay now. It was a simple blood clot causing the pain."

His attempts at consolation were falling on deaf ears, Jon knew this. Her face was a mask, tight lipped and cold, with hatred and defiance in her eyes.

There was no conversation on the way home. Periodically, Jon would ask, "Are you all right?" or "Are you in pain now?" There was no response.

Ellen waited anxiously for their return and ran to the door when she heard the car. She put her arms around Christy when she came in.

"Honey, are you all right? What was wrong? What did the doctor say?"

Christy pushed her mother's arms away. "I just need to go to my room and lie down, Mom. Daddy can tell you everything." Ellen looked a little hurt but let her go.

When Jon entered, Ellen was angry and jumped on him verbally. "I've been waiting here without any word from you about my daughter. Why didn't you call like you said you would? What's wrong with Christy? She doesn't look good."

"Hold on. She's all right. The doctor said she was having a difficult period and there was a blood clot that was causing the pain. It had to be removed. He said it was nothing to be overly concerned about and after a little rest, she'll be just fine."

Jon tried to walk away but Ellen grabbed his sleeve.

"I'm her mother. I should have been with her. How dare you keep all this from me! What ever possessed you to get involved? This is a mother's job."

"I'm sorry, Ellen, I acted without considering you. I was so worried about Christy that I thought of nothing else but getting help. Will you please forgive me?"

After a long, hard stare, she said, "Probably, but only if you promise never to keep anything from me again. It's almost like you and Christy have shut me out. She keeps telling me to talk to you."

"Ellen, do we have to go on with this interrogation? I said I'm sorry." He started for the kitchen. "I'm going to make myself a drink. Would you like me to make you one?"

She didn't answer.

Ignoring Jon's admonition to let Christy rest, Ellen went directly to Christy's room to see her daughter. Christy wasn't quite asleep, and when her mother asked how she was feeling, Christy meekly murmured, "Okay, Mom."

"Can I do anything for you, dear?"

"No, Mom. I'm so tired, I just want to sleep."

Christy was still experiencing pain and it was building.

"Please, honey, how can I help you?" Ellen asked.

Christy only mumbled incoherently.

Ellen pulled the covers over Christy and touched her cheek and smoothed her hair back from her forehead. Christy was warm but not feverish. Since she was unresponsive, Ellen decided to let her sleep.

"Sleep tight, my baby," she whispered as she left the room and closed the door. Jon tried to talk to Ellen when she came downstairs, but she ignored his attempts at conversation. She went to the kitchen, made herself a cup of tea and carried it up to the guest room. Ellen couldn't sleep through the night. She got up a couple times during the night to check on Christy. Nothing had changed. Christy was in the same position and seemed to be sleeping soundly.

When morning came, Ellen's first thought, immediately upon awakening, was of Christy. Putting on her robe, she went directly to her daughter's room. When she entered the room, Christy had kicked off the covers and was lying in a bed soaked with blood. Ellen screamed and dashed to the bedside. Christy was unconscious. Jon heard the scream and ran down the hall.

As he ran he yelled, "What's happening?"

"Jon, call an ambulance! Christy's bleeding!"

Jon entered the room and when he saw Christy, he yelled, "Oh, my god!"

The ambulance arrived fifteen minutes later. Ellen sat by the bed sobbing hysterically, saying "My baby, my baby," while Jon paced the room wringing his hands helplessly. His only thought was, *What have I done? What have I done?*

The ambulance attendants advised them to follow in their car. Jon grabbed his jacket and as he took his keys from the hook next to the kitchen door, he yelled to Ellen, "Let's go! Just put on a coat over your robe."

They were wheeling Christy in through the emergency entrance when Jon and Ellen got to the hospital. Ellen ordered, "Stop the car, Jon." He did and she jumped out. It was only a matter of minutes before Jon had the car parked and was inside standing next to Ellen.

Christy was moved into one of the cubicles where a doctor was waiting. He turned to Jon and Ellen as he closed the curtain and said, "There's a waiting area just down the hall. Please wait there. I'll let you know how she's doing as soon as I get her stabilized."

Jon and Ellen walked to the waiting area and sat down on a long, cushioned, wooden bench. Jon put his arm around Ellen but she slid away from him and snarled, "Don't touch me!" They waited silently, Ellen frequently dabbing her eyes and blowing her nose.

"For god sake," she finally whispered, "Why is it taking so long?"

"I'm sure they know what they're doing, honey."

"Oh, shut up!" she spat.

They saw the doctor walking towards them and stood up.

"How is she, doctor? Is my baby all right?" Ellen asked anxiously.

The doctor wasn't smiling. He hesitated then said, "She had an infection that created a weakness in the wall of an artery in the uterus. She lost too much blood. The transfusion we gave her didn't help. I'm so sorry."

"What do you mean, you're sorry?" Jon exclaimed angrily.

"Your daughter died just five minutes ago. We did everything we could. I'm so sorry."

"No! No!" Ellen tore away from them and ran to the cubicle. She threw herself on her daughter and screamed, "Christy, Christy, my baby. Don't leave me."

Jon walked to the other side of the bed, took Christy's hand and fell to his knees. He began to sob. "My beautiful daughter, what have I done?" He muttered over and over. The words didn't register with Ellen. She was lost in her own disconsolate misery. Much later, Ellen would recall those damning words.

CHAPTER 26

The sky was overcast, as a thunderstorm was imminent. In the distance an occasional loud thunderclap could be heard. The day was dark for so early an hour, and brightened only when brief flashes of lightning sliced their way through the clouds. A light rain began to fall, resulting in a monotonous hiss, as it spattered on the leaves of the surrounding trees and bushes.

Jon Malcolm stood a little beyond the small circle of mourners. He stood with his head down, trying to hide his eyes under the broad brim of his hat. He had long since given up the struggle to restrain his emotions. Uncontrolled tears ran silently down his face. He sighed deeply and tried to force the memories of his sordid, selfish life from his mind, but to no avail. The past kept forcing its way in, bit by bit, hammering away at his brain. *There's no use remembering,* he thought. *Nothing can change the past. Nothing can change the future, either. Nothing can bring my Christy back to me. I gave her life and now... dear God, I've taken it away!*

Slowly, he raised his head and glanced around at the meager group of people standing by the open grave. This was nothing in comparison to the crowds that had flocked to the funeral parlor in order to catch a glimpse of Christy, who lay in her casket. Sweet Christy, whom he had killed with his stubborn arrogance. He was glad there were so few attending. At least they'd had sense enough to stay away from the burial giving her family the privacy to spending their last moments alone with her.

He looked over at his wife. Poor Ellen, how he wished he could have spared her this grief. She looked so lost and alone standing there; not at all like the strong, confident woman he'd married. She looked so much older. He had done this to her. He knew this meant the end of their life together. He knew she would never live with him again. How could he blame her? Anyone would feel the same if they'd been put through the torment she'd experienced. He would miss her terribly. If only he could put his arms around her and comfort her...perhaps bringing some comfort to him as well. But that would only make things worse. He wouldn't be able to bear the hatred and revulsion he was sure she had for him. "I'm sorry, Ellen," he whispered. "I'm so terribly sorry."

The words of the clergyman, which had seemed almost inaudible before, suddenly became very loud and clear.

"And forgive those who have trespassed against us. Open the gates of heaven, Lord, and receive this child into your heart and your sanctuary for she is innocent. Receive her spirit, for Thou art forgiving and kind to all who come before Thee. The Lord will bless her and keep her. The Lord makes his face to shine upon her and give her peace."

The clergyman's words faded again. After a while, Jon stopped trying to listen.

The rain was falling lightly but steadily now. He pulled his coat tighter about his neck. He wondered if the other people could hear what the clergyman was saying. He noticed that almost everyone had an umbrella and were sharing theirs with others who hadn't brought one. He wished now that he would have remembered to bring his. Certainly, the dark clouds had been sufficient warning. Ellen had always reminded him of things like that. Poor Ellen! Look at her. She had forgotten to bring one for herself. Martha, Ellen's sister, stood next to Ellen, with her arm around her, holding an umbrella over their heads. Jon had always liked Martha. She was several years older than Ellen but they were very close. Christy had loved Martha, too. Martha had no children of her own so she doted on Christy. Now Martha, too, was bereft of comfort.

Greg, Martha's husband, stood next to her. Then there was Ellen's brother, Joseph. Next to him, Ellen's younger brother, Steven, who stood grim-faced and angry. Ellen had told Steven what had happened. None of the family would talk to Jon now. There were other people there, some of them Christy's friends from high school, but he didn't know their names, had never bothered to learn them.

The pastor's voice droned on and on, forcing Jon's mind back to the days of his youth. The mirror of his soul was there before him and he had to look into it.

Everything seemed so very clear to him now, even the days that, for so many years, he had been successful in forgetting. He remembered something he'd heard or read a long time ago; it went… "Somewhere, from the depths of one's mind, circumstances bring about a chain of events that illuminates our past, revealing secrets long thought dead."

His pain made him dizzy. He couldn't stop thinking of the hurt he had caused others. Ruth's young face appeared in his mind. He really had cared for her, but he had been selfish. He knew his mother's threat of leaving him out of the will had been genuine. He'd had to let Ruth go, along with the child she was carrying; his child. He'd put all of that out of his mind a long time ago. There had been a few times when he'd thought about Ruth and wondered where she was. He wondered if his child was a boy or a girl. After the death of his mother, he was going to try to find them but suddenly having money and his freedom and being the playboy that he was, his friends had taken up all his time.

"Now, I am, most surely, reaping what I have sown," he said quietly to himself. "That's what Ruth said to Mother that day."

CHAPTER 27

The Parker house was like a tomb. Nothing anyone could say would have eased the tension.

Looking on helplessly, as her son struggled with pain that was verging on a nervous breakdown, Ruth felt overwhelmed with remorse. *Why did I ever go to my dad's house? Why did I have to meet Jon? Why did I have to run away? I know why. Because I couldn't bear living in the same town with Jon, so I had to leave. If I hadn't, Robert and Christy probably would have met as children, but Robert would have been teased and called a bastard, the child of a loose woman. That would have been almost as cruel.*

Ruth and Gene tried to console Robert but it wasn't working. He spent most of every day in his room and at night he would walk around the neighborhood or pace on the backyard patio for hours. He tried to reach Christy but he kept getting a recording that the number was temporarily out of service. Ruth thought she would bring him a little comfort if she walked with him.

"Mom, I know you think you're being helpful, but you're not. Please don't try. I need to be alone. I know I can't wait any longer to see if Christy's okay, so I'm going to her house. Her father will probably throw me out, but I need to know what's happening. I know her father is preventing her from getting in touch with me."

"I can't stop you from going, Robert, but I'll worry all the while you're gone. If you'd like, Dad and I will go with you, even though I never planned on seeing Jon Malcolm ever again."

"No, Mom. When I go, I'll go alone."

"Before you go, why don't we try calling the house? You've been calling Christy's number and that's the one that's been out of order. Let's go inside and I'll see if I can get their main number through Information."

Ruth was successful in getting the Malcolm's phone number. Without asking Robert's permission, Ruth proceeded to dial the number. The phone rang four times before a hoarse male voice answered, "Yes?"

"May I speak to Christy, please?"

"No! And don't call anymore. My daughter is dead." He slammed the phone down.

Ruth's eyes opened wide. She couldn't believe what she had just heard. The voice sounded like Jon's. Emotions rushed through her. It had been so long since she'd heard him speak. *Why did he say his daughter was dead? Can this be true? Or is he just not accepting any calls thinking they might be from Robert?* She turned to Robert who was standing beside her.

"That was Mr. Malcolm and he hung up on me. He said "my daughter is dead.'"

"I know what he's doing and I'm not going to let him get away with it. He's treating Christy like a prisoner. Give me the phone." His hand shook with anger as he took the phone from Ruth.

Jon was all alone in the big house, sipping wine and pacing. He couldn't face what he'd done. The consequences of his selfish act hurt too much to go on living. Destiny cascaded its way to his retribution with unbearable pain. Jon walked to his study and sat down at his desk. He slowly opened the bottom drawer and took out a gun. The phone rang. After several rings, Jon lifted the receiver from its cradle.

After dialing Robert heard the angry voice on the other end of the line.

"Who is this?"

"I would like to speak to Christy, please."

"I said who is this?"

"It's Robert, Mr. Malcolm, and I must talk to Christy!"

"Robert, I know who you are and you can't talk to my daughter."

"Why the hell not? What harm can it do?"

"The harm has already been done. My daughter is dead. We buried her yesterday." There was a long silence before Jon finally continued. "It's all my fault, all my fault." He was sobbing now.

"What do you mean, she's dead?" Robert shouted into the phone.

"You're just saying that to keep me away. It's not going to work. I still love her, even though you're trying to mess it up for all of us."

There was no response from Jon. Robert heard him put the phone down. Another minute of silence passed but Robert did not hang up. He heard a clicking noise, and the shot that set his ear ringing.

"Mr. Malcolm! Mr. Malcolm!" Robert yelled.

"What is it?" Ruth asked. "I heard that noise. It sounded like a gunshot."

"I'm sure it was a shot, Mom. I think Mr. Malcolm just shot himself." Robert turned to his mother. "He said Christy is dead and that it was his fault. Christy can't be dead. She's carrying our baby."

The next morning, Gene brought the paper in from the front porch.

"Robert, you'll want to read this," he said, handing the paper to his son.

Robert read the first line and looked up at his father. "This says Jon Malcolm, eminent industrialist, committed suicide."

"Keep reading," Gene said.

Robert read on. "He could not face the sudden death of his only child, a daughter named Christine."

Robert suddenly burst into tears, dropping the paper. He fell to his knees, his legs no longer able to support him. "She's dead. Christy is dead!" he sobbed.

EPILOGUE

Ruth stood on the patio and smiled. It was a balmy evening. The moonlight shown silver white as it splashed on the bushes and grass, illuminating a beautiful yard and flower garden. Years of serious maintenance and love had paid off with grateful blossoms.

The evening was too beautiful to pass up. She could see Gene's and her labor in every foot of the yard. She'd just had to step outside for a little while. She wished Gene could be beside her but after a long and stressful day, he'd retired early. His position on the board of directors at the hospital sometimes proved to be too much at his age. Ruth had adjusted to this and was fine with it. They had been so close through all the years that, even when they were apart, they were together. Their thoughts were always of each other.

Ruth's gaze fell on the yellow rose bush growing at the corner of the house and rested there. This bush had needed more tender care than most of the others but it had finally made it to maturity.

When she thought about it, like tonight, she could still hear laughter and the clanking of spades coming through the kitchen door. She could see the two young lovers outside enjoying the task of planting something beautiful together. *Will the pain never end?* She wondered.

Ruth thought of her daughter, Pauline, now happily married to an architect and living in Oklahoma City. She had made her parents the proud grandparents of two beautiful children. Ruth looked at the Sweet William that she'd helped the grandchildren plant on one of their visits. Their shouts of pleasure at the end of that task still rang in her ears.

Pauline and her family and Robert still came home for holidays. That brought joy to her and Gene. Ruth remembered their last visit. The children had made the holidays fun again.

Most of all, she thought of Robert. He was doing well as an attorney and living in Texas. His letters seemed cheerful enough, but they didn't convince Ruth. Sometimes, he would bring a friend home with him, but they'd never see the woman again. There was a sadness about him that never seemed to go away. He would laugh and tell jokes, but the melancholy never left his eyes. *I don't think other people notice, but I do,* Ruth thought.

Robert did a lot of pro bono work and told Ruth and Gene that someday he'd find Martha Travis and Dr. Roman. Ruth encouraged that thought but, privately, felt that those two were probably dead by now. If Travis and Roman hadn't been found, they were at least out of business. The FBI is relentless about that kind of criminal activity.

Ruth wondered if Robert would ever find another love like he had for Christy. Perhaps he would. She hoped he would. On occasion, Ruth would ask if he was having a serious relationship with anyone, and he would always answer, "Some people are destined to have one great love in their lives. I've already had mine."

THE END